A MOMENT OF VULNERABILITY ...

Jane bowed her head and covered her face with her hands. She started to turn away, but Anthony gripped her upper arms. "It's good to cry. You needn't feel ashamed." His heart went out to this young, brave girl caught up in a tragedy. Before he knew what he was doing, a force beyond himself caused him to draw her into his arms. She did not pull away. Instead, she buried her face against the side of his neck, where he could feel her warm, moist breathing. They stood there, she emitting not a sound, he becoming increasingly aware of the faint scent of lilac in her hair and the softness of her full bosom brushing against his chest.

"Ah, Jane," he murmured, and when she pulled her head back to regard him questioningly, his hands involuntarily locked against her spine and drew her closer. Nearly all reasoned thought left his head as he became acutely aware of every one of her soft curves molding to the contours of his body. His heart started hammering. A tremor shot through him as he felt her soft thigh pressing against the hardness of his. He felt an overwhelming urge to kiss her. . . .

The
London Belle

Shirley Kennedy

A SIGNET BOOK

SIGNET
Published by New American Library, a division of
Penguin Putnam Inc., 375 Hudson Street,
New York, New York 10014, U.S.A.
Penguin Books Ltd, 27 Wrights Lane,
London W8 5TZ, England
Penguin Books Australia Ltd,
Ringwood, Victoria, Australia
Penguin Books Canada Ltd, 10 Alcorn Avenue,
Toronto, Ontario, Canada M4V 3B2
Penguin Books (N.Z.) Ltd, 182–190 Wairau Road,
Auckland 10, New Zealand

Penguin Books Ltd, Registered Offices:
Harmondsworth, Middlesex, England

First published by Signet, an imprint of New American Library,
a division of Penguin Putnam Inc.

First Printing, September 1999
10 9 8 7 6 5 4 3 2 1

Dedicated with love and affection to
three fans I know I can always count on:

Brent Hayes
Melissa Hayes
Gina Cannamucio

Chapter 1

At the Duchess of Ponsonby's ball, held at her palatial mansion on St. James's Square, London, in June of 1817, two strangers caught sight of each other across the crowded ballroom floor. One was Anthony, Lord Dashmont, who had just returned from his sugar plantation in the West Indies. The other, Lady Jane Sperling, eldest daughter of the Earl of Hedley, was the belle of the ball. When their eyes locked, each felt a jolt.

"Who is that?" inquired Lord Dashmont of his affable friend, the Honorable Tatton Fulwood, second son of the Earl of Harlestone. He nodded toward the tall, willowy girl across the room.

Tatton followed Anthony's gaze. "The one in blue, next to Lord Slingsby? That's Lady Jane Sperling. She's well into her first . . . no, I believe, her second Season." Tatton scratched his head. "Perhaps her third, actually."

"Third?" Anthony inquired suspiciously. "Is there something the matter with her?"

"Nothing, except she's rather a haughty chit. But then, why shouldn't she be? She's beautiful, as you can see, and quite lively. See how the dandies flock around? Fine dowry. Countless offers, but thus far, she's having none of them." Tatton jokingly raised his short self on tiptoe. "I, myself, would have offered, had I been able to look her square in the eye." He sank down again and remarked, "The little blonde in white is her younger sister Christabell, who's just out. That's her aunt, Lady Eugenia Fanshawe, standing next to Slingsby." Tatton grimaced. "I would as lief take on a pair of tigers as that old harridan."

"She's not so terrifying as she looks." Anthony gave a nod of recognition toward the stout, white-haired lady dressed in elegant black, sparkling with diamonds, who stood ramrod straight and whose imperious expression appeared permanently affixed upon her seasoned face. "I could hardly forget Lady Fanshawe. She came calling regularly when my wife was alive."

Tatton continued, "There's Lady Jane's older brother, Edmund. You might know him as well."

"I saw him gambling at Brooks often enough before I went away."

"Interested?"

"In Lady Jane?" Anthony firmly shook his head. "She's not bad looking by half, but another silly goose, I daresay, and I surely don't want another—" He stopped abruptly, aware he was about to step into his own forbidden territory.

Tatton had the good sense to ignore his friend's obvious reference to his deceased wife. Instead, he appeared relieved. "All to the good. I was hoping you wouldn't crave an introduction."

"Not by half," Anthony answered in a voice both firm and final. "I have no interest in birdbrained young chits with nothing on their minds but catching a husband." He paused before lightly inquiring, "But why would you not wish to introduce us?"

"You've lost touch." Tatton gave a whiff of disgust. "I warned you not to run off to the West Indies."

"Had I not, I could well be rotting away in Newgate as we speak. Besides, I was seeing to my holdings and—"

"—and losing track of everything that counts in London," Tatton interrupted indignantly. "Gone two and a half years! And doing what? Cutting sugar cane? Broiling in the hot sun? Look at you. That tanned skin you've acquired is *not* the mark of a gentleman."

Anthony's firm mouth curled with a touch of humor. "Incredible though it may seem to you, Tatton, being a gentleman isn't everything in Jamaica."

"No doubt. Well, I can assure you, you'll never find me on that hot, uncivilized little island of yours."

"I would never find you more than a mile from St. James's Street."

Tatton sighed. "No sense arguing. You've always done exactly what suits you." He paused, as if searching for just the right words before continuing. "I hear you've brought your son up from Kent."

Anthony nodded and said curtly, "David is here for a short visit, along with his aunt and grandmother."

"Is he . . . improved?"

"David's condition hasn't changed. He's still withdrawn and uncommunicative, as he has been ever since his mother's death." Pain flickered in Anthony's eyes. "I had planned on returning to Jamaica shortly and bringing David along. I had a vision of his growing up there, just as I did. He would have learned the meaning of tenacity and hard work—a far cry from the indolence and depravity you see in London."

"How the leopard has changed his spots," Tatton exclaimed. "Do my ears deceive me? You, the former rake of London, are now accusing *us* of indolence and depravity?"

Anthony laughed aloud. "Rest easy. I have given up thoughts of returning to Jamaica any time soon, now I know David should remain here. So I'll be visiting my old haunts again, wenching and debauching with the best of them." He grew serious. "I've resigned myself. David will never change. I shall visit him from time to time, but he's happy enough, and will lead a serene, if dull, existence at Fairfield Manor with Georgiana's mother and sister."

What a pity Tatton thought, but remained silent. Poor child, having to grow up under the iron thumbs of those two dour, humorless women. A worse fate he could not imagine. But his friend had gotten that stubborn look in his eye, and he had best get to another subject. "'Twould be best to stay away from Lady Jane Sperling."

"Stay away? But why?" asked Anthony.

"Because there's the most hideous rumor going around—"

"Tatton, my dear!" A young woman with dancing curls and cherub lips emerged from the crowd, grabbed Tatton by the arm and fluttered her eyelids. "Where have you been hiding? I shall die of thirst if you don't fetch me some punch this instant."

Anthony watched idly as his friend willingly allowed himself to be led away. He glanced across the room again, to where that most boring of fellows, Lord Slingsby, was engaged in animated conversation with Lady Jane. Anthony could not take his

eyes off her. She was slender, taller than most, light brown hair
piled high into some sort of Grecian affair, except for little tendrils of curls falling about her delicate face. She wore a high-
waisted blue satin gown that swirled delightfully around her
slim, curved figure, and was low cut enough to reveal a most
generous amount of creamy white bosom. As he watched, she
fluttered her fan, tilted her head back, and laughed with delight,
as if Slingsby had just delivered the most witty of ripostes.
Ridiculous, of course. Nothing that oaf Slingsby ever said
could be even half that amusing. She had a nice neck, long and
slender . . . swanlike, some love-dazed poet would call it.
There. She was looking at him again. For an unnerving moment
their eyes locked before she looked away. He wondered what
Tatton's hideous rumor was, and why Tatton thought it best
they not be introduced. Not that it mattered. He had set his
plans for the future. He would remain here indefinitely and par-
take of those delights one could find only in England, all sorely
missed after he, out of dire necessity, had fled to Montclaire, his
plantation in Jamaica. Most especially, he missed the gambling.
How he had yearned for his gentlemen's clubs in St. James's
Street!

Some day he would return to his island. He would settle
down and marry sturdy, sober-sided Isabella Wentworth, the
daughter of Jamaican planter Tybalt Wentworth. She would be
of great assistance in running his plantation. Not that he loved
her, or ever could. But he had not married for love the first time,
either. Now, at thirty-two, he had grown wise enough to realize
that he must marry for practical purposes and never again
marry another flighty, empty-headed London belle. Never. Not
after Georgiana . . .

"Who is that?" inquired Lady Jane Sperling of Archibald,
Lord Slingsby. Only with great difficulty had she managed to
pull her gaze from across the ballroom floor where a dark-
haired man, lean face bronzed by wind and sun, stood regarding her with black, piercing eyes. "See? That man staring at
me."

Her brother, Edmund, a handsome young man, tall and even-featured like herself, overheard. "Have you not enough admirers?" he asked.

"Can I ever have enough?" she retorted, fluttering her fan.

"It appears you have lost one." Edmund glanced toward the dance floor, to where their younger sister had just begun a quadrille with a tall young man resplendent in an elegant double-breasted wool frockcoat. "I note our fashionable Lord Beckford has been most attentive to Christabell this evening."

Jane placed her fan in front of her lips so Slingsby couldn't hear, and murmured, "I could lure him back in an instant if I wanted, brother dear."

"Such conceit!"

She laughed. "But 'tis true. Why should I pretend otherwise?" She looked across the floor again. "So who is he, Edmund?"

Edmund idly scanned the crowd. When he spied the gentleman in question, he scowled. "That, dear sister, is Anthony, Lord Dashmont, the most notorious rake in London—or at least he was before he took himself off to the West Indies some time back. Supposedly to see to his sugar plantation, but rumor had it he was escaping the law because of a duel. He's just back, I understand. Widower. His wife died four . . . five years ago, so he—"

"Such a tragedy," interrupted Lady Eugenia Fanshawe, Jane's great-aunt, who was bold enough, and ancient enough, to interrupt any conversation without trepidation. "Poor, dear Georgiana. Terrible, the way she died."

"A rake you say?" asked Jane, oblivious to her great-aunt's tittle-tattle. She risked another quick peek over her fan at Lord Dashmont, who at last had summoned good manners enough to look away. He was not particularly tall, she observed, but the whole of him was so well put together that height was of no import. Broad shoulders . . . flat stomach . . . slender waistline . . . And the way he was standing. Hand resting idly on his hip, as if he disdained the whole gathering and cared not a wit what anybody thought. Strange, she had professed to liking only men who towered over her, but she found it of no consequence that this Lord Dashmont could be only two, possibly three, inches taller than she.

Jane snapped her fan shut and turned to her brother with curious eyes. "So he fought a duel. Why else do you call him a rake?"

"The usual reasons," Edmund answered blandly, "gambling—drinking—the theater—actresses—a fair share of our beauteous Cyprians. Also, if *on-dit* serves correctly, he cut quite a swath through the affections of some of London's most distinguished ladies of rank. All that, of course, before he fled England."

"There's no reason to believe Dashmont has changed," Lady Fanshawe observed scornfully. "He was *not* raised a gentleman. His father kept him on that little island far past the time he should properly have been sent to England for his education."

"But did Lord Dashmont not lose his wife?" inquired Jane. "Perhaps it was grief that lead him into debauchery."

"Dashmont is long past his so-called grieving," Lady Fanshawe replied, "if, in fact, he ever grieved at all for dear Georgiana. I used to go calling upon the poor young woman. Her main complaint was that her husband appeared to be avoiding her." Aunt sniffed. "The man is still ridden with despicable vices, besides which, he has a young son whom he hides at his estate in Kent and totally ignores." She pressed her lips closed and bobbed her head, secure in the knowledge that she, one of the pillars of society, ought not be contradicted.

But Edmund protested, "Not so, Aunt. At this moment his son is visiting him in town. Besides, Dashmont is not so wicked as he's painted."

"Humph," declared Lady Fanshawe, "how can you judge him when you are as debauched as he?"

"Touché," Edmund answered lightly and gave a slight bow.

Aunt was wrong, thought Jane. At twenty-two, Edmund had habits not dissimilar from those he had attributed to Lord Dashmont, but she knew he kept his so-called wicked ways in moderation. "You are *not* debauched, Edmund," she laughingly protested, "although I suspect you want us to think you are."

Edmund's blue-gray eyes, the exact shade of Jane's, lit amusedly. "You are absolutely correct. I'm no Dashmont, although I strive to be. But I've yet to fight a duel on Putney Heath and be compelled to flee the country because I nearly did in Sir Lucian Sykes."

Lady Fanshawe remarked disdainfully, "If memory serves correctly, Sir Lucian accused Lord Dashmont of cheating at cards."

"It was never proven," asserted Edmund. "Sir Lucian erred. Anthony is a gifted card player—he has no need to cheat."

"*Anthony*, is it? So you know the rascal?"

"I may have played a game or two of whist with him at Brooks from time to time. Indeed, Papa has known him for years." Edmund added thoughtfully, "I find Dashmont quite tolerable, despite his reputation. He's not so much a rake as he is a man who says and does exactly as he pleases, society be damned." He directed a meaningful look at Jane. "Dashmont would make a fine catch."

"No gambler is a fine catch," Jane retorted. Bitterness welled in her throat. Although she loved her father dearly, she had to say what she felt. "Papa's the perfect example."

"Jane is right, Edmund." Lady Fanshawe's many chins quivered indignantly. "Lord Dashmont might be a widower, and rich as Croesus, but, alas, he is a gambler and thus, completely ineligible." She placed a protective hand on her grand-niece's shoulder. "Look away, my dear. Your mother would faint if she knew you were even considering such a dangerous man." She awarded a warm glance to Lord Slingsby, who had been standing by listening with rapt attention. "Is that not so, m'lord?"

"Indeed, so, madame," eagerly chimed bland-faced Lord Slingsby, a tall, thickset, balding man in his early forties. He cast an adoring look at Jane. "I liken Lady Jane to a delicate flower. Her innocence must be sheltered at all costs from such a villain."

Delicate flower indeed! Jane smothered a smile behind her fan, not daring to risk a glance at her brother. But she must play her role, so she smiled coyly and murmured, "You are too kind, sir."

"You must come to tea on Thursday," Aunt Eugenia informed Lord Slingsby, an invitation that sounded more like a command. "Chalton House in Regent Street."

"Indeed, I am well acquainted with the beautiful mansion in

which you and your family dwell, Lady Fanshawe," gushed Slingsby, "and I am truly delighted to accept." The adoring look he cast Jane made her heart sink. She was well aware her family's patience was wearing thin. Slingsby would be proposing soon, and she, after hedging for three Seasons, and letting, in Aunt Eugenia's words, "perfectly splendid suitors escape," would have to accept.

"Introduce us, Edmund."

The strange voice Jane heard at her shoulder was soft, yet deep and forceful. Even before she turned, she knew, from the scandalized lift of Aunt's eyebrows, that it was the man who had been staring at her from across the room.

"With pleasure, Dashmont." Smooth as silk, Edmund managed the introductions. ". . . you remember my aunt, Lady Fanshawe, of course, and may I present my younger sister, Lady Jane Sperling?"

With equal smoothness, Jane dipped in a fleeting curtsy as Lord Dashmont performed a graceful bow in return. "Delighted," he said lightly, gazing at her with those piercing dark eyes. The orchestra erupted into a rousing waltz. "Would you care to dance?"

Beside her, Jane felt, rather than saw, her great-aunt stiffen. "Remember what I told you," Aunt whispered into her ear in alarm, "you cannot—"

"I would be delighted, sir." Jane was not the least fearful of risking Aunt's ire. Aunt was disapproving, no matter what she did.

Lord Dashmont showed the trace of an amused smile as he led her onto the dance floor, then placed his arm around her waist while she rested her hand on the shoulder of his superbly cut gray waistcoat. She did not have the impression he was laughing at her, though; he appeared to be laughing at himself. The next thing she noticed was his hand. It wasn't pudgy and soft like a dandy's, but hard and rough, as if he had actually engaged in some sort of manual labor. And whereas whiteness of skin was highly prized among the *ton,* his face was deeply tanned, with little crinkly lines around his eyes that indicated he'd been much in the sun. *Most unusual.*

They began the dance, his right foot forward, her left foot

back, from the very start in perfect symmetry, as if they had danced together all their lives. They began to dip—turn—float around the dance floor, lost completely in the darting flurry of the waltz. Soon she was thinking, never had she had a partner so smooth—so light-footed—so graceful—and so totally in charge. He was silent as they danced, an inscrutable look replacing his slight smile. She, too, remained silent, wrapped in the bliss of stirring music and a skilled partner, for once not feeling the need for silly chitchat.

But as they danced, she began to experience feelings she had never felt before. Perhaps it was the enticing musk of his honey-water cologne teasing her nostrils, or his arm around her waist, so sinewy hard, so unyielding. Perhaps the feel of her small hand enveloped in his larger, rough one, or it may have been the appeal of his handsome, lean face, tanned or no, with those chiseled lips, that enticing cleft in his chin, and those worldly-wise eyes. She had danced with boys all evening, but this was different—this was a man. Despite herself, she became so intensely aware of his presence that she became short of breath. She could not fight the need for a giant gulp of air. To disguise it, she burst forth with, "Lovely weather for June, is it not, Lord Dashmont?"

"Indeed it is, Lady Jane," he replied.

Had she detected a trace of derision in his voice? Well, she could hardly blame him. The weather—such a stupid remark. But she still felt unsure of herself, and so must carry on. "So I hear, Lord Dashmont, that you have recently returned from the West Indies."

"Last week," he replied with studied politeness. "What else have you heard?"

In the manner she'd been taught, Jane demurred with a flutter of eyelashes and exclaimed, "Why nothing, sir, why ever do you ask?"

He leaned back and regarded her with barely concealed scorn. "Coquetry does not become you. Save the silly chatter for someone who appreciates it. Lord Slingsby, perhaps?"

This was not the type of insipid dance conversation to which she was accustomed. For a moment she was so taken aback that no ready response leaped to her lips. "Well!" she managed, then lapsed into silence, concentrating on the dance, struggling to find a suitably scathing reply. But she could find none, mainly because, she had to admit, the man was right. Her reply had been silly, fatuous, and worst of all, a lie. But that was how she was supposed to act. Mama—Aunt—everyone had made it clear that to catch a husband a girl must act the silly fool and never in the world let on she had a brain. At first she had questioned their advice, but after three Seasons, during which her parents were becoming increasingly anxious, she had long since accepted her role as the empty-headed debutante.

But then, she decided, what with his wicked reputation Lord Dashmont did not qualify as a suitor. He deserved a good put-down. Why not be honest and tell him exactly what she thought?

She tilted her head back and smiled warmly. "Since you invite the truth, sir, I heard that before your departure for the West Indies, you were quite the rake, inclined to drinking, gambling, fair Cyprians and actresses, as well as highborn ladies. Not only that, you were compelled to leave the country because you fought a duel at Putney Heath and nearly did in Sir Lucien Sykes, who had accused you of cheating at cards."

There she went again, speaking honestly, her worse fault, according to Mama and Aunt Eugenia. Although she kept a straight face, the moment the words flew from her mouth, she regretted them, aware that whether they were true or not, and whether Lord Dashmont could be considered a suitor or not, he could well be gravely insulted. She had no need to worry, though. After a pause, wherein he obviously was letting the words sink in, Lord Dashmont tilted his head back and burst into laughter.

"What refreshing honesty," he managed after his laughter died. "Much better than that silly prattle you were giving me." How annoying he is, she thought, but before she could answer, he continued lightly, "And I hear that you, Lady Jane, are into your third Season."

"Quite so," she answered in a tone to match his own, then further challenged, "what else have you heard?"

Instantly he answered, "That you are rather a haughty chit.

And also, if memory serves correctly, you've had countless offers and will have none of them."

It was her turn to burst into laughter. "You are correct, sir, although extremely rude to say so."

"Rude, am I?" Mockingly he continued, "You've cut me to the quick." He dipped and whirled her around before he inquired, "Still waiting to be struck by Cupid's arrow?"

"Not at all," she answered, this time seriously. She made a sweeping gesture around the room. "Look about you and what do you see? Nothing but dandies, so taken up with themselves they've no thought for anyone else. And I'm expected to fall in love with one of these fops? Ha! I think not."

"Really?" Anthony feigned surprise. He nodded toward a tall, exceedingly handsome gentleman waltzing by. "What about Lord Farley here?"

"He has a silly laugh."

"Well, then, what about Viscount Landsdale over there? Such a handsome devil, and most elegantly attired."

"Are you serious? Have you not noticed the sloppy manner in which he ties his cravat?"

"Then Lieutenant Heathcart?" He nodded toward a young naval officer resplendent in a gold-braided blue cloth coat, white waistcoat and breeches, as well as an epaulet on his shoulder, cross belt, and sword.

"Never! He's balding and he wears too much cologne." Jane wrinkled up her nose. "Not only that, he pads his calves with sawdust so his legs won't look so spindly in his breeches."

"What an astute judge of character you are," Anthony observed with a humorously arched eyebrow. "How perceptive of you to detect such major flaws."

Jane was aware she had deliberately made herself sound shallow, which only showed how little she cared for Dashmont's opinion. She lifted her chin defiantly. "Laugh if you like, but I assure you I am well past the point where I foolishly expect my own true love to appear."

"But don't all young girls dream of love?"

"Not this one." Jane nodded with resolve. "I have determined I can have a fine life even if I never find true love." She flashed a self-satisfied smile. "Of course, I shall marry well, to someone who's at least halfway tolerable, with enough wealth and high enough title to please my parents. Then I shall have lots of children and be the best mother in the world."

"An admirable ambition. It appears you know exactly what life has in store for you."

"I do," she answered firmly. "Then the rest of the time, I shall do what pleases me."

He regarded her solemnly. "And what pleases you, Lady Jane? Painting flowers? Embroidering samplers?"

Bristling, she answered, "What do you take me for, some featherbrain?"

He looked surprised. "I was only describing the legitimate pursuits of young ladies. If I insulted you, my apologies."

She didn't feel like forgiving him. "You reflect the thinking of the times, Lord Dashmont." Before he could reply, she plunged ahead with, "Really, sir, that I could possibly have a brain in my head and want to accomplish something other than embroidering a sampler must seem a foreign notion to you."

His brow furrowed. "I suppose it does. So what did you have in mind?"

She took a moment to consider whether or not she wanted to answer, deciding that with his insulting attitude, he did not deserve an answer. Besides, hardly anyone knew what she truly had an interest in. Surely she should not reveal it now.

She regarded him with fluttering eyelashes and assumed her well-practiced demure smile. "My needlework is exquisite, my watercolors are superb, and my piano playing a positive delight. Now are you satisfied?" She stopped dancing. Glancing toward the edge of the dance floor, she toyed with the notion of simply marching off the floor, leaving this arrogant man to stand here alone as he deserved.

He appeared to read her mind, however, and demanded quickly, "Don't even think it. Finish your dance with me."

How dare he give orders, as if she were a common scullery maid. But her feet refused to move, and when he placed his arm around her waist to draw her closer, she discerned the raw power that lay directly beneath the thin veneer of his civility. For a moment she was spellbound. Here was a real man, not one of her namby-pamby suitors, and she had no idea how to handle him. It was almost frightening. No sense making a scene, she decided. She would simply finish the dance and never speak to the overwhelming Lord Dashmont again.

They resumed waltzing. As they twirled past her family, Lord Dashmont remarked with a chuckle, "It appears your aunt disapproves of your dancing with me." He pivoted her around so she could view Aunt's fierce face over his shoulder. "If looks could kill, I should be lying stone cold dead at Lady Fanshawe's feet this very moment."

"Aunt cannot abide gamblers. She considers you a rake, sir," said Jane, still fuming over his insult, "as do I." The music ended. They stopped dancing and broke apart.

"Better a rake than one of your foppish suitors," remarked Lord Dashmont equitably. He gave her a slight bow, said with a grin, "You dance tolerably well, Lady Jane," and walked away, quickly disappearing into the crowd.

He had left her breathless, stunned that he had departed so quickly, and angry, not only because he had seen through her pretensions and shallow facade, but because he had considered her naught but another ignorant London belle.

"Jane, do come here," demanded Lady Fanshawe. When Jane approached, she went on, "How could you have danced with that man?"

Before Jane could reply, her mother appeared. A small, sweet-faced woman with prematurely gray hair, she was quite pale, clutching her fan with one hand, the other spread over her heart.

"Mama, whatever is the matter?"

"'Tis nothing," Lady Sperling answered faintly, and gave a nervous laugh. "Except the silliest thing—I fear I have been snubbed."

"But how is that possible?" Jane was totally perplexed. No one dared snub the Sperlings. They were solid members of the *ton*.

"I do not know, Jane, but it happened, nonetheless. I had gone up to pay my respects to the Duchess of Ponsonby. When she saw me coming, she deliberately turned her back, as did Lady Howard, with whom she'd been conversing."

"But there must be some mistake. I shall go myself and have a talk with her."

Jane started away, chin lifted indignantly, but her brother came up and gripped her arm. "Let it go."

"But—"

"Let it go." Edmund's grip tightened. He drew her aside, his usual cheery face somber. "You don't understand." They stood frozen. For a moment they looked into each other's eyes, she, questioning, he looking pained as he struggled to frame an explanation. "It's . . . not a good idea," he finished lamely.

"Why?"

"I had not realized the rumors had spread this far . . ." Edmund continued, still stumbling, ". . . best not confront Her Grace, else you, too, could be snubbed."

"But *why*, Edmund?" Jane demanded, "you *must* tell me." If there was anything she hated, it was shilly-shallying.

Sighing, Edmund regarded the ceiling. Finally, with an expression of resignation, he looked her squarely in the eye. "'Tis Papa. Rumor has it he's on the verge of bankruptcy." With irony he continued, "If you think our dear friends in the *ton* would stand by us, think again. They are poised, ready to pounce like vultures, over such juicy *on-dit* as this. Lady Ponsonby's slight is just the beginning. If Papa were to lose his fortune, they would desert us in droves."

Jane gasped. "But we've always been so rich. We're the Sperlings. It's unthinkable we could be"—she could hardly choke the words out—"poverty stricken."

"You know Papa is an incurable gambler."

"How could I not? He's hardly ever home, and we know he's at his clubs every night. But so are his friends. They gamble as often as he, but *they're* not ruining themselves."

"But they don't gamble as much as Papa. He cannot stop himself."

"But he's always been so good to us." Jane felt a sick feeling in the pit of her stomach, as if she had been kicked. "He's the dearest Papa in all the world. I know he loves us. If he can't stop himself, can you not stop him?"

Edmund, who was never one to display his true feelings, allowed a bitter laugh to escape his lips. "You think I haven't tried? Papa is totally out of control. I wager even as we speak, he's at White's, or Brooks, playing fast and loose with the family fortune."

"How much has he thrown away?" she asked, afraid to hear the answer.

Edmund shrugged. "You think he would tell me? You know how secretive he is. But I hear it's sometimes thousands of pounds in a night." He took Jane's hand reassuringly. "Try not to worry. He would never touch your dowry, or Cristabell's, and he would never touch Chalton House or Hedley Hall."

Jane frowned. "It's not me I am worried about, it's Mama. She would never survive such a disgrace."

Edmund managed a faint smile. "Mama is tougher than you think. She would have to be after bearing ten children in fourteen years and only six survived. All the while, mind you, married to a man who's occupied with horses all the day, and whist and faro all the night."

"But what shall we do?"

"Do?" Edmund's faint smile held more than a touch of irony. "There's not a thing we can do, except pray Papa will come to his senses."

"Surely he will," Jane said brightly. She had lived in luxury all her life. The thought that Papa could gamble away all their money was inconceivable. "How could he do otherwise?"

"Indeed," Edmund concurred and took on a more cheerful countenance. "Of course you're right. I was looking at the dark side. At Brooks I have seen men ruin themselves in a single night—gamble away their coaches and fine horses, their estates—everything, down to their last farthing. But Papa has more sense, despite his weakness for gambling."

"Of course he has. You worry needlessly."

"May I have the next dance?"

Jane felt like cringing. Percy, Lord Bradbourne, stood before her, a man she could not abide. Tall and gaunt, with a pasty complexion and small, crafty eyes, he was much older than she, at least fifty, with thinning hair, a slit of a cruel mouth, and an air of superiority only thinly disguised. He had a funny smell about him—musty—as if he slept each night in a catacomb. Worst of all, she loathed his fingers, which were exceedingly long, bony, and maggoty white. Jane forced herself to smile. "I would be delighted, sir."

While they danced, they exchanged small pleasantries, he holding her closer than she liked. Mercifully, the dance was short. At the end, he led her back to her aunt, who wasted no time in fawning over him. Jane could hardly keep from making a face when Aunt, with near quivering obeisance, inquired, "My dear Lord Bradbourne, would you honor us by coming for tea tomorrow?"

"Delighted," Bradbourne replied in his stilted fashion, with a stiff, unyielding bow. He caught Jane's gaze. "Until tomorrow, my dear," he said, peering at her intently in a manner both bold and frankly assessing.

"Aunt Eugenia, how could you?" Jane demanded after he had bowed again and backed away.

Lady Fanshawe returned a reproving gaze. "The man is rich, Jane. We must move quickly. His third wife died just recently. I warrant he'll not be single long."

"I have no intention of becoming number four." Trying to disguise her pique, Jane continued, "Really, Aunt Eugenia, you appear to be collecting men on my behalf this evening in a most blatant manner. I wish you would not. And I wish—"

"'Tis for your own good, child," Lady Fanshawe interrupted. "You simply must find a husband soon."

Why the urgency in her aunt's tone? Jane wondered. But she said no more, and was soon lost in the pleasures of the music, the dancing, the glittering surroundings, and her natural confidence in herself, brought about by the knowledge, though she was not consciously aware of it, that she was young, rich, beautiful, and an undisputed member of the Polite World. What she *did* know was that it was fun to have half the young blades of London at her feet. *Even though I want none of them,* she reflected wryly.

By the end of the evening, Jane had nearly forgotten Edmund's concern about Papa's gambling. She had danced every dance, flirted outrageously, and been told how beautiful she was at least a dozen times. The only flaw in her evening was that she had failed to put Anthony, Lord Dashmont, out of her head. She could not forget his fluid grace, his lean, taut body, and when he smiled, how strikingly white his teeth were against his deeply tanned face. Of course, it was most annoying, the way his shrewd eyes had cut straight through her pretenses, surveying her with mocking thoroughness, seeming to see into her real self.

But what is my real self? she wondered. *I'm happy with my life, yet I'm discontent. Sometimes I think there must be more to life than beaux and parties and beautiful clothes.*

But what on earth was she thinking? It was that scoundrel, Dashmont, who had stirred up such rebellious thoughts. Well, she hoped she would never see him again. He was a handsome devil, she had to admit, but much too blunt, and above all else, was a gambler, just like her father, and she would never entertain the notion he was suitable. *Unless I crave a life of misery,* she told herself wryly, thinking of her mother. *But I shall soon forget the dashing Lord Dashmont. He's only a passing fancy.*

Chapter 2

It was after midnight. The family was heading home, packed into their large town coach decorated with the ornate Sperling crest on the door, lulled by the steady clip-clop of the team of four matched grays. Jane and Edmund rode backward. Squeezed in across were Aunt Eugenia, Mama, and Christabell, glowing with excitement as only a belle in her first Season could glow.

"What a thrill to be in London," she exclaimed. "The soirées—the balls—the beaux—isn't this all too marvelous? Did you see me dancing with Lord Beckford? Did you see how he looked at me? I vow, if Jane doesn't marry soon, I shall *die* from impatience."

Jane gave a pat to her sister's knee. "Rest easy, Christabell. I shall marry soon, *loath* though I am to find a mate." She cast a mock accusing glance at Mama, knowing Mama couldn't see it in the dark.

Christabell protested, "But you were the belle of the ball tonight, suitors flocking all about you. You can take your pick. I cannot understand why you're so reluctant to marry."

"Well, I am," Jane replied. Was it her conversation tonight with Dashmont that made her realize how much she had been dissembling? "But I won't meet my true love among those foppish dandies on the dance floor. I may never meet him."

"How can you say that?" asked Christabell, astonished.

"Let it go, my dear," Mama swiftly interrupted. Jane discerned her chastising tone. Mama continued, "Is Lord Beckford special, Christabell?"

In a mock despairing voice Christabell lamented, "Yes, but what's the use? *Jane* must marry first, but she keeps saying no.

What if she never says yes? Then I shall waste away to a withered, old, unmarried crone."

"Nonsense," proclaimed Aunt Eugenia. "Why, just tonight I extended invitations to two fine possibilities—Lords Slingsby and Bradbourne. The latter, of course, being by far the better choice."

"It won't do any good, Aunt," said Jane. "I detest Lord Bradbourne."

"Old Bony Fingers," said Christabell, "that's what we call him."

"She's right," Jane continued, "I cannot abide those long, bony fingers of his, besides which, he smells like a musty old catacomb."

"Best not speak too hastily, Jane," Mama interceded in her usual placating voice. "Lord Bradbourne possesses a better title and ten times the fortune as Lord Slingsby."

She sounds so tired tonight, thought Jane. Ordinarily Mama remained cheerful, despite physical difficulties brought on by bearing so many children in such a short time.

Jane sighed with impatience. "Lord Bradbourne is a widower three times over, Mama. None of his wives died in childbirth. Are you not curious as to why they all died so young?"

"Point well taken," remarked Edmund. "I've played cards with Bradbourne at Brooks. He's a cold fish, all right. I've never seen him laugh, or even smile, except when he's getting the better of some poor fool who's about to go under. He's a scoundrel when it comes to cards. Come to think of it, I've even seen him beat Papa a time or two."

Edmund's words were followed by a long, uncomfortable silence. It was as if the very mention of Papa's gambling had cast an instant cloud of gloom. In the darkness of the carriage, Jane heard Mama heave a heavy sigh. She felt a pang of unease again. Could Papa's money problems be that serious?

Christabell distracted her thoughts by asking, "Isn't there a third possibility, Jane? I saw you dancing with Lord Dashmont. I must say, he looked exceedingly graceful, as well as devilishly handsome. You appeared to be enjoying yourself."

"That rake," Jane exclaimed. "Not even remotely is he a possibility. I found his lack of manners most intolerable."

Edmund guffawed. "Didn't appear so to me. Chrissy's right. You looked positively blissful dancing with the handsome widower. He's outrageously rich, you know. Not only from his estate here in England, but he makes immense profits from his sugar, some of which he turns into an exquisite dark rum that he ships to Boston."

Christabell asked, "Edmund, tell us how his wife died."

Thank you, sister, Jane thought to herself. She, too, was curious, but would never deign to ask.

"Terrible tragedy," recounted her brother, "all brought on by Georgiana's reckless self-indulgence. What a spoiled little chit she was. Had to have a high-perched phaeton so she could drive through the park and impress the *ton*. At first Anthony forbade it, as well he should. Such an unstable design. But she wheedled and cajoled, claiming if Lady Archer could handle her High Flyer by herself, than so could she. Finally, Anthony gave in, even though Georgiana possessed no skill with the whip and refused to learn. Not long after, when she was racing recklessly through the park one afternoon, mind you, with her small son by her side, the phaeton flipped. She flew out, landing beneath the wheels of a passing dray. Alas, the poor creature was killed instantly, all of it witnessed by the boy."

"Was he hurt?" asked Jane, distressed by the tragic story.

"He was uninjured, though to this day has never been the same."

How horrible, Jane thought as the carriage rolled to a stop in front of the grand Corinthian portico of Chalton House. But her thoughts were distracted when she heard her mother sadly murmur, "Do you suppose Papa has come home?"

"The odds are against it," Edmund answered in a troubled voice. "No doubt he's still at his club."

Gambling. Jane felt the pleasure of the evening suddenly slip away.

"The night is young, Anthony," Tatton remarked as they fought through the after-the-ball crowd to his four-wheeled Landau with its two matching bays. "Are you on for a trip to Brooks? Or perhaps a visit to your dear old friend Brilliana would be in order."

"I don't think so," Anthony replied, unenthused.

"What this?" Tatton asked, feigning astonishment. "Could it be you have forgotten those nights of bliss?" He jabbed Anthony in the ribs. "As I recall, many's the tale you used to relate about Brilliana's liveliness and most affectionate nature, not to mention—"

"Not tonight," Anthony interrupted tersely.

Tatton was silent a moment, deep in thought. "That little chit you danced with—Lady Jane."

"What about her?"

"You seemed taken with her."

Anthony scowled. "I found her a silly girl with no depth to her at all."

"But aren't they all? These little chits go to great lengths to conceal whatever intelligence they possess when we're around."

And Lady Jane has none, Anthony reflected sourly. He recalled her supercilious statements about the men he'd pointed out. Lord Farley had a silly laugh. Heathcart was doomed because of sawdust in his breeches. Poor Viscount Landsdale considered himself the fashion plate of London, but she, ruthless creature, had skewered him over the way he tied his cravat.

It was galling that he had been unable to put the silly baggage out of his thoughts this evening, to the point he was distracted and had no desire to visit Brilliana, whose vibrant nature and warm enthusiasm, especially in bed, he vividly recalled. That must quickly change. "I'm still tired from the journey, Tatton. But starting tomorrow, I shall be back to my old haunts again."

Tatton looked relieved. "I was beginning to wonder if you were regretting your return to England, wishing you were back on that dismal island again."

Dismal? Anthony had been born on Jamaica. His father, a raucous giant of a man with giant tastes, kept him home long past the age other plantation owners sent their sons to England for their education, most never to return. But William, the fifth Earl of Dashmont, insisted his only son ride by his side each day, overseeing the green, slightly rolling fields of Montclaire. Anthony had easily absorbed all there was to know: how to

oversee the six hundred workers with a fair but firm hand; how
to schedule work; how to exercise sharp judgment as to
whether it was more profitable to send a shipload of surplus
molasses to England or to Boston. Growing up lean and sinewy,
Anthony knew he could never reach the physical stature of his
father, but he grew up just as hard, just as tough. "Hard work
makes the man," his father would bellow. "Be tough. Believe in
yourself. No matter what the turmoil, keep your balance. Never
question what you've done. If you did it, it was right. You're
daft if you ever waste a moment on regrets."

Anthony never did. When he was sixteen, the family was
compelled to return to its vast estates in England because of his
mother's health. He went reluctantly, but soon fell in with the
delights of *haut ton* living, and never returned until out of necessity, two and a half years ago. But now, thinking of his
beloved Jamaica, he remembered a spot not far from the big
house where far vistas could be seen: the Atlantic to the north,
the Caribbean to the west, each body of water a sparkling blue,
edged with swaying palm trees and white sand. *Dismal? No,
never.* But Tatton had never been there. Tatton would never
know.

Chapter 3

Late the next afternoon, Jane stood by the fireplace in her spacious green-and-white bedchamber. Idly, she gazed at the white porcelain elephant that was part of the giltmetal clock on her mantel. She had loved this clock from as far back as she could remember—first at the family's country estate, Hedley Hall, now here in London. The elephant stood upon an ornate gold base. Across its back hung a tapestry molded from the porcelain, painted with delicate pink and green Japanese figures. The clock itself was mounted atop the tapestry in a round, giltmetal frame, its glazed enamel dial set within a Japanese porcelain case. The elephant was young, with a merry twinkle in his eye, and appeared almost to be smiling. As a small child, Jane had named the elephant Timmy, and thought of him as her good luck piece. How often had she gazed upon Timmy with delight when she was little? Sometimes through tears, she thought wryly, when she had been sent to her room as a punishment.

Which happened often, she thought, remembering what an obstinate little girl she had been and the trouble she had caused her nanny.

Jane gave Timmy a rub for good luck, then turned to her harlequin desk, where lay one of her ancient manuscripts, the secret interest which she had almost revealed to that rake last night. Thank goodness, she had not. No doubt he would have laughed at her, just like her family, and informed her that for a highborn young lady such an interest was most unseemly.

She sat at her desk, eager to examine the last of the ancient books she had brought with her from Hedley Hall. It came from a whole trunkful of such manuscripts, all inscribed by Cistercian monks in the eleventh and twelfth centuries. They had been acquired by Robert, Lord Sperling, first Earl of Hedley, her great-great-great-great-great-grandfather. He had rescued them from Stanholm Priory, which for centuries had existed not far from Hedley Hall. But in 1537, Stanholm Priory was looted and burned to the ground, a result of the Great Suppression instigated by Henry VIII, whose desire was to destroy every monastery in England. Thank heavens, the first Lord Sperling had possessed enough good sense to intervene in time to save the manuscripts from going up in flames. She had wondered if he was motivated by greed and concluded, probably. According to ancient catalogs, many of the manuscripts had been embellished with gold, jewels, and enamels, matching the splendor of the altar vessels. But the more ornate ones had all disappeared—sold, most likely, by the first Lord Sperling or his descendants. Perhaps she should not condemn him. For all she knew, his motive for saving the entire monastic library wasn't greed at all, but a prescient sense of history.

She would never know. And it didn't matter. All that counted was her joy and pride in rescuing what remained of the precious manuscripts that had lain in a musty trunk in the attic all these years, until one day she had found them. Only the plainer ones were left, but even they were leather-covered, some with exquisite tooling, and with ornate clasps. From the age of twelve, when she began learning Greek and Latin, she had toiled over these manuscripts. It had not been easy. She had no expert to advise her, and her family didn't care. As best she could, she had taught herself to catalog the ancient manuscripts, then translate the text to English from their original language.

"At it again, eh?" Edmund's voice. He had come up behind her and laid a friendly hand on her shoulder.

"Look at this one, Edmund." Eagerly she pointed to the cover. "See the fancy tooling?" With care she unhooked the gold clasp and opened the ancient volume. "It's similar to *The Book of Hours*. See how it looks three-dimensional?" She pointed to a gold, blue, and purple decorated letter on the first page of vellum. "Much, I should say, like a psalter made at Winchester in the time of King Athelstan. Notice the blue. It's so deep it must be mixed with lapis lazuli." Eyes alight, she twisted in her chair to look directly at Edmund. "Do you realize lapis lazuli is one of the most exotic minerals in the *world*? It comes only from Afghanistan. The mines there were described by Marco Polo, who visited them at the end of the thirteenth century. Think of it!"

"Oh, indeed, I think of it constantly," replied Edmund, straight-faced, with only a hint around his lips that he was teasing. "It's positively exhilarating. I'm so thrilled—"

"Fie on you," she replied and gave him a playful shove. Edmund had not the slightest interest in ancient monastery manuscripts. But at least he attempted to support her interest, as opposed to the rest of her family. Not only that, she would be eternally grateful that he came to her defense years ago when she had professed that her heart's desire was to learn Greek and Latin.

"Not suitable for girls," Papa had roared, and pointed to a much reworked sampler Jane had just completed. "The girl needs to improve her needlework."

"What matter whether my tutor teaches one pupil or two?" Edmund had reasoned, finally so convincing that Papa had relented.

"But you are to keep it to yourself, Jane," Aunt Eugenia had warned. "Young ladies have no need for Greek and Latin. 'Tis most unbecoming."

But unbecoming or not, Jane had learned both languages and loved them. She pointed to the ancient manuscript again. "Sad to say, this is the last of them—"

Suddenly Christabell burst into the room. Jane noticed immediately that her wide blue eyes, usually sparkling with gaiety, were clouded with worry. "Whatever is the matter?"

"I am most upset." Dressed in a blue-ribboned gown of white muslin, Christabell boosted herself onto the four-poster bed, clasped her hands, and dangled her feet in their soft blue leather shoes. "Mama and Papa are quarreling. I would not have believed it, had I not stood outside their chamber door and heard it with my own ears." A look of wonderment crossed her face. "Arguing!"

Jane looked skeptical. "Mama never quarrels. Have you ever

known a time when Mama didn't acquiesce, and Papa didn't get his way?"

"No longer," declared Christabell. "All I know is, she shouted at him."

"But I have never in my whole life heard Mama shout, or even raise her voice."

"I know what I heard."

"What were they arguing about?" asked Edmund. "Was it money? What did Papa say?"

"Hardly a word." Christabell flung her hands out in astonishment. "They were talking about money, near as I could tell, and Mama was doing all the talking. Fancy Papa with his mouth shut, allowing Mama to berate him." Her face clouded. "I'm afraid something terrible has happened."

Jane saw that her younger sister was close to tears. She turned to her brother. "Say something to reassure her, Edmund."

"How can I do that?" Edmund asked with a cynical raise of his eyebrows. "I do not wish to alarm you, Chrissy, but it's quite possible Papa's gambling losses are so heavy he's close to bankruptcy."

Christabell gasped. "That cannot be."

Jane shot a cross look at her brother. "Of course it cannot be. You know how Edmund tends to exaggerate."

"But think of it, Jane," Christabell cried, "what if it's true and Papa's fortune is gone? We would have no dowries, no fine clothes, or jewels, or lady's maids. We would be obliged to leave London and live in some dreary hovel alongside the peasants in the countryside. I would find such a fate totally unendurable."

"You?" exclaimed Edmund, "what about me? I'm the first and only son, remember? I stand to lose my entire inheritance. For all I know, I could be out on the streets tomorrow, hawking fish in Leather Lane."

Jane sat on the bed beside her sister and put a comforting arm around her shoulders. "Don't worry, they're probably quarreling over something silly. Doesn't Mama have a right to lose her temper after all these years? Besides, 'tis none of our business, and you should not have been eavesdropping. Now ring for

Sarah and tell her to lay out a bonnet and walking dress." She paused, making sure her voice sounded light and carefree. "I have just decided we need fresh air. I'll wager a stroll through Hyde Park will raise your spirits." She glanced at her elephant clock on the mantel. "Nearly five o'clock. Perfect. We shall arrive at Hyde Park in time for the fashionable hour."

Christabell brightened. "What a marvelous idea. We shall indeed don our very finest and impress the *ton*."

Jane's spirits also lifted. How silly to be concerned with such trivial problems.

"'Tis time for our ride through the park, Anthony," Lady Cavendish announced in her shrewish voice.

"I am aware of that, madame."

Standing in the front entry hall of his spacious London town house, Anthony had, as usual, to make a conscious effort to conceal his dislike of his deceased wife's mother, who stood before him now, her straight-backed, thinnish figure gowned in dreary black bombazine, her black reticule gripped in her skinny fingers, dangling just so. Every move she made was just so, Anthony reflected glumly. He wondered if his mother-in-law, who was both humorless and unaffectionate, had ever performed one carefree, uninhibited act in her entire adult existence. Not likely. Lady Amanda Cavendish had a rule for everything except breathing. No doubt she would regulate that, too, if she could.

"I am ready, Mama," said Hortense. Georgiana's only sister was a colorless little creature who seldom smiled. She had been "sickly" all her life, or so her mother claimed, and at twenty-one was still under Mama's heavy thumb with not a prospect of a life of her own. A pity. She could actually be attractive if she did something with her hair, and if her mother did not keep her bundled up in those dreary, dark clothes. Hortense's plight had been bad enough before Georgiana died, but now was even worse, what with Lady Cavendish's unrelenting overprotection of her only remaining child.

Georgiana . . . at least she'd possessed a bit of spark, Anthony mused, albeit not much else in her selfish little head.

"We shall spend exactly one hour in the park," Lady

Cavendish decreed in her tight-lipped manner, "after which we shall return for tea." She reached down and gripped her grandson's shoulder. "How does that sound, David? I should imagine you'll be highly pleased to see all the *ton* dressed to the nines for the fashionable hour. Hyde Park at five in the afternoon is the grandest show in London. The Prince Regent himself might come riding by."

"Yes, Grandmama," David mumbled, then pressed himself against her skirt and stuck a thumb in his mouth.

Lady Cavendish continued, "We shall take your hoop and stick along, David, in case you want to play."

Not likely, thought Anthony. His mother-in-law hardly inspired fun and frivolity.

"Shall you be riding in the carriage with us, Anthony?" inquired Hortense.

Ride with those two dreary women? Heaven forbid. "Thor is in need of exercise," he quickly replied. "I've sent instructions to Timmons to saddle him up." *Thank God for my horse,* he thought. The farther he could distance himself, the better. He smiled down at David. "Would you care to ride with me, son? I can set you in front of me on the saddle."

"No," the little boy cried, cringing closer against his grandmother's skirts, jamming his thumb further into his mouth. A tear rolled down his cheek. "I'm scared of horses."

Anthony could only suppress a "Damme!" by gritting his teeth. He looked down at his delicate, sandy-haired son and cringed inwardly. *My only child a coward.* Gone was the little boy who could carelessly track mud across a Brussels carpet and haven't a care; who could brazenly filch a biscuit from Cook despite stern warnings; who knew not the words docile and obedient and when thwarted, stamped his foot. That little boy had disappeared the day Georgiana died. *I must accept the fact,* Anthony told himself for at least the thousandth time. He should be accustomed to the pain by now and accept what he could not change. More than once, he had questioned his decision to place David in his dour grandmother's care. But it had seemed wise at the time. Now it seemed too late to change. David was Grandmama's good little boy now, hardly saying a word, obedient, silent, withdrawn, afraid of his own shadow. *Totally without spirit.*

Not only that, Lady Cavendish, along with Hortense, had firmly entrenched herself at Anthony's opulent estate. She would never admit it, of course, but she was in her glory as mistress of Fairfield Manor, and would abhor returning to her drafty, in-need-of-repair country house in Cornwall.

Anthony looked into his small son's fearful eyes. "Very well, David," he replied evenly. "You may ride with your grandmama and Aunt Hortense. I'll ride alongside. 'Tis a lovely day for a ride, do you not agree, Lady Cavendish?" *One more day,* he thought as he forced a smile. Then the three of them would be gone again, back to Fairfield Manor. What a relief to be rid of them. A heaviness centered in his chest as he realized what he had been thinking. *But it's true—I love my son dearly, but can scarcely tolerate the sight of him.*

The fashionable hour was at its height. As Anthony's town coach rolled slowly, majestically, through Hyde Park, Anthony followed close behind, mounted on Thor. *To think, there was a time when I accepted this,* Anthony mused as he bowed to the Duchess of Rutland, driving swiftly by in her two-wheeled *vis-à-vis.* Today he was finding his only enjoyment lay in viewing the dazzling display of horses, some said the finest in the world, all coddled, these prime bits of blood, and groomed to a high gloss. Indeed, smart rigs with matching, high-stepping horses were all the crack. He took great pleasure in seeing them trot swiftly by.

As for the rest, he had never cared a groat for "the finest show in London," and had only joined in for Georgiana's sake. He had never cared to join the simpering dandies in their blue, brass-buttoned coats, their white cravats so stiff and deep they couldn't possibly see their boots while standing. Nor had he ever been impressed by the highborn ladies in their ornate carriages, or the young ladies on horseback preening in their finest feathers to impress the *ton.* And especially had he never been impressed by the sumptuously bedecked Cyprians, all on the lookout for a wealthy protector. Doubtless he would soon recognize one of them—he had not been gone *that* long—and could easily seize the opportunity to renew old acquaintances. Somehow the thought did not excite him. But for what other reason had he returned to England, other than his son, of course, except to gamble at his old haunts in St. James's Street and revisit the delights of the beautiful actresses and Cyprians he had known? *But suddenly I don't care,* he thought with a jolt. *Give me the green fields of Montclaire any time.*

He had just surprised himself. *I must still be tired from the voyage,* he assured himself as he rode along. *Should not have attended the ball.* Which reminded him, a question had been nagging at him all day. *What compelled me to dance with the Sperling chit?* A vision of the tall, slender girl in the blue satin gown danced through his head again, as it had done continuously since last night. He could find no good reason why he had impulsively crossed the dance floor and asked Edmund to introduce them. Curiosity, he supposed.

Halfway through the park, Lady Cavendish exclaimed with a haughty sniff, "Look there. See those two young women walking toward us?"

Following his mother-in-law's gaze, Anthony caught sight of two young females strolling along the winding pathway beside the road, followed by their lady's maid in gray. One was a pretty blonde in a peach-colored gown and matching poke bonnet. The other looked absolutely smashing in a pink-and-white silk strolling gown trimmed with roses, on her head a bonnet of pink velvet topped with an ostrich plume. *Lady Jane.* To his surprise, his heart lurched at sight of her. *But whatever for?* Considering her impudence last night, and her vain, empty-headed demeanor, there was no reason.

"It's the two older Sperling girls," his mother-in-law continued. "How can they dare even show their faces after that disgraceful *on-dit* flying around?"

What on-dit? Anthony pressed Thor close to the carriage. He was loathe to ask—to give credence in any way to the vitriol that constantly dripped from mother-in-law's lips—but he had to know. "Rumors about the Sperlings? What do you mean?"

"Well you should ask," Lady Cavendish informed him smugly. " 'Tis beyond rumor. Sperling has gambled away much of his fortune. He is on the verge of bankruptcy."

How appalling, thought Anthony, not allowing his personal feelings to show. Still sitting easily astride his mount, he watched the two young ladies approaching ever closer.

Christabell was the first to spot him. Clutching Jane's sleeve, she cried, "Oh, look, sister, 'tis Lord Dashmont, that 'dreadful' man you met at the ball last night."

"Indeed it is," Jane said, trying to sound offhanded, although her heart had just taken a small leap. As the carriage rolled closer, she noticed Lady Cavendish, a woman she had met once or twice, so she smiled and nodded.

Anthony watched closely. Just as he suspected, Lady Cavendish did not return the greeting, but instead turned to her daughter. "You shall not nod when we pass by, Hortense. We do not acknowledge a family that is in disgrace."

"The devil you won't," exclaimed Anthony, fighting back instantaneous rage. He was off his horse in an instant, striding toward the two young women now standing in the middle of the path, looking rather confused. "And a good afternoon to you, Lady Jane and Lady Christabell," he said with a sweeping, exaggerated bow.

Why is he being so friendly? Jane wondered. Christabell smiled brightly and bobbed a curtsy, whereas Jane answered with a perfunctory greeting and a near imperceptible dip.

But if Lord Dashmont was aware of Jane's cool greeting, he took no notice and called toward his carriage, "Just look whom we have encountered, ladies." To Jane and Christabell he said, "Come, have you met my family?"

They followed Lord Dashmont to his carriage. While he opened the door and performed the introductions, it did not escape Jane's notice that he cast a piercing gaze at his mother-in-law, seeming to warn her she had best be polite. But how could that be? Jane wondered, and when Lady Cavendish and her daughter both gave their nods, she convinced herself she had not been about to be snubbed, even though both nods were brief and unsmiling. The young boy was unsmiling, too. How strange, she thought. A child this age should be spirited and lively, not somber-faced and cringing against his grandmama. But still, all little children delighted her heart, so she bent into the carriage, took up his hand, and shook it warmly. "Good afternoon, David, I am honored to meet you."

The boy remained silent. Jane pretended not to notice. "How old are you?" she inquired with a smile.

"He's nine," Anthony said quickly. He did not want David mumbling, sucking on his thumb again. Loathe to see the child press further against his grandmama, Anthony reached into the carriage and swung David to the ground.

The boy stared past Jane, but she went on gamely, "And what are you studying, young man?"

Silence. Finally, repressing a sigh, Anthony answered, "Among other things, he is beginning the study of Latin, but is having some difficulty." He looked sternly at David. "My son is not fond of his tutor, but I am searching for a new one so that he *will* continue, and he *will* learn both Greek and Latin."

"Ah," she exclaimed, and to David said, "*non omnia possumus omnes.* Do you know what that means?" The boy shook his head. "That is Latin for we can't all do all things." She glanced at Anthony. "Perhaps he's not ready for a foreign language."

"Perhaps," Anthony answered noncommittally, while inside he was thinking, *does this young chit know Latin? Astounding.*

Something is wrong with this child, Jane thought sadly. How she wished she could get through to him. "Well, David," she continued, "*nosce te ipsum.* That means know thyself, which your father wishes you to do. You must decide what you want in life, for now is the time to prepare for it." She noticed the hoop lying on the floor of the carriage. "Are you good at rolling hoops, David?" Silence. The child simply stared, his large gray eyes regarding her suspiciously. *Well, I'll fix that,* she thought, finding the sad young face tugging at her heartstrings. She put out a cautious hand and said, "I have always wanted to learn how to roll the hoop. May I try?"

The boy shrugged indifferently. Jane reached for the hoop and stick and set the hoop upon the pathway.

Christabell started giggling. "Jane, you're not really—?"

"Of course I am. How hard could it be?"

Jane glanced into the carriage. Lady Cavendish was positively glaring, her lips pressed tight. Finally, she opened them enough to state indignantly, "This is most unseemly, Lady Jane. What if the Prince Regent came riding by?"

"Let him," Jane merrily replied, and set off with the hoop down the path, hitting it with the stick, but making sure it wobbled and fell. Not easy, because she had been quite good at rolling the hoop when she was a child. Her design now, though, was to fail miserably. Christabell, who obviously had discerned what she was doing, joined her, and for a time the two of them ran up and down the path, laughing and giggling as the hoop wobbled and fell time after time. Finally, Jane received the desired result. David appeared at her side, regarding her with a scorn that was ill concealed.

"You are not doing it correctly," he informed her with nine-year-old solemnity.

"I'm not?" Jane feigned astonishment. "But I thought I was doing rather well."

"Girls don't know how to roll hoops." David took the hoop and stick away from her. "Here, I'll show you."

Anthony watched fascinated as the three ran down the pathway, Jane and her sister laughing, David leading the way. Then David tripped slightly, and the hoop went wildly rolling across the lawn.

"Ha! You can't do it either," teased Jane, and to Anthony's astonishment, David laughed and, running after the hoop, called back over his shoulder, "Oh, yes I can!"

"He laughed," Anthony, who was still next to the carriage, declared aloud in amazement.

Lady Cavendish lifted her nose. "Lady Jane's antics are most unseemly. She's no lady when she dares behave like a nine-year-old. And during the fashionable hour, no less. Her mother should be told."

My son laughed. Anthony hardly noticed the stinging words of his mother-in-law, but instead, slid off his horse and headed toward the little group that was now winded and resting. By the time he reached them, David was solemn-faced again, declaring, "I'm tired. I want to go back to the carriage."

Christabell took his hand and started away, leaving Anthony staring down at Jane. Her cheeks glowed. Her eyes sparkled. Little tendrils of shiny brown curls had escaped her bonnet and hung in shiny ringlets around her face. Although her dress was modest, the fast little breaths she was taking made her full breasts heave up and down beneath the silk. *God's blood!* He could hardly keep his eyes off them. Something stirred within him. *Damme. I'm acting like an eighteen-year-old. I must pull back, or I'll act the fool.* He was hard put to sound casual, but he managed as he coolly remarked, "That was kind of you, Lady Jane. The boy is not easily drawn out."

"It was my pleasure, sir," she answered with equal aplomb and wiped a bit of dampness from her brow. She glanced at his carriage and inquired with mock solemnity, "I trust the Prince Regent did not ride by?"

Anthony laughed and answered, "I do not believe so, but he would have enjoyed the spectacle if he had." He grew serious again. "It appears you know Latin."

"I speak and write both Greek and Latin." She grinned up at him. "Are you surprised?"

"After last night, I would never have guessed. I mean . . ." He paused, aware he had not been overly tactful. "What an accomplished young lady you are."

"That's high praise coming from someone who thinks I'm such a featherbrain," she said, a meaningful gleam in her eye. She backed away. "I must leave now. High time I returned home to embroider my sampler."

Anthony folded his arms and stared at her. "You are an enigma, Lady Jane."

"In what manner, sir?"

"Last night you took great pains to act the flighty chit without a brain in her head. So I treated you accordingly, and you resented it. Now I find you really do have a brain in your head, but you seem loathe to admit it. So which is it to be? How should I treat you?"

"Your question really requires no answer," she said. "It's doubtful our paths will cross again. If they do, we are only acquaintances, so you needn't be concerned about how to treat me."

"Anthony, come," called Lady Cavendish, "we are behind our schedule."

Anthony deigned not to answer his mother-in-law. Instead,

he bowed to Lady Jane and in an amused voice replied, "But of course, we are indeed just acquaintances."

With not another word he turned and strode away.

"But why were you so rude?" asked Christabell. They were strolling toward home, and Jane had just described her parting conversation with Dashmont. "He's terribly handsome, and rich, and you must admit he was the soul of politeness."

"He's a gambler," replied Jane.

"Do you suppose Hortense has set her cap for him? I should think there's a match her mama's trying to push."

"Hortense can have him," Jane replied.

Christabell cast her sister a scornful glance. "You don't fool me, you goose. I know you're interested."

Jane was silent a moment, then decided to be honest. In a soft, sad voice she began, "Lord Dashmont is a gambler, just like our father. Think back, Christabell, to how our mother has suffered all these years from Papa's negligence. Do you think I would wish to be left alone every night while my husband haunted the halls of Brooks and Boodle's and White's and wherever else? And worse, how could I marry a man who might lose the family fortune, just like—" Jane stopped abruptly. No sense worrying Christabell unnecessarily.

"Just like Papa," Christabell finished for her. "You don't have to coddle me."

"I still say it will never happen." Biting her lip, Jane looked away, wondering how she could be so sure.

Chapter 4

It was past midnight when Anthony, Tatton by his side, mounted the steps at sixty St. James's Street, where stood their gentlemen's club, the exclusive Brooks.

"Good to be back to your old haunts, eh?" Tatton remarked as they passed through the black-and-white marble hallway toward the Great Subscription Room, the center of the club's night life, including gambling. With a jab to the ribs, Tatton continued, "When we are done, perhaps a visit to Brilliana? 'Tis high time."

Anthony didn't answer. Instead, he paused, taking in his first view of Brooks for two and a half years: the marble busts, the magnificent painted ceiling, the fine paintings that many a young nobleman had brought back from his European tour and donated to his favorite club. "Strange, Tatton. While riding my sugarcane fields, blistering under the hot Jamaican sun, I dreamed of the day I would be headed toward the gaming room at Brooks again. So here I am, but I find I have lost my enthusiasm."

Tatton shrugged. "Give it time. You looked enthusiastic enough last night when you danced with Lady Jane."

Anthony found Tatton's remark annoying, perhaps because he had been thinking continuously about that surprising young woman since last night, and especially after the accidental meeting in the park this afternoon. "She was pleasant enough, but may I remind you—?"

"That if you ever marry again, it will be that plantation owner's daughter," interrupted Tatton impatiently. He frowned in concentration. "Let's see . . . what's her name now? . . . ah, yes, Isabella Wentworth. 'Sturdy' you called her." Tatton flicked a glance of mock inquisitiveness. "Tell me, what exactly does sturdy mean? Fat, perhaps? Or does it means hefty and well muscled? In which case, 'sturdy' should come in handy on your plantation in case one of the oxen gets sick."

"Enough," Anthony declared lightly. "What she looks like is none of your concern."

As they neared the gaming room, he heard the well-remembered rattling of the dice box and the constant, low murmur of excitement. Despite his declaration of boredom, he felt the old rush of excitement. There was nothing like this in Jamaica.

"What shall you play? Faro?" Tatton inquired.

"For fools."

"Macao?"

"That, too." Anthony paused thoughtfully. "A few hands of whist should do it, and not for high stakes, since I am out of practice."

"Would that it were so," scoffed Tatton. "Regardless of how long you've been away, there's no one in the club tonight could beat you . . . except"—he frowned thoughtfully—"Lord Bradbourne, perhaps."

"Do tell," said Anthony with a skeptical raise of an eyebrow.

"The scoundrel's at the top of his game," Tatton replied appeasingly. "He's been playing at Brooks every night for at least a month. Perhaps he has no wish to return home, which is quite understandable. Who would not want to escape that cold, drafty castle of his in North Wales?"

An old gambling crony of Anthony's, the venerable Sir Godfrey Hatton, came tottering by, engrossed in counting his markers.

"Good evening, Sir Godfrey," said Anthony, "I see you've won again, as usual."

Sir Godfrey's ancient face lit with delight. "Dashmont! Delighted to see you back again. Yes, I've won again tonight"— his smile vanished—"in contrast to Robert, Lord Sperling."

"What do you mean?"

"The man's done up." Sir Godfrey shook his head in sad disbelief. "The fool's been losing heavily these past few weeks, but managed to retain at least part of his fortune. Not after this evening, though. Never have I seen such a sickening sight. He has reduced himself from wealth to near-beggary in a single night. Taken at faro by that scoundrel, Bradbourne. What a fool's game."

Tatton said, "Surely not his entire fortune."

"The knave took all. Sperling's gambled his entire estate away, down to his last guinea. Chalton House? Gone. His fine horses? Gone. His carriages? Gone, every last one. Even his daughters' dowries—"

"My word!" Tatton looked horrified. "Along with all else, Sperling has lost his mind."

Anthony thought of Lady Jane. Much too haughty and sure of herself, but dear God, she didn't deserve this.

Sir Godfrey continued, "At least he's hung on to his estate in Kent. That's all that's left as of now, but he's still in there, and heaven only knows . . ." His voice trailed off, as shaking his head he continued on his way, muttering, "Pity poor Sperling."

"Pity his family," Tatton exclaimed. They entered the gaming room, beautiful with its domed ceiling, elaborate scrollwork, and enormous chandelier, beneath which countless fortunes had been lost at the turn of a card. Nothing had changed, Anthony reflected. Oil lamps and beeswax candles still illuminated men with faces blank except for hungry eyes, playing whist or crowded around the hazard and faro tables. Immediately Anthony sensed tension. Although play went on, all eyes kept surreptitiously turning toward the faro table, where Bradbourne, acting as banker, sat behind stacks of bank notes and markers, plus two heaps of loose gold piled high upon the green baize. Across, sat Lord Sperling—or, more accurately, the quivering wreck of the man Anthony recalled as Sperling.

"Good Lord, look at him," exclaimed Tatton.

Anthony was shocked. He remembered Sperling well, had played whist with him at Brooks many a time. Sperling had been a large, imposing figure of a man, supremely arrogant, with a lionlike head, sharp blue eyes, squared chin, and full head of wavy blond hair. Tonight, however, he was deathly pale, his face tight with tension. He even seemed smaller somehow, as if he'd shrunk into his chair. His expression was blank, of course, as befitted a gentleman, but a patina of fear glistened on his forehead. He seemed in a daze as he signed a marker with shaking hands and shoved it across the table toward his opponent. "Take it," Anthony heard him say in a despairing voice, "that's the last of it."

"Not quite," replied Bradbourne, insufferably insolent.

The room fell deadly still, no one even bothering to pretend disinterest in the tragedy unfolding at the faro table.

"What do you mean?" asked Sperling.

It would have been inexpressibly bad form to smile, yet Anthony was sure he detected a slight twitching at the corners of Bradbourne's mouth. "Have you forgotten Hedley Hall?"

Sperling turned yet paler, if that were possible. "My estate? I . . . I . . . don't think . . ."

Bradbourne sat easily back in his chair and raised an eyebrow. "Giving up so soon, old fellow? Out of pity for your plight, the spirit of generosity has struck me. I feel compelled to offer you the opportunity to regain your fortune."

Sperling whispered, "How?"

"One more hand of faro. You must put up your estate in Kent. If you win"—Bradbourne made a sweeping gesture across the stack of gold, bills, and markers—"you'll have it back. If you lose . . ." He shrugged, leaving the rest unsaid.

"Sperling had it coming," Tatton whispered. "Never liked the fellow. Much too smug—prone to brag and swagger."

"He's not swaggering now," said Anthony. Tatton was right, yet tonight, with Sperling's total disgrace at hand . . . "I take no joy in seeing the ruination of the poor wretch." He thought of Lady Jane again, of that first moment he'd seen her in the blue dress across the dance floor, confidence brimming in the proud tilt of her chin as she wasted her dazzling smile on that oaf, Slingsby. Now she'd have nothing, not even a dowry, and if Bradbourne won Hedley Hall, not even a roof over her head. She most certainly would not have Slingsby, who had many a time declared he must marry well. "That rogue," Anthony muttered under his breath. "Such downright greed and avarice. Someone should . . ."

"Should what, Anthony?" asked Tatton, mildly surprised at his friend's vehemence. "Naturally, 'tis my inclination, too. Bradbourne should be dragged from his chair and pummeled thoroughly before getting chucked into the Thames, and furthermore—" Tatton froze. He had glanced toward the entryway. "Good lord, it's young Sperling, just in time to say farewell to the last of his inheritance."

Anthony also glanced toward the entryway, where stood Edmund, a sick expression on his face, apparently already apprised that the fortune he was to inherit was gone. Seeing Anthony, the young man approached. "Is it true?" he inquired in a broken whisper.

Nodding, Anthony rested a sympathetic hand on Edmund's shoulder. "He's lost all to Bradbourne except your estate in Kent. Now that, too, is on the table."

"That scoundrel!" Edmund clenched his fists. His face reddened. He moved to charge toward the faro table, but was quickly grabbed on either side by Anthony and Tatton.

"You cannot make a scene," Tatton whispered fiercely. "Control yourself."

Before Edmund could answer, they were again drawn to the drama taking place at the faro table. Looking half in a daze, Sperling had been staring across the green baize at his lost fortune. "Hedley Hall against all you've won tonight?" he finally managed.

"That's the wager." Bradbourne's eyes were hard as granite. "Take it or leave it." A cruel smile twitched his lips. "What's it to be, Sperling? Quickly. I haven't all night."

Not a glass clinked. Not a coin rattled. The attention of the entire roomful of gamblers was riveted upon the two men at the faro table. Even Edmund had stopped struggling, and, like the rest, stared at the two faro players as if in a trance.

"Well, Sperling?" Bradbourne drummed his fingers impatiently.

"He cannot," Edmund whispered under his breath despairingly.

"Steady, Edmund, he can," Tatton said. Aside to Anthony he whispered, "Bad enough Sperling has tossed up his entire fortune, but the family home as well? Good God! Aside from Edmund, the man's got Jane, Christabell, and the three little girls still at home."

Where would they go? Anthony wondered. What of Lady

Jane? He pictured her lighthearted manner, that proud tilt of her head. Strange, he ought to be laughing at the downfall of such a vain young creature, but instead he found himself feeling nothing but sympathy. She, who had been the belle of the ball, fending off suitors right and left—how would she cope with losing all, including her dowry?

Sperling was about to speak again. He appeared to be having difficulty choking the words out. "All right, Bradbourne, I agree. One more hand of faro." He picked up a chip and moved it indecisively back and forth over the complete suit of cards, in spades, enameled on the green felt. Upon which card should he drop the chip? Anthony could well understand the dilemma causing Sperling's vacillation. The right choice would redeem him. The wrong choice meant the utter ruination of the entire Sperling family.

"The six," said Sperling finally, dropping his chip on the six of spades. "To win."

"No doubt for his six children," Tatton whispered. "A pity he didn't think of them sooner."

Anthony was too absorbed in the scene to answer. He knew Bradbourne. Had, in fact, gambled with him early on, but then avoided the man because he suspected him of being a Captain Sharp. *Takes one to know one,* he thought uneasily. Not that Anthony had ever cheated, contrary to the opinion of Sir Lucien Sykes, but he knew all the tricks and ways to cheat, and had long been wise to Bradbourne. Nothing he cared to prove, though. He had simply avoided the man, and thus had never been pressed to call him out.

"Do you think he will cheat?" Tatton asked, as if reading his thoughts.

"With a hundred pair of eyes upon him?" Anthony's mouth pulled into a sour grin. "Perhaps . . . in fact, he probably will, but he's so adept I warrant no one will catch it."

Anthony found himself holding his breath as the play began. Fascinated as the rest, he watched Bradbourne shuffle a new deck of cards, then present them to Sperling for the cut. He discarded the top card, the "soda," which was never used. Now came the suspense. It was a simple game. Bradbourne would deal two cards at a time, face up, one to the right, one to the left.

If any six appeared first to the right, Bradbourne won. Any six first to the left would bring Sperling's salvation.

Bradbourne slapped a card to the right. An eight. A visible sigh of relief swept the room. He slapped a card to the left. A three. No one had won or lost.

Tension mounted as Bradbourne went through three more rounds: An ace, a four—a five, a queen—a nine, an eight.

"Still four sixes in the deck," Tatton tensely whispered, "I vow, my heart's pounding. It's got to be soon."

Anthony felt his own heart pounding. He looked at Sperling, who sat with shoulders hunched, face tense and drawn, gazing with anguished eyes as each card was laid down. Anthony had never much cared for the man, whose superior air he found quite annoying. Truth was, if not for Sperling's family, he'd not shed a tear for a man who was fool enough to toss up his entire fortune. *But his family. Lady Jane. Come on, Bradbourne, give us a six to the left.*

"I cannot bear this suspense," Tatton murmured again. "Where are the sixes hiding? It's got to be the next play."

All those in the room seemed to know it, too. There was a collective holding of breath as Bradbourne slipped the next card off the deck, turned it, and dropped it to his right.

A six.

Bradbourne had won, to a collective gasp of dismay.

Looking as if he had seen the gates of hell, Sperling stood, so abruptly his chair tipped back and crashed to the floor. "I shall have my solicitor draw up the papers," he announced in a numb voice, and, looking neither right nor left, headed toward the door. At the entryway, Edmund blocked his path.

"Papa, how could you?" Edmund shook his head in shocked disbelief. "All is lost. My God, what will Mama do? And Aunt? And where will my little sisters go?"

"Stop it, I cannot bear to hear this," Lord Sperling cried in torment. Covering his eyes with one hand, he stumbled from the room, a broken man.

Tatton shrugged and commented, "Someone had better keep an eye on him. More than one man's blown his brains out for losing far less than Sperling just did."

With alarm, Anthony realized Tatton was right. Without another word, he spun on his heel and abruptly left the room. He must find Sperling. The man carried a pistol, and there had been a look of complete hopelessness in his eyes.

Sperling had not left the building, the doorman informed Anthony. With frantic haste, Anthony retraced his steps up the main hallway, swiftly opening each door. At last he opened the door of a small anteroom and found Sperling, tears streaking down his face, standing in the middle of the room holding a pistol to his head.

Anthony froze. "Don't be a fool, Robert," he said in a soft, controlled voice.

Sperling kept the gun to his temple. "Why not?" he cried. "What have I left to live for?"

"Your wife . . . your children . . ."

Sperling laughed bitterly. "Live to see them reduced to poverty?"

"So you're taking the coward's way out."

Sperling's hand trembled, yet he did not move the pistol. "Fortune has deserted me. You don't understand."

"But I do. I have known grief, same as you. But I never thought of killing myself."

"You ran away instead."

Anthony nodded. "Yes, I did run away, although you're the only man on earth I've ever admitted it to. That silly duel wasn't the only reason I sailed to my plantation in the West Indies."

"How can I run away? I've lost my horses, my carriages"— he laughed bitterly—"I've not money enough to hire a hackney to the docks."

"If nothing else, can you not think of your family?" Anthony entreated. "They face financial ruin tomorrow. Must they also learn you've blown your brains out, too? For God's sake, man, be rational. Run away if you must . . ." He suddenly remembered—"Here's a thought, Sperling, I understand there's a ship at the West India Docks, making ready to set sail for America."

For a long, agonizing moment Sperling didn't move, then slowly lowered the gun. "America . . ." Anthony saw a glimmer of hope in the broken man's eyes. "I could get a new start . . . make my fortune . . . return to England some day."

"Of course you can. But I daresay you must hurry. The ship sails at first light."

Sperling put the gun away and drew his shoulders back in resolute fashion. "I shall need your assistance, Dashmont, if you don't mind. I'll need to stop by my home, my solicitor's, then on to the docks." With an ironic twist he added, "I'll need a lift, since I no longer own a horse and carriage. And also, old friend, could you see fit to loan me the fare to America?"

Anthony assumed his blank face. "I shall gladly give you a lift, the fare, and a little extra." It would be bad form to comment further on Sperling's attempt at suicide, so he said nothing, concealing his great relief that he would not be witness to a man ending his life before his very eyes.

They started for the front door, Sperling ahead. Tatton came up beside Anthony, saying low, "I heard you. You saved the poor wretch's life. That was remarkable, old man."

"Thanks, Tatton," Anthony replied grimly. The tragedy of the scene had put him in no mood for compliments. "Have the doorman bring our carriage around. We must get Sperling on his way to America."

Chapter 5

It was still early morning when the butler appeared at the door of Anthony's dressing room and announced Mister Tatton Fulwood had arrived. Tatton, gray eyes bleary, entered close behind, declaring, "I vow, I am still not awake after chasing about with you and Sperling half the night." He threw himself into a carved beech armchair, stretched, and yawned. "I had two hours sleep at most."

"I, too," Anthony absentmindedly replied, "but we must get to Chalton House early, before the news gets out." Standing in his knit footed drawers and spotlessly clean muslin linen, he addressed his valet. "I had better dress to the nines today, Haskins. My green frock coat and nankeen britches . . . the Hessian boots . . . leather gloves . . . beaver hat . . . silver handled walking stick." He frowned and sighed. "I don't relish this. You are not obliged to accompany me, you know."

Tatton sniffed. "What else would get me up at this ungodly hour? But why should *you* be the bearer of such ill tidings? Surely Sperling's solicitor will be going round to Chalton House this morning. Why not give the letter to him?"

"I gave Sperling my word that I would personally deliver his letter into the hands of his wife, and so I shall," Anthony replied in a voice that did not invite further comment. With his valet's help he donned his morning outfit. Done, he stepped back and examined himself in the mirror.

"Simple but elegant," commented Tatton. "Lady Jane will no doubt swoon at the sight of you."

"If she swoons, it will be because her father's run off, the family fortune's squandered, and her life ruined," Anthony replied tersely.

"But there's nothing more you can do," Tatton argued as he followed Anthony down to the breakfast room.

"I am aware of that." Anthony realized his answer was more sharp than intended, but he was finding himself hard put to be civil. The burden of bearing such tragic tidings to the Sperling family had enveloped him in gloom this morning, but no sense taking his anger out on Tatton. How many friends did he have who would present themselves at his door at this hour, just to be of help?

But his friend could not keep his mouth closed. After they seated themselves at the breakfast table, Tatton reminded him, "Also, as I recall, you promised you would do what you could for Sperling's family. Now, there's a hazardous trap if ever there was one."

Anthony glared. "You need *not* put in your oar, Tatton."

"But surely you're not obligated. Good Lord, man, what were you thinking of? Is it Lady Jane? Are you smitten with her? I vow—"

"Utter nonsense." Anthony threw down his napkin. He would have said more, but the butler appeared to announce the arrival of an uninvited guest. "Slingsby? At this hour? Oh, well, send him in."

Lord Slingsby entered, looking quite the dandy in his brown double-breasted cutaway frock coat with velvet-lined collar and sleeves that were cut full, almost puffed, at the shoulders. *Lord help me if I ever dress as foppishly as that,* thought Anthony. He noted Slingsby's usually vacuous face was flushed with excitement.

"Is it true?" Slingsby inquired without so much as a greeting.

"Good morning, Slingsby. Do sit down. Would you care for some breakfast?" Anthony indicated one of his German gilt-wood side chairs and took a leisurely sip of tea before inquiring, "Is *what* true?"

His visitor seated himself and eagerly continued, "It's all over London that Sperling lost his entire fortune at Brooks last night and has fled England. Is he truly dished up? Has he really taken ship to America?"

"He has lost everything," Tatton interjected. "Sperling is as broke as a ragged beggar on the streets."

"Good Lord!" Slingsby sat back in astonishment, but managed to inquire, "And the dowries? Are they also gone?"

"You mean Lady Jane's, of course," Anthony commented in an ice-edged voice.

"Of course." Slingsby seemed oblivious to Anthony's enmity.

"No dowries. Lady Jane is without a farthing, as is Lady Christabell."

"What a pity," Slingsby exclaimed. "My heart goes out to them, of course. I am devastated."

"You conceal it well," Anthony commented. "One would never guess that underneath that brave facade you are awash in misery."

Slingsby did not appear to have caught Anthony's contempt. "I had my eye on Lady Jane. Matter of fact, her great aunt, Lady Fanshawe, had invited me to tea today. I shall send my regrets, of course. Damn shame. I had been counting on it."

Anthony struggled to show no indication that beneath his smooth demeanor he yearned to grab this silly beggar by his fancy frock coat, give his matching breeches a good swift boot, and toss him out the door. Instead, he managed, "How deucedly inconvenient for you, old man. My heart bleeds. In fact—" He felt a nudge beneath the table. It was Tatton, warning him not to lose his head. His friend was right, of course. No earthly good would come from insulting pudding-headed Slingsby, who could not begin to comprehend stinging sarcasm anyway.

"What a strange mood you're in," Tatton commented after Slingsby, still in a dither, had departed.

"And I'll be in this mood until I deliver Sperling's letter, so let's get on with it, shall we?" Anthony thought of Lady Jane—no doubt still asleep at this early hour—and what a horrible shock was in store for her when she awoke. Of course. That's why he had been thinking of her so much. It was only pity.

An errant ray of sunshine teased Jane awake. For a minute or two she snuggled deep into her quilts, thinking of plans for the day. She, Mama, Aunt, and Christabell were going to pay a call this afternoon at the magnificent mansion of Lady Claridge. Oh, good. She would wear her new plum velvet spencer over her white muslin gown . . . the matching plum velvet slippers, of course . . . her embroidered bag with tassels . . . her tucked silk bonnet with lace frills and a ribbon bow knot over that Titus hairdo that Sarah always did so well.

This morning she would work on the last manuscript from Hedley Hall, and also . . . she couldn't think what, but there was something else . . . something warm and tantalizing tucked away in the back of her head that would be enjoyable to think about . . . ah, yes, Lord Dashmont. *Wicked man.* Never would she take up with a gambler. But still . . .

He loved his son, obviously, and yesterday in the park he had been most courteous and kind. Also, she admired the humorous gleam in his eye, and the way he dressed—not all fopped up like the dandies, but elegant, though simple. She liked the tiny smile that seemed to lurk at the corners of his mouth, showing he did not take himself too seriously. It seemed, too, that in the park his eyes had lit at the sight of her, though she may have been mistaken.

But I had better not spend too much time thinking about him, she scolded herself. Lord Dashmont was a reckless gambler, just like Papa. Mama might put up with that, but *she* never would.

She was about to arise when she suddenly realized the house was deadly quiet. She lay still and listened. *How strange.* Chalton House was always bursting with activity at this hour. Breakfast trays rattling . . . parlor maids hauling buckets of water, shoveling ashes, scurrying up and down the back staircase. But there were none of the familiar sounds this morning, only silence.

Sarah, her maid, entered. But instead of her cheery "How did you sleep, m'lady?" she was long-faced, uttering not a word. Jane swung out of bed, wrapped her night dress around her, and demanded, "Sarah, what is wrong this morning? Why is everything so quiet?"

"Nothing's wrong, m'lady," Sarah mumbled. She gazed at an invisible spot on the floor, carefully avoiding Jane's eyes.

"Are you sure?"

Sarah could only dumbly shake her head and avert her face further.

Jane quickly dressed in a gray chintz morning gown with a ribbon-bound scalloped button closure down the front. When her toilette was complete, she hastened down the hallway to Edmund's room and knocked lightly. He didn't answer. She peeked inside. His bed had not been slept in, but she was not in the least surprised. She was not supposed to know that Edmund occasionally dallied overnight with one of his ladybirds, but of course she did.

Downstairs in the breakfast room, Mama, Aunt, and Christabell were sitting at the table, looking uneasy, no one saying a word.

"Good morning, everyone, this house is like a mausoleum this morning," Jane commented as she slid into her place.

Christabell nodded. "Bridget was quite rude to me this morning. And look, my breakfast is all burnt."

Mama gave a puzzled shrug. "The servants are acting in a most peculiar fashion, as if they know something we do not."

"Where is Papa?" Jane inquired.

Aunt sniffed with disdain. "My dear brother has probably not returned from his club yet. You know how he is."

"Mama, ask Croft," Jane whispered, "he knows everything." She nodded toward the sedate white-haired butler who was busy at the rosewood sideboard, overseeing their breakfast.

Mama crooked her finger and beckoned the butler. "Do you know the whereabouts of his lordship?"

"He is not here, madame," Croft replied in his usual stiff fashion.

"I can see that, Croft." Mama was not easily annoyed, but she had answered crossly. "Well, if he's not here, do you know where he might be?"

Croft hesitated, as if deciding whether or not to say more, then plunged ahead. "Lord Sperling appeared briefly in the middle of the night—approximately one o'clock in the morning, I should say—accompanied by Lord Dashmont and Mister Tatton Fulwood. He directed me to pack a small valise, with the barest of essentials. When I finished, he took it, and the three departed posthaste."

Jane felt her heart sink. "Did he say where he was going?"

"He did not reveal his destination."

"Oh, dear." Mama put her hand to her throat. "Something is terribly wrong."

They finished their breakfast in either gloomy speculation or dismal silence, then adjourned to the morning room. Soon Croft entered with a note on a silver platter, which he presented to Lady Fanshawe. "This just arrived by messenger, m'lady."

Aunt opened the note and read the contents. "How peculiar. Due to 'adverse circumstances' Lord Slingsby will not be coming to tea today. He sends his regrets."

Ordinarily, Jane would have been delighted she would not have to endure a boring hour with Slingsby. Instead, she felt numb. Two nights ago Slingsby would have crawled to the ends of the earth for an invitation to tea at Chalton House, but now "adverse circumstances" kept him away? What was *wrong*? Papa gone . . . Edmund gone . . . the servants acting strangely . . . and, most mysterious of all, Slingsby was sending his regrets.

Jane noticed she was not the only one upset. Mama's face was taut with anxiety, her brow increasingly furrowed.

The butler reappeared. "Lord Dashmont and Mister Tatton Fulwood to see you, m'lady."

"At this hour?" exclaimed Mama.

"It would appear so, madame." Only a slight twitching of Croft's nose indicated his opinion of persons who would dare to call before the day was half done.

When the two visitors entered the morning room, Jane was struck by how solemn-faced they both appeared. This morning there was no humorous gleam in Lord Dashmont's eye. Instead, he caught her gaze briefly, barely acknowledged the rest of the family, and proceeded straight to Mama, who was seated on a couch next to Jane. Holding a letter, he gave a slight bow and said, "Lord Sperling instructed me to put this directly into your hands, madame. It is not good news. You may wish to read it in private."

Mama shook her head. "That won't be necessary. I keep no secrets from my family."

"Then we shall stay if you like, or withdraw, whichever suits you."

"No, stay." Mama's voice was strained. Ever mindful of her

manners, she nodded toward a mahogany couch covered with striped green silk and asked them to be seated. Carefully, she unsealed the letter and read aloud:

> *My dear Henrietta, Because I have suffered a temporary loss of funds, I regret to inform you that by the time you receive this I shall be on the high seas, having taken ship to America . . .*

With an anguished cry Mama fell back on the couch, allowing the letter to flutter to the floor. "Read the rest, daughter," she cried, "for I cannot bear to."

Jane's own sudden anguish almost overcame her, but she managed to take up the letter and in a stricken voice continued:

> *Rest assured, I shall return as soon as I have regained my fortune. Meanwhile, I have instructed Mister Beckworth, our solicitor, to acquaint you with pertinent details. Sorry, my dear, it appears we have lost all. My love to the children. You may expect my return at the earliest possible moment.*
>
> *Sperling*

Jane let the letter fall to her lap. As if in a dream, she looked about her. Her mother's face was deadly pale. She still lay prone against the back of the couch and appeared too stunned to talk. Aunt Eugenia was merely staring, tongue-tied, while tears were already streaming down Christabell's anguished face. Jane's first reaction was disbelief. Papa could never do such a thing. It was inconceivable they had lost all. Surely something had been salvaged.

But before Jane, or anyone, could speak, Croft announced the arrival of Mister Beckworth.

Lord Dashmont half arose. "Perhaps we should take our leave, Tatton."

"No, no," cried Lady Sperling, "I want you to stay. There are questions . . ."

"Good morning, madame . . . everyone." Mister Beckworth, the pinch-faced, always businesslike family solicitor, wore a solemn expression that hinted at painful embarrassment as he seated himself and pulled a sheaf of papers from his valise. "Pity . . . pity," he began, "you have my sympathies, Lady Sperling, as . . . ahem! . . . does the rest of your family. Now let us see . . ." He began thumbing through his papers. "It would appear Lord Sperling lost heavily at gambling last night"—he nodded briefly at Dashmont—"as I presume you have informed them. It further appears Lord Bradbourne is now in possession of the entire Sperling estate."

Christabell cried harder. "There's nothing left?" she wailed.

"I fear not. Bradbourne won both Chalton House and Hedley Hall, complete with all furnishings, along with all your carriages, horses, and equipages. Not to mention every farthing your father ever invested." Revealing his discomfort, Beckworth tugged at his cravat and cleared his throat before continuing. "I have talked to Lord Bradbourne. He has most kindly agreed to allow you to stay until the end of the week. At that time, you must vacate the premises, leaving all behind, with the exception of your personal possessions, such as your clothes and articles of toiletry."

"End of the week?" cried Christabell, "why, that only gives us three days."

"Have we nothing left?" asked Jane in a deadly quiet voice.

"You are penniless."

Beckworth paused a moment, in deep thought. "However, I seem to remember . . . ah, yes, I do believe he managed to hang on to a small yeoman's cottage near Hedley Hall." With a hint of a wry smile he added, "Must have forgotten it in the confusion, no doubt, or it, too . . ." He collected himself and left the rest unsaid.

Jane remembered the cottage. It was little more than a run-down farmhouse with a thatched roof and primitive conditions. "At least it's a place where we can go, but where will we find money for food . . . clothing? How can we survive? How can—?" She stopped abruptly, acutely aware that Lord Dashmont and Tatton Fulwood were witnessing this humiliating debacle. She looked to her mother, but Mama still appeared to be distraught, as were Christabell and Aunt. *I must take charge,* Jane thought. Despite her own anguish, she stood, smoothed her skirts, and said with dignity, "I thank you for delivering my father's letter, sirs, but could you leave us alone now? We have much to discuss."

Anthony rose, as did Tatton, and bowed to her and Lady Sperling. "I do understand. We shall leave immediately."

Mama gathered herself up, stood, and said, as if in a trance, "I, too, thank you for your help, sirs."

"They did indeed help," Beckworth interjected. "Why, if it were not for Lord Dashmont, Sperling would not be on his way to America."

Jane stared wide-eyed at Dashmont. "*You* helped my father leave England? Would you kindly explain yourself?"

Anthony faced her squarely. "There is not much to explain, Lady Jane. Since your father was without funds, I provided transportation to your home so he could pack his valise, then on to Mister Beckworth's home to sign some papers, and thence to the East India Docks, where I paid his fare to America, as any friend would do."

Jane persisted, "But whose idea was it that he sail to America? He never even mentioned such a journey before."

"It was mine."

"*You?*" Jane glared at him with reproachful eyes. "So we have you to blame for this? My father may have lost all, but there was no need for him to leave the country. Why didn't you stop him?"

A strange, grim look passed between Dashmont and Tatton. Tatton began, "You are not aware of all the circumstances, Lady Jane. You see, your father—"

"No," Anthony exclaimed, nudging Tatton's arm. Stony-faced, he bowed deeply to Lady Sperling. "Again, my deepest sympathies, madame." He looked at Jane. "I cannot answer. 'Tis best we leave."

Anthony and Tatton had barely left the drawing room when Anthony heard Christabell, close to hysteria, cry, "What shall we do?"

"Do not despair, little sister," he heard Jane reply. "We shall ask Edmund. He heads the family now."

Anthony paused for an agonizing moment. There was one sad fact he had forgotten—or had he simply been reluctant to be the purveyor of even more bad news? He returned to the morning room and faced Jane. "Apparently no one told you. Your brother was at Brooks last night, privy to the spectacle of seeing his entire inheritance gambled away. Like your father, he, too, was in great distress. And so"—how he hated to devastate this family further—"Edmund is with his father. He, too, is on his way to America."

The second they were out the front door, Tatton started to berate him. "Why did you not explain that Sperling was holding a pistol to his head? God's blood! When you counseled him to sail to America, you saved his life."

"I could *not* explain," Anthony said firmly. "How would his family feel if they knew Sperling nearly took the coward's way out? Better they think ill of me than to compound their grief." He smiled wryly. "There is no honorable way I can defend myself, Tatton."

"But it's an outrage. How could you allow Lady Jane to address you in such a manner?"

"I haven't a care what Lady Jane thinks." Within himself, his words did not rest easy. *Am I lying?* Anthony wondered. But before he could examine his feelings, a triumphant Lord Bradbourne appeared, practically strutting up the marble front steps of Chalton House.

With arrogant satisfaction, Bradbourne began, "Ah, Dashmont. Come to console the Sperlings? They'll be gone by the weekend, so I am here to inspect my new property." He struck a pose, gripping a hand boastfully around his lapel. "Not bad, eh?"

Anthony gritted his teeth. "Let us pass. I have no time for braggarts."

"You need not feel sorry for the Sperlings," Bradbourne commented in a voice smooth as oil. "I'm here to propose to Lady Jane. Naturally she will accept. What choice does she have? I already have her dowry." With a gleeful laugh he proceeded up the steps.

A fury swept over Anthony. He had just decided to charge up the steps after that scoundrel when, for the second time today, he felt Tatton's warning nudge. "Must I drag you away?" his friend whispered. "There is absolutely nothing you can do. As for Lady Jane, do you remember when I asked this morning if you were smitten with her? If I recall correctly, you answered 'utter nonsense.' Then prove it—walk away."

Tatton was right. *I have fulfilled my obligation to Lord Sperling,* Anthony reminded himself. *No sense getting further involved.*

With great difficulty, he ordered himself to turn his back on Bradbourne. "Let's drop by Tattersall's," he said, forcing the words out. "I'm in a mood to see some fine horseflesh today."

Chapter 6

•

A fter Anthony and Tatton left, Jane sat stunned, along with the rest of the family, as Mister Beckworth droned on, it seemed forever, thumbing through his papers, torturing them with endless descriptions of all the possessions they did not own anymore. Upon his departure, Jane's exhausted, grief-stricken mother could only repeat in a ragged whisper, "Robert is gone. Edmund is gone. Whatever shall we do?" Jane and Christabell helped her to her room, where she lay limp upon her bed, a cold compress covering her forehead.

Meanwhile, Aunt had retired with a "dreadful headache," asking not to be disturbed. Jane and her sister each retired to her own room, Christabell gushing endless torrents of tears. As yet, Jane had remained dry-eyed, but after she closed her door, she caught sight of her Ormolu clock upon the mantel. *Oh, Timmy.* Even her beloved porcelain elephant belonged to Bradbourne now. She fell on her bed and gave way to wrenching sobs. Where would they live? How would they eat . . . buy clothes? Oh, the irony. Hers and Christabell's dowries . . . the family fortune . . . Chalton House . . . Hedley Hall . . . all lost over a few senseless games of cards. Worst was knowing that her father had betrayed them. No. Worst was that Papa and Edmund were at this very moment sailing to America, no doubt never to return. So who was going to help them? Certainly not Mama. She was much too ill and distraught, aside from probably being in a family way again. Christabell and the younger girls were far too immature to rely on, or give any kind of useful advice. Nor could Aunt Eugenia, who was financially totally dependent upon Papa. In fact, she had seemed to fall apart at the dreadful news. *But surely there must be someone who can help us.* Jane attempted to dredge up the names of male relatives. There were only two, as she recalled—cousins, neither of whom were wealthy nor lived close by. So there was no one she could turn to. Smothering a sob, she wondered, what should she do? She, who in her whole life had never been compelled to make a decision beyond choosing what color ribbon should adorn her curls. How could she even begin to make decisions now? Impossible. Another sob racked her as she buried her head in her pillow. She would think about it later. In the meantime, surely someone would step forward to help.

Jane heard a discreet knock on her door and a soft call of "m'lady?" It was Croft.

She quickly wiped her eyes, sat up, smoothed her hair, and swung her feet to the floor. "Please come in," she called.

"Lord Bradbourne is downstairs. He wishes to see you."

Bradbourne? How dare he even come here. He was the last person on earth she wished to see. Besides, hadn't he already made his wishes known through Mister Beckworth? So what more could he possibly want? How she hated the thought of uttering one more word to him, but at present there was no one else in the family to handle the matter. *But Mama would be polite no matter what the circumstances,* she told herself. *And so must I.* "Inform his lordship I shall be down directly."

Jane waited for the butler to take his leave, but he remained where he was standing, an inscrutable expression upon his face.

"Will there be anything else, Croft?"

"Yes, m'lady." The butler self-consciously cleared his throat. "I assume you are in charge, since Lady Sperling is indisposed, and both Lord Sperling and Lord Edmund are . . . ahem! . . . not available. Therefore, I must inform you that at the end of this day the servants will no longer be in your employ. Some may stay on in the house, of course, in hopes Lord Bradbourne will hire them, but as for any continuance of service to the Sperlings"—he allowed a tight smile—"you do understand."

"Oh, no," she cried, leaping to her feet, "how could you do this?"

Croft shrugged. "How could we not? Unless, of course, you have the means to pay us." He cast accusing eyes upon her. "As it is, we shall lose our back wages."

This was dreadful. She could not imagine how the family could do without servants. "But surely—" she began, then fell into silence. He was right—there was no money. "I . . . I understand, Croft. The servants are not to be blamed . . . under the unfortunate circumstances." What more could she say?

After Croft left, she wondered if she should summon Sarah to help her change her dress before receiving Bradbourne. No, she decided. The girl had been surly enough this morning. Now she would probably refuse to come. The dress she was wearing would have to do. In fact, gray was a fitting color for this terrible day.

When Jane walked into the formal drawing room, she found Percy, Lord Bradbourne, standing by the fireplace. She sickened at the sight of his tall, black-clad figure—his long, usually dour face now lit with a triumphant glow. Most enraging was the sight of his repulsive fingers wrapped around a blue, ormolu-mounted Sevres vase—one of Mama's favorites—which ordinarily stood upon the mantel. *It belongs to him now. So unjust. But I'm speaking for the family, and I daren't show my anger.* She swallowed hard, trying not to allow her true feelings to show, and even thought of forcing a smile, but decided under the circumstances, that would be beyond the necessary. "Good afternoon, sir. You wished to see me?"

"Sevres, is it not?" Bradbourne inquired coolly, gazing at the vase in his hands. He turned it over, examining it closely. "Such fine workmanship on the pierced foliate lips and cherub handles."

Mama's vase. Never had she felt such rage. "Why are you here, sir?"

With maddening slowness Bradbourne replaced the vase on the mantel. "I shall need to do an inventory," he said, supposedly in an offhanded manner, but she sensed the calculated cruelty behind his remark.

"Why are you here, sir?" she demanded again, this time not trying to mask her enmity.

Bradbourne laughed lightly. "Mercy, such hostility. Well, I shall not fault you today, poor child. You and your family have suffered a terrible loss. But you would be well advised to curb your animosity. I am here to offer you a means to prevent the ruination of the Sperlings."

Her heart sank. Already she knew what he was going to say. Retaining her outward calm, she clenched her fists secretly within the folds of her skirt, looked him in the eye, and declared, "Explain yourself, sir."

A chilling smile curved Bradbourne's lips. "Since your attitude does not invite words of flattery nor flowery phrases, I shall get to the point. I plan to take you for my bride. If you consent, you and your family will be well cared for. If you do not"—a glint of evil arose from the depths of those hard, passionless eyes—"what a shame to see the Sperlings homeless, humiliated, without a farthing to their name." He paused for a feigned "tsk-tsk" of sympathy. "How inconsiderate of your father to flee the country. And Edmund, too? So it would appear the burden of survival is on your small, and if I may say so, helpless shoulders."

"Stop," she commanded, "that is quite enough." She could say no more, but stood shaking in rage and fear. How she would love to tell him what a heinous villain he was, and that she would not marry him if he were the last man on earth. *You cannot say no,* a cautious voice advised her. But her other, far more independent voice, asked, *But how can I say yes to this loathsome man?* She couldn't stand him, could not imagine being in his bed, those long, bony white fingers stroking her, those thin, cruel lips kissing her . . . what a horrible thought. She controlled a shudder.

Bradbourne laughed with contempt. "I shan't need your dowry, since I already have it. If you are in need of a further inducement, out of the kindness of my heart I shall return Hedley Hall to the Sperlings."

Hedley Hall—how thrilled and happy Mama would be to get it back. Mama, Aunt, and her three younger sisters, could live in a luxurious home, and quite well, too, off the tenant rentals. Ice gripped Jane's heart as she realized nothing but her marriage to Bradbourne would save them. She opened her mouth to choke out her words of acceptance, but a lump rose in her throat and the words refused to come. Was there no alternative? She would need further time to sort it out. "I shall consider it, sir. You shall have your answer by . . . Friday."

"Best not wait too long," Bradbourne answered in a mocking tone. "You are penniless and without a dowry. Ask yourself, what man in his right mind would marry you now? Friday is too late. You must decide by tomorrow."

Chapter 7

That night, the fate of the Sperling family lay heavily on Anthony's mind. As he dined with Tatton at Brooks, he tried to enjoy himself, but could not.

"Why are you so concerned?" asked Tatton.

"We should have stopped Sperling. We could have, easily, before he tossed the lot."

"Stop a man from gambling? I hope you know how ridiculous that sounds." Tatton regarded Anthony suspiciously. "Why have you suddenly developed a conscience?"

Anthony sighed. "Don't forget, 't'was I who persuaded Sperling to ship to America."

"What I won't forget is, you're the one who stopped Sperling from blowing his brains out."

"I find no satisfaction in being right."

"Besides," Tatton continued, "you needn't worry about the Sperlings. Lady Jane is bound to save the day by marrying Bradbourne. She has no choice. So all's well that ends well. The Sperlings receive their fortune back, or part of it"—Tatton frowned—"depending, of course, on Bradbourne's generosity."

"What do you mean?"

"Rumors abound about the man. I have heard he's reluctant to part with so much as a farthing. Even worse are the tales told concerning his first three wives."

Sir Godfrey Hatton, dining at the next table, had overheard. He stopped his fork in midair, leaned confidentially toward Anthony, and whispered, "You want to know about Bradbourne?" Sir Godfrey stabbed his fork toward a portly gentleman dining alone in a far corner. "Talk to Dudley over there. His daughter, Emily, was Bradbourne's first wife. She died two . . . three years into the marriage. 'T'wasn't childbirth. Funny business, that. Don't believe I ever heard the cause."

Over Tatton's objections, Anthony immediately rose from the table and was soon seated across from Lord Dudley, a white-haired, sad-faced gentleman in his early sixties who was just finishing his dinner.

"My apologies for interrupting, sir," said Anthony, "but there's a question I must ask concerning Percy, Lord Bradbourne."

Dudley's features promptly hardened. "That villain! That scoundrel!"

"Would it disturb you to speak of Bradbourne's marriage to your daughter? I ask not out of idle curiosity." Without revealing names, Anthony explained he was concerned for a young woman whom Bradbourne was considering for his fourth wife.

"I shall be glad to expose the truth, sir," Dudley began. His voice taut with emotion, he continued, "Directly after my daughter and Lord Bradbourne were married, he took her to that dark, gloomy estate of his, up in the most remote part of North Wales. Kept her virtually a prisoner. Though I have no proof, 't'wasn't long before he was mistreating her in the most vile, unimaginable ways. If you could see some of the letters she wrote! She was much too modest, too frightened, to describe the beastly manner in which he was treating her, but I could read between the lines."

"Did you not try to see her?" asked Anthony.

"By God, of course I tried. Driven by fear for her life, I traveled to North Wales. I shall never forget the bleak remoteness of Bradbourne's estate. It was situated miles from the nearest village, amidst awesome cataracts and enormous mountains. The castle itself was vast in its dimensions, at least six hundred feet in length, with massive, black limestone walls, so dark and gloomy I shuddered when I first caught sight of them." Dudley clenched his fists. "He would not allow me to see her. Said she was ill, that I should go away."

"Did you?"

"What else could I do?" Dudley shook his head in despair. "She was his wife—his property. There was nothing I could do but leave. Shortly after, that blackguard sent me word of her death. He never gave a cause, nor a reason, only that she had contracted some mysterious malady and had already been buried beneath those dark castle walls." Dudley took a moment to collect himself and added in a broken whisper, "Not an hour passes I don't think of how my Emily lies buried, so cold, so lonely, in that godforsaken land."

Anthony allowed a decent interval to elapse before he gently asked, "Do you know what caused the death of his other two wives?"

"Rumor has it the second did away with herself. The third, so I've heard, suffered the same fate as my daughter's." Dudley's face twisted with pain. "Pray, save that young woman from becoming his fourth wife. The man's a sadistic monster. Only he and God know the tortures he put my dear Emily through."

A troubled Anthony soon returned to Tatton and described his conversation with Dudley. "She shall not marry him," he declared, a muscle quivering in his jaw.

"But is this your business?" asked Tatton.

"Since I am at least partly responsible for Sperling's flight to America, I feel it is my duty to help his family."

"Indeed?" Tatton scoffed, "you mean to tell me you have no feeling for Lady Jane except duty?"

Anthony bristled. "That's exactly what I mean." But within, Anthony questioned himself. Did he feel nothing but pity for the poor, unfortunate girl?

"So what do you intend to do?" Beneath lowered eyelids Tatton leveled a sly gaze. "You could marry the chit."

"Are you daft? I plan to marry Isabella Wentworth."

"Ah, the plantation owner's daughter." A devilish look came into Tatton's eyes. "Pray, tell me more about the wondrous Miss Wentworth. Aside from 'sturdy,' is she beautiful? Warmhearted and generous? Oozing with graciousness and charm?"

Anthony bristled. "Miss Wentworth is sturdily built and in good health. She possesses a serious disposition, and though she seldom laughs, I find her a welcome change from my first wife, who, as you may recall, giggled night and day. Also, she has inherited a certain penurious nature from her father. As a consequence, she is not in the least extravagant. She will make a decent wife and fine mother."

Tatton sat back aghast. "Sturdy and in good health? Penurious? That's the best you can say? What I'm hearing is she's fat, dull, and stingy. For God's sake, man, if you're looking for the opposite of Georgiana, then temper your search with moderation. Otherwise, you'll end up with a wife you cannot abide." Tatton stopped for a quick chuckle. "Have you ever thought of marrying for love?"

"Even if I were to fall in love, which is most unlikely, I swear I would never marry another London belle, which brings us back to Lady Jane." Anthony's mouth twisted wryly. "She is not exactly fond of me, convinced as she is that it's my fault her father and brother fled to America. Not only that, she heartily disapproves of gamblers. One can understand, of course. So marry me? I suspect she would prefer the devil himself."

When Jane came downstairs the next morning, she faced by far the most terrible day of her life. Today they must pack their belongings. But where would they go? No one had yet said a word. She was still stunned, and had come to no decision concerning Lord Bradbourne. As it was, she could barely accept that life as she had known it was gone forever.

It appeared no one in the family had even begun to cope with plans for the future. Christabell was moping in her room. Mama was still feeling ill and lying down. Perhaps Aunt Eugenia would be her old self today and would know what to do.

Jane checked the breakfast room. Just as Croft had proclaimed, there was no food, nor even table settings. What should she do? It occurred to her that never in her life had she not been served breakfast. She should go to the kitchen, she supposed. She could at least find bread, butter, and perhaps some fruit. *Perdition!* She had never been in this kitchen before. It was different at Hedley Hall. Growing up, she had gone where she pleased, and could remember long, friendly visits beside the huge kitchen fireplace while sitting on Cook's ample lap. Only later, when she grew up, did she learn that as a lady of the house she must never deign to enter the kitchen.

"Henrietta? Jane? Christabell?"

Jane recognized Aunt's voice. She returned to the entry hall, where she saw the elderly woman making her way cautiously down the curving staircase, aided by a cane, which Jane had never seen her use before. Aunt, dressed for visiting, declared, "Estelle was not there to help me dress this morning. I must report this to Mrs. Lester," she said in bewilderment, referring to the housekeeper.

Jane commanded herself to sound calm. "Good morning, Aunt Eugenia. Surely you're not going out today."

"Of course I'm going out." The proud old lady gazed at her imperiously. "Tell Croft he must instruct Jenkins to ready the carriage by one o'clock. I shall leave my card with Lady Robsart before we call on Lady Claridge." She proceeded toward the breakfast room.

Jane felt heartsick. "Aunt, there is no breakfast this morning, but wait and I shall fetch you something from the kitchen."

Lady Fanshawe drew herself up and cast a scornful gaze at her niece. "No breakfast? Are you daft?"

"Aunt Eugenia, Estelle is gone, as is my Sarah. Cook is gone. Croft's gone. They're all gone."

"But who will fix our meals? Who will hitch the carriage? Who will drive us?"

"Aunt, I am terribly sorry, but there is no carriage. You cannot go to Lady Robsart's or anyplace else today."

The old woman seemed to crumple before her eyes. "Then I shall return to my room," she said feebly. "You may tell Croft I do not wish to be disturbed."

"I shall bring you up some bread, fruit, and tea, Aunt Eugenia," Jane called after her. She thought her heart would break as she watched her aunt wearily make her way back up the staircase, leaning heavily on her cane. In the past, she had resented Aunt's overbearing attitude and, in particular, her unsolicited advice. But now, what wouldn't she give to hear her aunt berate her again—take charge—announce in that grand, imperious voice what the family must do. But it wasn't going to happen. Thanks to Papa, proud Aunt Eugenia had changed into a confused old lady overnight.

Jane rummaged through the silent, empty kitchen and was able to find bread, butter, milk, and some apples. She took a tray to Aunt, and placed the rest on the rosewood side table. When Mama and Christabell finally came downstairs, it was more than enough, since they were so distraught they could hardly eat.

Christabell, red-eyed and devastated, declared, "Lord Beckford will have nothing to do with me now."

"Assuredly not," Jane answered. No sense lying. Christabell, the whole family, must face the truth.

Mama was still extremely pale and drawn. "I am sure you know I am with child again," she admitted. "What will become of us all, and now"—she laid a trembling hand upon her stomach—"another mouth to feed. How can we buy food? How can we find a roof over our heads?"

Jane had no answers. She, herself, could hardly eat. After a few nibbles of bread, she returned to her room and, in despair, flung herself on the bed. How could Papa have done this? Bitterly, she remembered his penchant for gambling that had brought them down. Gamblers . . . how she hated them all, including Lord Dashmont. Especially Lord Dashmont, who had aided and abetted her father and brother in sailing off to America.

She spied her beloved manuscripts, still lying on her harlequin desk. Were they Bradbourne's now, or could she take them with her? What did it matter? She would never have the heart to look at them again, even if she married Bradbourne. And if she did marry him, would she ever have children? Probably not. None of Bradbourne's three wives had produced a child.

Nothing had been resolved when, later in the morning, Jane, who had been engrossed in sorting through her books, looked up at Christabell, who had just entered her bedchamber and announced, "You would never guess who's come to call."

Jane asked, "Another merchant come to collect his bill?" News of Papa's flight had spread like the wind. One after another this morning, merchants had come pounding on the door, eager to collect their money, angry when they departed empty-handed.

"Not a merchant this time," said Christabell, "though I confess, I am loathe to open the door for fear it will be. Oh, Jane, I am not accustomed to opening the door all by myself. What shall we do without Croft?"

"We shall manage," Jane said stoutly. "Now tell me, who's come calling?"

"Lord Dashmont."

"What?" Jane slammed down the book she was holding. "How dare he? After I—"

"No, no," Christabell hastily interrupted, "he did not ask to see you. 'Tis Mama he wishes to see."

"Did you inform him Mama is indisposed?"

"Yes . . . no . . . not exactly . . . oh, Jane, I don't know what to do." Christabell's face twisted with anguish. "I cannot *believe* Papa gambled away my dowry."

"But he did, little sister," Jane replied softly, "I'm so terribly sorry."

Christabell collapsed onto the bed in tears, burying her head in the pillow. "Will he ever come back? And Edmund . . ." Thoughts of her brother provoked a new onslaught of tears. "Do you think they'll get rich in America? If they do, will they return some day?"

"I would not depend on it." This was no time for fairy tales, Jane thought grimly. "Chances are they will never return."

"Then I shall never have a dowry, so I shall never marry," Christabell declared between sobs. "I shall end up old and ugly and alone."

Jane sat on the bed beside her sister and stroked her hair. "There, there, Christabell, 'twill all be better soon."

"I don't see how," came her sister's muffled reply.

Neither do I, unless . . . In all her nineteen years Jane had never felt so wretched and alone. What a bleak, hopeless future lay ahead of them. *But no, all can be saved. I have only to marry Lord Bradbourne.* After all, her family came first in her heart, far beyond any selfish desires or negligible inhibitions of her own. And what other choice did she have? Without a dowry, no other acceptable man in the world would marry her now. And at least she would know that Mama, Aunt, and her younger sisters would have a home. Surely Lord Bradbourne would provide Christabell's dowry. *Though I may have to beg,* she thought grimly, remembering Bradbourne's reputation for stinginess.

"What would you think, Christabell, if I married Lord Bradbourne?"

"You cannot." Christabell burst into tears again. "Oh, Jane, I never for a moment wished for you to marry Old Bony Fingers."

"Well, if I did, it would all be fine," Jane replied in a soothing voice. *All would* not *be fine,* she thought, *all would be absolutely horrible.* She could hardly choke the words out: "It wouldn't be so bad."

Christabell kept arguing, but they came to no agreement. After a time she gave up and asked, "What shall we do with Lord Dashmont? He's downstairs waiting."

"Mama can see him," said Jane.

"She's in no condition to see anybody." To Jane's surprise, Christabell sat up and wiped her eyes. "But I shan't cry anymore," she announced, attempting a smile and lifting her chin bravely. "You're the head of the family now. You've enough troubles."

Jane was deeply touched by her sister's gathering her courage. *Head of the family.* Jane hadn't thought of it before, but with Papa and Edmund gone, Mama paralyzed with grief, Aunt helpless, no male relatives to rely upon . . . The truth finally sank in. *The family's future is up to me, and I know what I must do.* But first, she must get rid of the unwelcome visitor.

"Where is Lord Dashmont?" Jane firmly inquired, "in the study?"

"Yes, in the study, but he was most insistent he wanted to see Mama."

"Then we must get her, and Aunt, too, though I cannot imagine why that dreadful man is even here. Meanwhile, I shall go down and see what he wants, and try to get rid of him as soon as possible."

After Christabell left, Jane touched her hair, felt its straggly state, and realized she must fix it before receiving their guest. "Sarah?" she called, before remembering her lady's maid was gone. She went to the mirror, picked up the comb and struggled for several minutes to form ringlets about her face and tuck her hair up in a bun. *How easy it looked when Sarah did it. Why did I never attempt to arrange it myself?* Finally, her throat aching with defeat, she decided she had done her best and tossed the comb down, vowing later she would practice until she had it right. She applied a touch of lilac cologne to her hair, then donned a green sprigged morning dress, for the first time ever having to reach around to the back herself to fasten the ties.

When she finally descended the main staircase, she told herself this was only Lord Dashmont, a man she could not abide, and she really didn't care how she looked. Marveling over the irony of it all, she wondered: was it only two nights ago she was floating in Lord Dashmont's arms, carried away by his charms? But that was a lifetime ago, and another girl entirely. That was a girl who had no thought in her head beyond what she would wear to the ball the next night, and the number of dandies who would beg her for a dance. Her spirits sank even lower as the truth struck home: that silly, carefree girl was gone forever.

Jane entered the drawing room with firm, proud steps and saw Lord Dashmont standing next to the window, staring out at the street. She bristled at the sight of this unrepentant gambler who had sent her father off to America. Only with an effort did she manage to maintain composure enough to say coolly, "Good morning, Lord Dashmont."

He turned, a look of compassion warming his dark, handsome face. As he crossed the room, she couldn't help but notice the quick, sure, lean grace of his strides. *Handsome on the surface. Evil underneath.*

"Good morning, Lady Jane." Today the rich timbre of his voice held no derision, only kindness.

I shall not have him pitying me. She raised her head high. "Mama will be down shortly. Would you care for some refreshment? I'll ring—" She had started toward the bellpull before remembering that Croft, all of them, were gone. How humiliating. She left her sentence hanging and stood indecisively, for once not knowing what to say.

"Best not disturb Croft." Amusement flickered in Lord Dashmont's eyes. "No doubt he's busy perusing the job advertisements in *The Times.*"

Her first impulse was to laugh, but she stifled it. Laughing was forgiving, and she would never forgive this man. "You find humor in our misfortune, sir?"

"A touch of humor can lighten the most terrible of calamities."

"Nothing can lighten this," she declared, her voice near shaking with intensity. "But how would *you* know?"

"I am not unacquainted with adversity," he answered evenly.

His wife, she remembered suddenly. Much as she disliked him, she must apologize. "How thoughtless of me. Of course, you must still be grieving for your dear wife."

"Perhaps I grieve because I don't grieve," he responded with a wry smile, and continued swiftly, "but that's another matter. May I ask if your family has made plans?"

She felt herself stiffen. Not bothering to hide her contempt, she answered, "Why should I discuss our plans with *you*? If not for you, we would not be in this predicament in the first place."

She waited warily, knowing she was being unfair. He could easily lash back by pointing out that Papa had not been tied to his chair in Brooks when he lost his fortune. And furthermore, it was Lord Bradbourne, not he, who had bankered the faro game that cost the family all.

Lord Dashmont remained silent for a time, regarding her with an unfathomable expression in his shrewd dark eyes. Finally, he spoke calmly, as if nothing untoward had occurred. "I take it then, that you have not become betrothed to Lord Bradbourne."

"If you think that's your concern, sir, I must tell you I think it is *not*. And I would like to suggest—"

"Lord Dashmont, how kind of you to call." It was Mama, entering the room with Aunt, supported by Christabell. Dressed in a dark, long-sleeved, muslin day dress with few frills, she was managing a wan smile.

After he had returned the greeting, Lord Dashmont said, "I desire to have a word with you in private, Lady Sperling."

Jane spoke up firmly. "Whatever you have to say, you can say to all of us."

Mama nodded. "Jane is quite right, sir. I have no secrets from my family, especially in the midst of this catastrophe. I would prefer you speak to all of us. Won't you sit down?"

They all seated themselves, except Anthony, who insisted upon standing. He began pacing up and down and without further preamble said, "Lady Sperling, I have a proposal for you. There is a caretaker's cottage on the grounds of my estate in Kent, where I should be happy to have you and your family stay. Furthermore, I should be happy to provide a small stipend . . . er . . . you might say a token of thanks . . . for, say, one hundred pounds per annum for your necessities. Also, I wish to replace the dowries of your eldest daughters."

After a stunned silence, Mama asked, "Why are you doing this?"

"Before he went away I assured Lord Sperling I would do what I could for his family." Dashmont cast an odd glance at Jane. "And since I do feel in part responsible for your husband's flight, I wish, in some small way, to make amends."

Jane, seated on the flowered chintz couch next to Mama, drew herself up. "It's more than a 'small way,' sir." She glanced at Mama, who was nodding in agreement. "We may be facing poverty, but we haven't sunk low enough to accept your charity."

Anthony shook his head in disagreement. Addressing Mama, he continued, "This is far from charity. In exchange, I request the presence of your daughter at Fairfield Manor, my estate in Kent. As you may know, my young son, David, resides there, along with his grandmama and aunt. He is in need of a tutor"— Anthony stopped and corrected himself—"a *companion* who can teach him Greek and Latin." He bowed toward Jane. "Yesterday in the park I could not help but notice how well my son took to your daughter. She actually brought a smile to his face—most unusual, I can assure you. So I am requesting she acquiesce to becoming an honored guest at Fairfield Manor for a time. What with her skills in Greek and Latin, and her obvious love of children, you would be doing me a tremendous favor if you allowed her to come."

Aghast and furious, Jane cried, "You are proposing I become a governess, sir? A . . . a . . . *servant*?"

"Not at all," Anthony responded patiently. "You will be given every consideration as a guest, *not* a governess. You will have the authority to do what you think best for my son. You will dine with the family. You will stay in one of our finest guest rooms, most certainly not in the servants' quarters."

"This is nonsense, Jane." Aunt Eugenia, who had remained uncommonly silent, was finally speaking up with some of her old verve. "You must marry Lord Bradbourne. 'Tis the only way. Even if we were to accept Lord Dashmont's offer, we would still be poor. Just think, Jane dear, there's your mother and I, you and Christabell, and the three little girls at Hedley Hall. That's seven mouths to feed and an eighth on the way. Where will the food come from? We *must* have servants—carriages—horses, but how can we afford them? The small stipend Lord Dashmont proposes is not enough. We cannot possibly exist in such a manner unless, of course, you want us all to live in abject poverty." She glared meaningfully at Jane. "Our only salvation is in your marriage to Lord Bradbourne, who, I am sure, will support us in the style to which we are accustomed."

Jane felt a flush of embarrassment. They were discussing the family's most intimate secrets in front of practically a stranger. "Aunt, can we not discuss this later? I am quite certain Lord Dashmont is not interested in every financial circumstance of this family." She glared at Anthony. "Suffice to say, sir, we thank you for your offer but must refuse."

"Quite right," stated Aunt Eugenia. She frowned at Anthony. "Although well intentioned, I'm sure, your gift is hardly necessary. Lord Bradbourne will be more than generous with the fortune he appropriated from my brother. Is that not so, Jane?"

Jane did not immediately answer. This was the moment for decision. Could she endure Bradbourne? Fearful images built in her mind, but she quickly quashed them. *Yes, I can endure him. And when I'm in his bed, with his horrible fingers upon me, I shall squeeze my eyes shut tight and transport myself to Hedley Hall, where I'll look down on Mama, Aunt, and the children, all warm and safe and secure.* She tried to speak, but her voice wavered. She tried again, looking Dashmont squarely in the eye. "Aunt is right. I *do* plan to marry Lord Bradbourne, so your help will not be necessary."

Jane watched curiously as Anthony, momentarily speechless, appeared to be struggling with himself to retain his composure. "Have I surprised you?" she asked, almost smiling.

Anthony did not smile back. Instead, he turned to Lady Sperling and sharply declared, "Madame, I must see you alone." He turned to Aunt. "You, too, Lady Fanshawe."

Jane opened her mouth to protest, but before she could, Dashmont stated in a flat, noncompromising voice, "This is not a subject fit for the ears of young ladies. Say no more. It will get you nowhere."

Jane stared, speechless with indignation, as the three disappeared into the library. She and Christabell could hear the murmur of their voices as they talked for at least ten minutes behind closed doors. When they returned, Lady Sperling, obviously upset, said to Jane, "Lord Dashmont has told us some things . . ." she paused, obviously adverse to putting her thoughts to words ". . . after what I've just heard concerning Lord Bradbourne, I do not wish you to marry him."

"But, Mama, it's the only way."

"No, no," Mama cried, "I have just heard the most vile . . . the most . . . oh, words cannot say. Jane, I shall not force you. The final decision is up to you, but I am pleading with you *not* to marry Bradbourne. If you do, I shall be sick with worry and not rest a moment. 'Tis far better that you go to Fairfield Manor as a guest of Lord Dashmont."

"But I do not want—" Jane began, then stopped abruptly, shaking with impotent rage. She had announced she would marry Bradbourne. How *dare* Lord Dashmont interfere? She tried to calm herself. What did it matter what she wanted? Her family was her first consideration, Mama's wishes in particular. Her own personal desires faded in comparison.

"All right, Mama." She turned wrathful eyes on Dashmont. "I shall be treated as a guest?"

"An honored guest, due every consideration."

"And you will send the stipend directly to my mother?"

"Whatever you wish."

Jane turned to her mother. "Where do you wish to live, Mama? In the caretaker's cottage at Fairfield Manor, or the old yeoman's cottage at Hedley Hall?"

"The yeoman's cottage," Mama answered without hesitation. Her eyes moistened. "At least it will be close to our old home."

Jane, keeping her face an unreadable mask, asked Dashmont, "Will that be satisfactory?"

"Of course."

Jane slowly pushed herself from the couch and stood tall. With many regrets, feeling she faced a lightless future, she said, "Then I accept your proposal."

When Anthony took his leave, he asked Lady Jane to accompany him to the front entryway.

She gave him a hostile glare as they reached the door. "What more do you want?"

Anthony looked into a pair of beautiful blue-gray eyes, which at the moment had darkened like angry thunderclouds. "I can see you are in no mood to talk sensibly."

"You are correct, sir," she snapped.

"Then I shall make this brief. Now that I have met my obligation to your father, you needn't fear I shall intrude into your life any further. You should be quite comfortable at Fairfield Manor. Mind, I haven't a care how you conduct yourself, other than tutoring my son."

"I shall never be comfortable in your home," she replied in a low voice taut with frustration. "Do you intend to check on me?"

"I visit Fairfield Manor but rarely. David is calmer with only his grandmother and aunt around."

Her mouth twisted wryly. "At last—one small blessing on this dark day."

Anthony bit his tongue. It could be razor sharp when he chose. He had used it many a time to crush an insult with words both contemptuous and cutting. Had Lady Jane been one of his fair Cyprians—or any other woman in the world, actually—he would have done just that. But he could not bring himself to castigate this young girl who was so bravely defying him, or reprove her in any way.

Why was he feeling like this? Just now, when she had walked into the drawing room, he'd felt this . . . this . . . smoldering attraction. Was his interest piqued by pity? Surely it could be. Judging from her disheveled appearance, it was obvious her maid had deserted with the rest. Not only was her dress hanging slightly crooked, the result, he would surmise, of her blindly tying it wrong in the back by herself, but her hair was a disaster. At the ball it had looked magnificent, coifed into that

Grecian upswept affair. But now, her obvious attempt to repeat this triumph had resulted in a scraggly bun with errant tendrils escaping every which way about her delicate face and down the back of her slender white neck. Calamitous, and yet . . .

How could a girl look so disheveled, yet at the same time enchantingly beautiful? He should be feeling nothing but pity for this poor creature who was in such disarray, yet . . .

She's standing in front of me and my pulse is racing. He felt a near-overwhelming urge to push each silky-soft tendril back in place, then take her in his arms and stroke away the frown of worry on her brow, and then . . .

You fool, what are you thinking of? Judging from the granite gleam in her eye, if looks were daggers, he would be skewered to the front door this very instant.

"I shall escort you to Fairfield Manor tomorrow," he stated flatly, "if that will be convenient."

"Do not trouble yourself, sir. I have no need of an escort. If you will but send your coach around, I am quite capable of making my own way to your estate."

"Very well, then. If you will be so kind, I should like you to deliver a letter I shall write to David's grandmother, explaining the circumstances."

"Of course. Now, if you will excuse me, I must go pack my things and—"

She suddenly stopped talking and stood staring at him with eyes that were fast filling with tears. He could almost sense the lump that was growing in her throat, and feel her desperation as she attempted to conceal it and act as if nothing were wrong and she was in control of her emotions.

"Lady Jane," he began, "I am so dreadfully sorry."

She bowed her head and covered her face with her hands. "You will forgive me, sir," came her muffled, shaking voice, "this has not been a good day, and I really must . . . must go pack my things."

She started to turn away, but he gripped her upper arms. "It's good to cry. You needn't feel ashamed." His heart went out to this young, brave girl caught up in tragedy. Before he knew what he was doing, a force beyond himself caused him to draw her into his arms. She did not pull away. Instead, she buried her face against the side of his neck, where he could feel her warm, moist breathing. Though he was careful not to hold her too tight against him, he could feel her shaking as she tried to stifle a sob. He waited for it to erupt, but it did not. They stood there, she emitting not a sound, he becoming increasingly aware of the faint scent of lilac in her hair and the softness of her full bosom brushing against his chest.

"Ah, Jane," he murmured, and when she pulled her head back to regard him questioningly, his hands involuntarily locked against her spine and drew her closer. Nearly all reasoned thought left his head as he became acutely aware of every one of her soft curves molding to the contours of his body. His heart started hammering. A tremor shot through him as he felt her soft thigh pressing against the hardness of his. He felt an overwhelming urge to kiss her, but had retained just enough sense to be aware that here, in the middle of the front hall, such an action would be utter madness. Still, he could not bear to let her go. Instead, he twined the fingers of one hand through her hair, above the back of her neck where those little tendrils hung down so enchantingly. Instantly, he was bewitched, not only by the smooth, silky softness of her hair, but by the warmth radiating from her skin, and that scent of lilac, all so unbearably tantalizing. Drawing in a ragged breath, he stroked her hair, and for a long, spellbinding moment ignored time, place, and the rules of society as he allowed himself the sweet, near unbearable luxury of holding her tight against himself, making no effort to control his fast, passionate breathing.

At first she did not resist, in fact, gave herself freely to his embrace. But soon he heard a muted protest and felt a small fist hammer on his shoulder. He let her go instantly.

She gasped and backed away. Her cheeks were flushed. Her chest was heaving. "I cannot believe this happened," she finally said.

"Neither can I," he responded, desperately trying to breathe normally again. "My apologies," he murmured as his mind raced. *What next?* He half expected her to slap him. He would have deserved it, too. He, who had always maintained iron control, had never lost it in this unseemly way.

"You needn't apologize," she said in a voice devoid of feeling. She had calmed herself and was regarding him with eyes that had become passionless again. "I allowed it, for reasons I cannot fathom. Can we pretend this never happened?"

"Of course." Lust and longing raged within him. It was almost unendurable—this wanting the moment to continue—this aching need to crush her soft, slender body against him—to claim her lips with a kiss so burning it would arouse her passion as his was aroused . . .

Impossible, of course. She loathed him because of her father. And of a more practical concern: they were standing in the main hallway for all to see. With the utmost difficulty he managed a shrug and an indifferent smile. "It appears I allowed your family's sad plight to cloud my judgment. My embrace began out of sympathy. My apologies that it . . . got out of hand. It was of no consequence." *Ha!* Whom was he trying to deceive? "Rest assured, it will never happen again."

Anthony left the house in dazed exasperation. How could he have behaved like such a fool? Why had he lost control like some green schoolboy? He must make sure this repugnant conduct never happened again. His mind raced. *I must get far away from her . . . of course! I shall return to the West Indies.*

He felt better already. Actually, he had planned to spend more time in England, enjoying a taste of his old life once again, but it had all fallen flat somehow. Perhaps at a later time, when his mood changed, he could enjoy it.

Meanwhile, a return to Jamaica would cause him to forget the very existence of the tempting but unsuitable Lady Jane Sperling. Indeed, he could forge ahead with his alliance to Isabella Wentworth.

Possibly. Come to think of it, I'm in no hurry.

Chapter 8

"Almost to Fairfield Manor, m'lady," yelled down the coachman.

It had been a dismal journey. Alone, pressed miserably into a corner of Lord Dashmont's carriage, Jane closed her eyes, as if to obliterate her painful parting from her family. To no avail. Her spirits sank to new depths each time she recalled those final farewells. Never had she seen her mother cry. Never had she seen sweet Christabell make such an effort not to cry. To compound her heartache, she had been forced to decide which of her cherished possessions to take with her and which to forsake forever—spoils to assuage Bradbourne's ignoble greed. In the end, she had been forced into utter ruthlessness, abandoning many of her lovely dresses, hats, jewels, fans, her beloved manuscripts . . . even the Ormolu clock had to be left behind. *Oh, Timmy, there was no other way.* Tears sprang to her eyes, but she blinked them back. She had shed her last tear and was not, she vowed, ever again going to cry over this terrible blow life had dealt her, no matter what.

She shuddered inwardly when she remembered her sudden qualm this morning when Lord Dashmont's smart black-and-gold coach rolled to a stop at the entrance to Chalton House at the appointed departure time. Perhaps, horror of horrors, he had changed his mind. Perhaps he was inside waiting, and would insist upon accompanying her to Fairfield Manor. A feeling of relief swept over her when she saw the coach was empty. She was further assured when the coachman presented her with a letter written by Dashmont, to be conveyed to his mother-in-law upon her arrival at his estate. Dashmont had kept his word. She would not be obliged to confront him again.

But how could she have lost her composure last night after maintaining it nearly to the end? Jane felt yet another blush creep over her cheeks. How humiliating to break down crying, right in front of the man she most detested in all the world. Until that moment of weakness in the entryway, she had held together so well. It was, she suspected, that gleam of sympathy in his eye that had softened her defenses. But whatever the reason, she had compounded her humiliation a hundredfold when he held her in his arms and fondled her hair. *And I let him.* She was furious with herself for allowing such an outrage. *Did I enjoy it?* Since yesterday she had asked this question of herself over and over. The logic in her brain said no, she could never have taken any pleasure from an intimacy with a man so despicable. Her heart kept saying yes, though. She kept thinking of those little tingles down her spine when he had entwined his fingers in her hair. How intimate had been their touch—how warm and comforting. And even beyond that . . .

She felt herself blush again, remembering how tightly he had held her—so tight she had felt every hard inch of him, in a manner she had never felt a man before. She caught herself, and laughed aloud at the irony. Despite the catastrophic turn of events in her life, here she was, musing over a contact with a man, which, though intensely intimate, was totally of no import. He had said so himself. Had she no pride? Dashmont had only held her out of sympathy.

And he had not even kissed her. Well, she had been kissed many a time, she would like him to know. Throughout her three Seasons, she had engaged in an occasional kiss, though not, of course, until after repeated begging and pleading on the part of one or another of her various beaux. In the far darkness of a balcony . . . behind a statue in a formal garden . . . in a deserted library. Each time, she had felt a delicious sense of peril, aware her parents would be scandalized, had they known. But even more exciting, in a world where men ruled women, and women did what they were told, she had delighted in her newly discovered power, aware that even the most conceited and arrogant of men would beg—plead—badger—cajole for a kiss and a touch of soft, young skin. In spite of herself, she smiled. Many's the proud young gallant she had teased unmercifully, fi-

nally offering her lips, but briefly, then ducking blithely away
as he, breath coming hard, hunger in his eyes, begged for more.

But Dashmont would never beg, she mused, suddenly de-
flated. That night at the ball he had laughed at her efforts at coquetry. A sixth sense told her she had no power over this rugged
planter from Jamaica who didn't fit the mold, and she never
would. He was not a man to play silly games like the dandies.
He was a man who would take what he wanted, if he really
wanted it . . .

And would I give . . . ?

Jane pressed her fingers to her lips and could almost imagine
that Dashmont had indeed kissed her and she could still feel the
warm moistness of his lips. At the base of her throat, she felt her
pulse beat faster, then swell. *Be honest.* Instead of acting like
her usual shallow, teasing self, she had willingly come into his
arms, overcome by the energy and power he projected. She had
loved the thrilling touch of his fingers in her hair. If the truth be
known, it was not outraged virtue that had made her pull away,
it was fear of discovery. Anyone, be it servant or family, could
have walked by and seen their intimate embrace in the entryway. Even so, it was all she could do to pound his shoulder with
her fist—not very hard, if she recalled correctly—and tell him
to stop.

You must forget him, she ordered herself sternly. She was
about to arrive at Fairfield Manor. There were much more
pressing matters about which she ought to be concerned.

With difficulty, Jane turned her thoughts to the problem at
hand. How she dreaded arriving unannounced. Dashmont's letter rested in her lap. She picked it up and ran her hand reflec-
tively over the thick parchment and glob of red wax impressed
with Dashmont's seal. He had promised she would be treated
like an honored guest, but even so, he could not guarantee she
would receive a warm reception. *And I won't,* she thought
grimly. She had only to recall Lady Cavendish's cold-eyed
smile that day in the park to know that both she and her daughter, Hortense, would be hard put to conceal their hostility. The
reason was obvious. From what she'd heard, Lady Cavendish
was firmly entrenched as the mistress of Fairfield Manor and

would remain so unless and until Dashmont married again. No wonder she would resent any girl Dashmont looked twice at!

I shall quickly convince Lady Cavendish that her lofty position is safe from me!

Jane sighed and looked out the window. *As if I would ever want him for myself. But they are obliged to treat me kindly,* she assured herself. *I shall do my best to become friends and always be pleasant, as a guest should be. I shall greet any kind of snub, or slight, with equanimity. I shall be good with David, who's such a fine little boy.* She smiled to herself. *My behavior shall be impeccable . . .*

With a great jangling of harness rings, the coach turned off the highway and started along a sunken drive lined with a dense screen of boughs and underwood. The remnants of Jane's smile disappeared as she anxiously peered through the window. The coach rounded a curve in the driveway. She gasped and said aloud, "How beautiful," as she gazed with delight upon Fairfield Manor, an enchanting seventeenth-century mansion that appeared to be sailing like some huge, proud ship above hawthorn hedges and ancient meadows.

She was captivated. No one had ever told her Dashmont's estate was so huge and breathtakingly beautiful. She knew he was rich, but this was incredible. Here was the quintessence of an ancient English manor house, built of beautiful plum-colored brick, with a host of gables on every facade, some straight, some crow-stepped, and some topped by pinnacles. The transomed windows were large and light, some stained with gorgeous colors, and the fine, tall, clustered chimneys were its crowning glory. There with acres of lawns and gardens surrounding it, a tiny lake with swans—was that a strolling peacock?—all against a background of heavily wooded hills.

The coach rolled to a stop in front of the north entrance portico located between tall, imposing marble pillars. *I'm here.* Jane smoothed her somber traveling dress of dark brown. She alighted from the coach, her face unreadable, her stomach clenched tight.

"How extraordinary," remarked Lady Amanda Cavendish as she carefully perused the letter from Lord Dashmont.

Jane sat fuming. Her trunks stood unattended in the entrance vestibule. Worse, she had not been offered tea, or any refreshment for that matter, and she was starving, not having eaten so much as a crumb all day. Her gaze swept the ornate salon, so beautiful with its splendid crystal chandelier and fan-vaulted ceiling. Across, seated stiffly on a giltwood tapestry settee, were the frowning Lady Cavendish and her dour daughter, Hortense.

Lady Cavendish finished reading her son-in-law's letter. With a sniff of her sharp, thin nose she dropped it like a hot coal from her fingertips onto the mahogany sofa table.

Jane began, "I trust Lord Dashmont's letter explains—"

"Oh, indeed," Lady Cavendish interrupted, her voice as cold as a grave. "His lordship has made everything quite clear. You are to be little David's governess."

Jane felt the anger sweeping through her, but maintained her calm. "Not governess, Lady Cavendish, simply a companion. I was invited by Lord Dashmont to stay as a guest for a while, and I—"

"Just what are your qualifications?"

Jane was finding it increasingly hard to remain polite. *She's talking to me as if she's interviewing a servant.* But she placed a smile on her face, vowing it would stay there, no matter what. "I am conversant in Greek and Latin, as well as French. Also, it seems little David took to me when we were in the park the other day."

"I see." Lady Cavendish glared daggers. "David most certainly has no need for another companion, what with myself and"—she nodded fondly toward her daughter—"Hortense here, who has done marvels for the boy." She shrugged elaborately. "But if his lordship sees the need for another . . . *companion*"—she had spit the word out—"then what can I say? Barkley?" she called to the butler. When he appeared, she continued, "Escort Lady Jane to her bedchamber."

Jane stood and inquired, "When can I see David?"

"Soon enough," Lady Cavendish answered shortly.

Hortense, who had not said a word thus far, glowered at Jane. "David has no need of you," she exclaimed, making no effort to hide her hostility. "I am the one who looks after David. He has no need for Greek and Latin. He—"

"That will be enough, Hortense," interrupted Lady Cavendish, though without conviction.

"Which chamber, m'lady?" asked Barkley.

"Hmm . . . that empty one on the third floor will do. Bridget's old room."

Third floor? Jane was thunderstruck. Third floor meant servants' quarters. She opened her mouth to speak, but without another word Lady Cavendish arose from the settee and walked briskly toward the door, followed by a smirking Hortense.

"David takes his dinner in his rooms," said Hortense, tossing the words nastily over her shoulder. "You shall see him in the morning."

Jane stood aghast, her mind racing. *Third floor? This must be some mistake.* In every country estate she'd ever been in, the third floor housed the servants. Surely it must be different here.

"This way," said Barkley. Trailed by two footmen carrying her two trunks and a valise, Jane followed the butler up the stairs. Not the front stairs, she realized to her horror, the back stairs. One flight—two flights—three. One look down the dark, narrow, uncarpeted corridor told her this was indeed the servants' floor.

Stunned and sickened, she asked, "Who was Bridget?" as she followed Barkley to the far end of the hallway.

"Bridget was a parlor maid," Barkley responded briefly, his attitude so aloof she dared not ask more.

"Bridget got herself dismissed," one of the footmen whispered with a snigger. " 'Twas the stable boy what got her in a family way."

Barkley opened a narrow door at the end of the hallway. In a cloud of misery Jane stepped inside, into a chamber so small there was hardly room to turn around. A single bed, a wooden chair, a dresser with a pitcher and basin on top made up the furnishings. On the unpainted walls there were pegs to hold her clothing. For a moment she could not speak over the lump of despair that had formed in her throat, then managed, "Thank you. I can unpack by myself." *But how stupid of me,* she thought as they hastily filed out. *They think I am a servant. They weren't going to help.*

It occurred to her she had not asked about dinner. She hastened to the door and called, "Barkley?"

The snobbish butler turned reluctantly. "Yes?"

Not yes, m'lady, she noted grimly, but for now she would let that bit of rudeness go. "What time is dinner?"

"The servants dine at six o'clock in the servants' hall, next the kitchen." He shrugged and added, "You've missed it tonight. But if you go down to the kitchen, Cook might—"

"I mean the family," she retorted, her head held high.

Barkley returned a gaze as chill as ice. "The family dines at eight o'clock promptly, but—"

"Thank you, Barkley," she cut in and quickly shut the door. Biting her lip, she wondered what she should do now. Part of her wanted to throw herself on the bed and cry—but no, she had vowed not to, and besides, crying would accomplish nothing except make her eyes red. Anger seized her. *That . . . that harridan.* How dare Lady Cavendish assign her to the servants' quarters when Lord Dashmont's letter clearly stated she would be treated as a guest. *But anger will get me nowhere,* she conceded. She sank to the side of the bed, telling herself she must think rationally. Obviously there had been some mistake. Perhaps Lady Cavendish had not read the letter carefully. *Yes, of course.* Suddenly Jane felt better. Lady Cavendish had simply misunderstood her son-in-law's instructions. Easily fixed, of course. When Jane came down for the family's dinner tonight, she would carefully explain she was *Lady Jane,* the eldest daughter of an earl, and thus expected to be treated accordingly. She would delicately point out that she must be moved to a new room, for most certainly she could not remain on the servant's floor. With the utmost tactfulness she would suggest Lady Cavendish read the letter again.

It must be almost eight o'clock now, she thought. No time to change. Besides, even if she had time to open her trunks and find a new dress, she would only have to repack when she moved out of this miserable room.

There was a knock on her door. One of the footmen handed

her a pitcher. "Thought you might like some water, miss," he said.

She thanked him, shut the door, and fought back tears. All her life she had been waited on hand and foot, never giving it a thought. Now, a mere touch of kindness in this cruel new world was almost more than she could bear.

Jane smoothed down her brown traveling dress, washed briefly from the pitcher and a basin on her dresser, and looked at herself in the small, cracked mirror above. *Oh, how awful.* The face peering back was pale, and pinched with worry. Her hair, which she had unpinned and which was now hanging loosely, was the best she could do but most decidedly lacked the skilled touch of her lady's maid.

Oh, well . . . it will all be better soon, she told herself bravely. *Once Lady Cavendish rereads Dashmont's letter.*

Jane was compelled to take the servants' stairway to the second floor. *But not the rest of the way,* she thought with defiance. An exquisite Elizabethan gallery stretched from the servants' stairs to the main stairway and was hung with a long line of ancestral portraits. As she sped past, Jane marveled at their beauty. Was that a Romney? Was this a Van Dyck? If she weren't so hungry and anxious to talk to her ladyship, she would stop to inspect them closer.

Jane reached the bottom of the main staircase and stepped into the awe-inspiring, barrel-vaulted entry hall where paintings, mostly of sporting events and horses, lined the walls. The savory aroma of roast beef and its accoutrements wafted into her nostrils. Her stomach churned. She was *so* hungry. Thank heavens, she would be eating soon. Which way? The house was so vast she had no idea which direction to go, but a passing parlor maid directed her to the dining room. When she found it, her first thought was how beautiful it was, with its rococo ceiling of pale blue and white, its crimson flock-paper, and the rose and brick red Axminster carpet covering much of the floor—old oak she could see around the edges. Then shock flew through her. Lady Cavendish and her daughter were already in their places at the long, mahogany table, which could seat at least thirty, but at the moment was set for only two.

There was no third setting.

Jane's knees grew a trifle shaky as she approached the table. A dead silence greeted her. Both mother and daughter seemed busy at their meal, but surely they were aware of her presence. Jane cleared her throat. "Good evening." The two abruptly stopped eating and stared up at her. "I . . . I have come for dinner."

Lady Cavendish's face darkened in a scowl. "You are expecting dinner here?" She sounded aghast.

"But of course." Jane took a deep breath. She must be bold. "His Lordship's letter most clearly states—"

"Did you read the letter?"

"No, I did not."

Sighing with annoyance, as if she had been greatly inconvenienced, Lady Cavendish continued, "If you did not read it, then how do you presume to know what was in it?"

"He told me I was to be an honored guest."

Hortense snickered. Jane ignored the rudeness and struggled on. "I was to be assigned a guest room, not one on the servants' floor. I was to eat here, with the family. Perhaps, if you were to read Lord Dashmont's letter again . . . ?"

Lady Cavendish awarded her a bleak, tight-lipped smile. "I know exactly what it says, Jane. You are to be David's governess. You are to be quartered on the servants' floor. You will take your meals in the servants' dining hall, or with the upper servants, if you wish, in the housekeeper's dining room."

"Surely not with us," Hortense squeaked, her nose twitching, as if she had encountered something extremely distasteful.

Lady Cavendish nodded in agreement with her daughter's sentiments and continued, "We did not invite you. If you do not wish to stay here, then for pity's sake, do not. His lordship's coach is here for the night and will return to London in the morning. Take it back if you like. Rest assured we shan't try to stop you."

In desperation Jane asked, "May I see the letter?"

Lady Cavendish abruptly pushed herself to a standing position, eyes ablaze with fury. "Young lady, I see I shall have to be bluntly honest with you. The letter is none of your business and has been destroyed. You are not welcome here. If you're hungry, you may obtain your meal in the kitchen, along with the rest of the servants. Then tomorrow I would strongly suggest you return to London, the earlier the better."

Jane stood where she was, at a loss what to do. She could not go back to London. There was nothing to go back to. By now, Mama, Aunt, and Christabell had begun their sorrowful journey to the yeoman's cottage, soon to be joined by her three younger sisters, who had been living at Hedley Hall. Even without her, the cottage would be dreadfully overcrowded. No, she could not, under any circumstances, return to her family. Besides, they needed the money Dashmont was going to provide for her services. Jane felt numb. Never in her life had she felt so weak . . . so poor . . . so powerless. *But he did promise me.* The answer came to her in a flash. *I shall send a letter to Dashmont. When he hears of what has happened, surely he'll come and set things right.*

"Lady Cavendish," she began, "I shall not return to London tomorrow, but I shall most certainly send along a letter to Lord Dashmont requesting he . . . he clarify his instructions in his letter. Perhaps if he came—"

"Don't bother." Ignoring Jane, Lady Cavendish seated herself, picked up a piece of bread, and slowly broke it in two. "More wine, please, Jeffrey," she commanded one of the footmen. As if she had just remembered Jane still standing there, she returned her attention. "There would be a certain difficulty delivering your message. As I recall, my dear son-in-law added a postscript to his letter, informing me that this morning he planned to leave London." Her mouth pulled into a sour smile. "As we speak, Lord Dashmont sails the high seas, well on his way to Jamaica." With a show of great composure, she took a sip of wine. "But don't worry, my dear. His lordship should be returning, perhaps in a year or two."

Jane spun on her heel and left the dining room without another word. Numb with shock, clinging tightly to the polished mahogany railing, she dragged her way up the main staircase to the second-story landing. At the top, as she paused to catch her breath, her knees went weak, then nearly buckled beneath her, just as her stomach cramped from lack of food. Jane grit her teeth. *Just let me get back to my room,* she beseeched, glancing

upward. Such irony. She had spurned that wretched little room
less than an hour ago, but now it was her only haven, to which
she could hardly wait to return. How she longed to fling herself
onto that lumpy little bed, pull up the covers and shut out the
world. *Now if I can just get back there . . .*

From the landing, Jane looked down the long, Elizabethan
gallery. Strange, it hadn't looked so long before, but now the
end of it seemed to disappear into infinity. She then must climb
another flight of stairs to the servants' quarters. Would she
make it? Her legs were shaking. She wasn't sure she could put
one foot in front of the other. Worse, she was feeling light-
headed. *I must make it. I cannot stand here all night at the top
of the main stairway.* She took a deep breath, but that seemed
to make her dizziness worse. Little black dots started swarming
in front of her eyes. *I cannot faint in the hallway,* she thought
with consternation, but despite herself, the black dots melted
into one big black blur. She sank to the top step, crouched over,
and covered her face with her hands. Her stomach cramped
again and she moaned, beyond all caring.

How long she sat huddled on the staircase she wasn't sure,
but she felt a sudden tap on her shoulder and heard a man's
reedy voice ask, "Here, here, girl, what are you doing on the
staircase?"

She felt too weak to lift her head up, but felt the tap again and
knew she would have to. Forcing her gaze upward, she saw a
white-haired old man in a blue damask dressing gown leaning
on his cane, supported on the other arm by his valet. "What the
devil is wrong?" he asked, scowling fiercely down at her.

She replied weakly, "Nothing's wrong."

"Who are you?" demanded the old man with no attempt at
courtesy. He was not a pretty sight, she noted distastefully. Hair
sprouted from his ears; ugly brown spots marred his hands and
face; bushy white brows grew in every direction over eyes that
once were probably bright blue, but now were dim and faded.
Before she could answer, he tapped her with his cane again, not
hard, but enough to arouse her indignation. "Speak up, girl."

"I do *not* need to be jabbed," she declared forcefully. She
thought to struggle to her feet, but decided against it. She still
felt dizzy, and there was a good chance she might collapse

again. But she couldn't just sit here, not with this horrible old man berating her . . .

With an effort she pulled herself to her feet. A new spell of dizziness attacked her, but she fought it back, saving herself by grabbing onto the newel post. "My name is Lady Jane Sperling," she managed faintly. "I am a guest of Anthony, Lord Dashmont. He wishes me to be a companion to his son, David, so I've just arrived from London—"

"You?" the old man interrupted waspishly, his eyes sweeping over her. "Come to teach David? Now there's a travesty if ever there was one."

Jane felt herself stiffen from the sheer offensiveness of the man. "And who might you be, sir?" she inquired coldly.

"I am Anthony's uncle, Lord Harleigh." He raked her with eyes full of contempt. "How old are you?"

"Nineteen."

"The Earl of Sperling's daughter, aren't you?"

She nodded.

"Sperling . . ." he mused, ". . . last I heard, he was tossing his fortune away with both hands. Has the fool got anything left by now?"

Such rudeness. Jane glared at him, not answering.

"So he tossed it all. Terrible waste. What idiocy." The old man gave her a withering gaze. "You're one of those bird-witted London debutantes, aren't you?"

She was feeling weak again and was forced to grab tighter onto the newel post. "I do not believe I have to stand here and listen—"

"Come to teach David," the old man ranted, "teach him what? How to tap your fan? How to flutter your eyelids at some empty-headed fop?"

Jane drew in her breath, aware she could not stay on her feet much longer. "Sir, I have traveled all day and am very tired. Also, I am exceedingly hungry. But since I have just learned I am supposed to eat in the servants' quarters, which I shall never, never do, I shall return to my tiny chamber up on the servants' floor, where, most likely, I shall starve to death. So with your permission, sir, I shall bid you *adieu.*"

"Think you're too good to eat with the servants, eh?" he flung at her.

If she'd sounded bitter, she didn't care. Without replying, and with as much dignity as she could muster, Jane turned away from Lord Harleigh and started down the hallway, informing herself she must walk a straight line and not, under any circumstances, keel over.

"Do her good to eat with the servants," she heard Lord Harleigh comment to his valet. "Those empty-headed London belles—all fluff, no substance. Snooty to boot. Haven't got the faintest notion what life's about. Well, she'll find out. Come, James, help me back to my room."

In the pitch black darkness, Jane lay curled on her lumpy bed, drained, hollow, lifeless. She had thought the low point of her life was when her father lost his fortune and sailed for America. Little had she known. Now her spirits had sunk to new depths. That tiny spark of hope she had sustained for her future had now been smothered—quickly, totally. Such a hopeless dilemma. She could not, under any circumstances, return to London, but if she remained here . . .

Jane pictured herself in the housekeeper's parlor, eating with the butler . . . the cook . . . *oh, dear God.* She would rather die than eat with the servants, upper or no. Her stomach cramped again, harder now, reminding her of the hunger gnawing at her vitals. With bitter irony she remembered all those fancy dinner parties where she had hardly touched her plate, blithely waving away Wesphalian ham and *vol-au-vent* of chicken, carrot *soup à la Geole,* compote of peaches, Nesselrode pudding and lemon cream . . .

Ah! Why even dream of such extravagances when right now she would settle for a crust of bread . . . a bit of cheese . . . anything. But she had her pride. Under no circumstances could she lower herself to sneak to the kitchen.

However, she must face reality. Without a care in the world, she had lived all her life in a cocoon of wealth and privilege, but those days were gone forever. If she remained here, she would be treated like a scullery maid at the hands of Lady Cavendish, her daughter, Hortense, and Dashmont's horrible old uncle, Lord Harleigh. *Oh, Papa, why did you leave me?* she silently cried. She tried to picture him and Edmund, safe at sea, heading for a new life in America. They were the lucky ones, she thought bleakly. She could also run away, but where? *I cannot go, I cannot stay.* Nothing but a dismal future awaited her, no matter what she did.

Dashmont's responsible for this, how I hate the man, were her final thoughts before she finally drifted into miserable, fitful sleep, hardly caring what tomorrow might bring.

Chapter 9

When Jane slowly awakened the next morning, her first thought was *food.* Half awake, she mused, *surely Sarah will bring my tray soon . . .*

Stark reality hit her full force as she fully awakened. No maid anymore—no friends, no family, she was all alone. Even if she died of starvation in this tiny, godforsaken room, there was no one to care. With despair she thought of that horrible scene last night in the dining room. How humiliating. How galling.

But whatever else, she must find something to eat, she thought, and struggled out of bed. It was early. Perhaps no one would see her if she slipped downstairs to the kitchen.

Hurriedly, she slipped into her plain brown traveling dress and smoothed her hair. Glancing out the window, she saw a splendid day dawning and gave a choked, desperate laugh. In her old life, each sunrise brought new promise. Her spirits always lifted at the sight. Not today, though. She came to a momentous decision: call it pride, foolishness, stubbornness—call it anything, including complete stupidity, but even if she starved to death, she could never bring herself to eat in the servants' quarters. *No.* She could not lower herself to rummage in the kitchen either—to grovel for food. She would not give Lady Cavendish the satisfaction.

What should she do? From her window she caught a glimpse of wooded hills. She stared at her four unpainted, scarred-up walls that seemed to be closing in on her and thought, *I am trapped here, I must get out.*

Perhaps a walk would clear her head.

It was so early few servants were stirring. Ignoring the gnawing of sharp hunger pains and her increasing weakness, she slipped quickly from her room and found a place to wash at the end of the hall. She hurried down the servants' staircase, out the back entrance, and drew in a breath of crisp, early morning air. She stood still a moment, her gaze taking in the vast acres of the estate. *How beautiful,* she thought again. The sun had just peeked above the wooded hills, causing dew to glisten on the vast stretches of verdant green lawn, and on the bluebells, primroses, and violets that lined a winding path. She chose to follow the path and first walked through a formal garden of yews and allées. Beyond it, she passed beneath an ancient stone archway with a Tudor gateway that bore several clear-cut coats of arms. After crossing another stretch of lawn, she reached a stand of dense wood where the path led toward the top of a hill. *Can I make it?* she wondered. Her legs were wobbling. *But I must.* She most urgently needed to find a lofty place where she could sit, think, and decide what to do. A hilltop would suit just fine.

She started up the heavily wooded pathway, her breath coming harder, her legs growing weaker with every step, but she would not give up, she told herself firmly. Finally she reached the top. Amidst a tangle of oaks, tall poplars, and the branches of small hazels, she glanced at the sight on the other side, and gasped in wonderment.

A small, green valley lay beneath her. By a gurgling brook, in the clearness of the early morning sunlight, she beheld gray, jagged, majestic stone walls that reached silently toward the sky. It was the ruins of an ancient, roofless church—a large one, she marveled. Around the church stretched acres and acres of ruins of what once must have been a busy monastery. She could make out the remains of many buildings: what must have been the chapter house, the stables, the remains of a garden, probably a bakery, the kitchen, perhaps a wool house, and many more. *That must be the cloister,* she thought—an open courtyard that was the heart of the buildings where the monks lived, from which alleys linked all the domestic buildings and the church. She gazed with delight upon the graceful arcades that lined the alleys. How delicate the arches, bases, and pedestals! What a miracle these fragile pieces of art had actually survived.

But the church itself was the most spectacular, with its high walls that bespoke of a time long gone. Sadly, a gigantic pile of debris covered the knave, mostly from the fallen roof, but also from the partially collapsed walls. She had no doubt this was an ancient, probably Cistercian, monastery that had been destroyed during the Great Suppression. In awe, she crossed her hands over her heart. What a marvelous surprise, and so unexpected.

"What are you doing here?" an old man's annoyed voice called from a distance.

She had thought she was alone. Startled, she looked down the hill, into the remains of the garden that lay by the old church. It was Lord Harleigh, that horrid old man she had met last night. How unpleasant to see him here. And why was he here so early in the morning? From a distance she discerned he was seated on a stone bench, one of several that formed a circle around an ancient sundial in the middle of the cloister garden. In front of him stood an easel with a canvas resting on it. On his one side were brushes and paints. On the other stood a small table. On it, laid out in orderly fashion on a white damask cloth, were a plate of bread, butter, and cheeses, a bowl of fruit, a pot of . . . it had to be tea. *Food.* Her stomach churned at the sight. It was simple fare, surely, but what wouldn't she give for just one taste.

In answer to his question, she called back politely, "I am out for a stroll, sir." Her voice was weak and shaky. She doubted her ability to conceal her hunger much longer and knew that if she was to retain her dignity she should leave immediately. Surely there was no use staying. From what she had seen of acid-tongued Lord Harleigh, he would most assuredly not wish to share his breakfast.

"Come down here," the old man called.

"I . . . I must get back."

"To what? Come down here," he repeated again, this time in a voice that did not invite protestation.

What had she to lose? She followed the rest of the pathway down the hillside, so weak by now she was compelled to make a conscious effort not to wobble about like some feeble old lady. Lord Harleigh hardly glanced in her direction as she approached. Dabbing at the canvas with his brush, he seemed concentrated on his painting. But when she arrived at the bench, he slanted a dubious gaze at her and asked, "Well, did you get something to eat last night? Or is your pride still causing you to starve yourself?"

Weak as she was, she could not help bristling. "The condition of my stomach is none of your concern, sir. I . . ." The enticing smell of freshly baked bread wafted past her nostrils. She closed her eyes and tried to think of something else, but to no avail. Despite her best intentions, she could not continue her bold answer to his lordship—could not, in fact, remove her gaze from his breakfast. *If I'm not careful, I shall start to drool,* she thought bemusedly. *I should run away from here immediately.*

"'Tis clear to see you did not eat." The old man was giving her his full attention now, gazing at her from beneath his bushy brows with probing eyes. "Best sit down, young lady"—he indicated a space on the other side of the bench, next to the food—"James has brought bread, cheese, and a bit of fruit. A modest repast, but perhaps you won't mind. Help yourself." He wiped out his empty cup and raised his pot of tea. "Enough for another cup, I think."

Food. Jane quickly seated herself on the bench and reached for a piece of bread. *You must retain your manners,* she warned herself, but it was all she could do to keep from cramming the entire piece into her mouth. *One bite at a time. Ah . . . how good. How wonderful.* After a few restrained bites, she picked up a knife and slathered the remainder of the bread with all the golden yellow butter she could pile on. When it slid down her throat, she knew there was nothing on this earth as beautiful, as joyous, as food.

Not a crumb of bread, butter, cheese, or apple remained when she finished and wiped her lips with a napkin Harleigh provided. She heaved a huge sigh of contentment. "Thank you, sir. That was wonderful." The thought struck her that never in her whole life had she truly understood what hunger meant. How horrible to be without food. Of course, she had heard of people starving, that it was a rather common occurrence, even in England. "I never knew what it was like to starve."

"Time you learned," the old man said bluntly. "Chits like you have no idea what goes on beyond your snobbish little world. Might as well live on the moon." Scowling, he scrutinized his painting and dabbed a touch of blue sky with his brush before he muttered, "London debutantes. Worthless." He glowered at her, thick brows bristling. "What was that nephew of mine thinking of? You'll not be happy here. Best get yourself back to London."

"I cannot go back," she answered firmly. Her gaze roamed over the old stone walls. "What *is* this place?"

"Merely an old ruin." Harleigh dipped his brush and started painting again. "You'd not be interested."

"But I am," she persisted, ignoring the old man's cynicism. "Surely this is one of the abbeys that was destroyed in the Great Suppression, but I cannot think which one."

Only a corner of Lord Harleigh's mouth twitched, but she knew she had captured his interest. "Great Suppression, eh?" he asked with feigned curiosity. "You must enlighten me."

"Gladly, sir." She would go along with his game, but if he thought he was fooling her, he was sadly mistaken. "Following the valuation of all church property in 1535, an act was placed before Parliament in 1536 that dismantled all religious houses with income of less than 200 pounds. By 1537, the wealthier houses fell, all of them pillaged and destroyed, including—"

"Enough, enough." The old man waved his hand impatiently. "So you've picked up a modicum of history. Good girl."

Again, she ignored his belittling words and asked, "Which one is this?"

"Linneshall," he answered tersely.

"Linneshall Abbey?" A shiver of excitement shot through her. "Why, Linneshall was one of the greatest—one of the richest. The lead from the roof alone was worth well over 1000 pounds." The enormity of her discovery sunk in. "And it's here—right here?" She was at a loss for words and sat gazing enraptured at the ruins, chin resting upon her clasped hands. Noticing a faded inscription carved into the stone rim of the sundial, she walked to it, bent, and read aloud, *"Tempus . . . edax . . . rerum.* I can just make the letters out. How appropriate."

Lord Harleigh slowly lowered his brush and stared at her with growing incredulity. "Translate," he demanded.

"Time, that devours all things," she replied without hesitation. "See, it is appropriate—especially when you look about you at these ruins." Seeing his look of astonishment, she fluttered her eyelids and gave him her well-practiced teasing smile. "My, my, however do you suppose she found such knowledge in her poor little empty head?"

The old man ignored her banter and sat silent for a time, as if in deep thought. "So you know Latin."

"Yes, and Greek, too. And French. Although how such a featherbrained debutante such as myself—"

"Silence!" Lord Harleigh gave her a searching look that swept her up and down, as if he were seeing her for the first time. "Why did Anthony send you here?"

"It's a long story." She leaned back comfortably on the stone bench and related the sad tale of how her father had lost the family fortune to Lord Bradbourne and had fled England, doubtless never to return. Briefly she mentioned how Lord Dashmont had aided her father and brother in their escape to America, and how, because he was contrite, he had come to invite her to Fairfield Manor.

". . . so that's why I am here, sir, to be a companion to little David and teach him Greek and Latin. The rest of my family have returned to a cottage close to Hedley Hall, our former estate." The words, *former estate,* still rankled and it was hard, keeping the bitterness from her voice. It was difficult, too, not to show her hostile feelings toward Lord Dashmont, although she had tried.

When she finished, Lord Harleigh addressed her with a shrewd look in his eye. "Don't like my nephew, do you?"

Tried, but not hard enough. "No, I do not like him," she answered honestly, and gave the reasons why. "And now this latest. He had said I would be an honored guest, but I am forced to sleep on the servants' floor and cannot take my meals with her ladyship and Lady Hortense."

"Ah, what a terrible life she leads," exclaimed his ancient lordship, rolling his eyes upward to address some deity on high. With a piercing gaze he asked, "Why are you whining? I can think of no duller way to spend the evening than dining with those two dimwits."

Had she been whining? Surprised, Jane answered, "It is quite obvious you do not tolerate whiners, sir, nor do I wish to whine. But still, Lord Dashmont and I had an agreement, which he has broken."

"My nephew is a man of his word," replied Lord Harleigh. "The problem lies elsewhere." He picked up his brush and started painting again. He had chosen to paint a section of the brook bordered by shadowed walls intertwined with ivy, and it was quite good, she observed. "That old crone," he mumbled. To Jane he said, "I, too, am an 'honored guest,' or I would protest on your behalf. But alas, Anthony has put Lady Cavendish in charge and there's nothing I can do." He muttered an oath and shook his head. "Look what she's done to her poor daughter. Criticized Hortense from the day she was born—keeps her coddled—tells her she's too fragile to lead a normal life, so the poor creature creeps around with the vitality of a snail. Miserable woman. Can't stand the sight of her."

"But can you not leave?"

Lord Harleigh shook his head. "I have lived at Fairfield Manor all my life—long before Anthony inherited it. He allows his old bachelor uncle to stay, though, and that's my preference, although I am far from destitute and could find excellent lodgings elsewhere, if I so chose. Then, too, I own Linneshall. The ruins you see about you are mine, not Anthony's, so you can see why I prefer living here, despite— ah, Brother William."

Jane followed Lord Harleigh's gaze to where the slight, brown-clad figure of an old monk stood quietly beside the gurgling brook.

Lord Harleigh summoned the old monk closer and performed introductions. "Brother William," he explained to Jane, "belongs to a small group of Cistercians—all that's left of the Linneshall monastery. They come here to garden." He nodded toward the long, neat rows of vegetables that took up part of the large garden.

"Lord Harleigh is too modest," said Brother William, bowing humbly to Jane, his arms crossed and invisible in the voluminous sleeves of his simple brown robe. With a kindly smile he added, "His lordship allows us the use of his garden, may God bless him."

Lord Harleigh snorted. " 'Tis the least I can do." To Jane he said, "Brother William and his humble flock live close by and feed half the countryside." His eyes suddenly twinkled with amusement. "Now, there's where you could have gone for a meal."

"Indeed," agreed Brother William. "We feed all who are hungry, and ask no questions. You are welcome anytime."

With a wave of her hand Jane indicated the surrounding ruins. "What a beautiful place this must have been. Do you ever feel bitter it was stolen from you and destroyed?"

"All those years ago?" Brother William shrugged and sighed. " 'Twas God's will, for reasons I am not privileged to understand. We can only give a humble thanks that God allows us to work in His gardens. And speaking of that"—with a merry gleam in his eye Brother William nodded toward his rows of vegetables—"God's weeds are growing tall. I must get to work."

After Brother William had gone to tend his garden, Lord Harleigh remarked, "My great-great- great-great-great-grandfather bought Linneshall directly after the Great Suppression. Pity. By all that's morally right, this property should still belong to the Cistercians."

"Then should you not return it?" asked Jane.

The old man seemed taken aback a moment, then guffawed. "Blunt little chit, aren't you? Well, if I were a saint, I would return it, but I'm not." He waved a hand grandly over the landscape. "Behold the ruins of Linneshall Abbey. Not just another plot of land, but a piece of England's precious history, which I am loath to part with. Lord knows, I will soon enough. Then it shall go to Anthony. God knows what he'll do with it. He has no love for ancient monasteries. Meanwhile, Linneshall Abbey has been, and always shall be, my life's work. Hundreds of manuscripts have been preserved from the abbey library—"

"Manuscripts?" Jane could scarce believe what she had heard. "You have manuscripts from Linneshall?"

"Hundreds." Lord Harleigh regarded her curiously. "But

surely a little chit like you would have no interest in ancient monastery manuscripts."

Such miracles, Jane thought as she returned to the manor. A miracle Lord Harleigh had invited her to take her meals with him. A miracle he had asked her to assist him with the precious manuscripts of Linneshall. She had awakened this morning in the depths of despair. Now, although she ached for her family and a life that could never be hers again, she felt a glimmer of hope, thanks to that grumpy old man. Perhaps living here might at least be tolerable, after all.

She returned to her humble room and unpacked her trunks. *I won't think of it,* she resolved as she hung her fashionable gowns on the very pegs Bridget must have used for her servants' dress. When done, she washed and changed from the wilted traveling clothes into a striped blue silk morning dress, her favorite with its nine rows of blue ribbon and a row of pearl buttons around the hem. Actually, it was a bit too fancy for a governess to wear, but she *wasn't* a governess, she was an honored guest and would wear whatever she wanted. She had always loved the cap she placed atop her head. It was a cornette of tulle, with rouleaux pulling in bouffants of white tulle. *A trifle elaborate,* she mused as she gazed into the tiny piece of mirror, teasing bits of curls from beneath the cap to lie on her forehead. But knowing she looked her best would help get her through this difficult day.

The problem was, she hadn't the slightest notion how to be a governess. David might well be difficult this first day. *What do I do?* she asked herself. She recalled Miss Ebersley, her longtime governess, who had been both stern and strict, yet at the same time had laced her lessons with warmth and humor. *I shall be just like Miss Ebersley.*

She found her way to David's classroom. When she entered, she witnessed David, pale and lifeless at his desk, halfheartedly writing with chalk upon a slate. Hortense, her face set in a frown, was standing over him, looking her usual dour self in a calico morning dress of dull tan that accentuated the sallowness of her skin. *She has an unfortunately high, rather shiny, forehead,* Jane reflected. *She could hide it easily with a few well-*

placed ringlets. But not the hint of a curl poked from beneath the drab, unadorned cap that perched atop Hortense's head.

Hortense stiffened at the sight of her. "We are doing sums," she said, her tone clearly indicating Jane was rude to interrupt.

"So I see," said Jane. She entered boldly, picked up David's slate, and silently examined the indifferent scribbles, thus giving herself time to think. This was no time for insipid politeness. Miss Ebersley would know it was imperative to send a clear message as to who was in charge. "David, we shall go over your sums shortly, but I can see already we need to work on neatness. Lady Hortense, I would appreciate your showing me how far David has progressed in studies."

Hortense bristled. "You must remember he is a very delicate little boy. His studies, of necessity, must be limited."

"Of course," said Jane, "but I'll need to give David some tests so that I might evaluate him."

David slumped farther into his chair and put his hand to his stomach. "I don't feel good."

No wonder, thought Jane. "I'm sorry you're not feeling well," she told him brightly. "We shall take a little walk shortly. Some fresh air and sunshine would do you good."

David's lower lip trembled in a pout. "Don't want to go for a walk."

Hortense put a protective hand on David's shoulder. "Mama says there are bad vapors in the air. With his delicate condition he is not allowed out."

Jane stopped herself from exclaiming, *nonsense!* and instead managed a mild, "But it's lovely out today. Surely—"

"No, Mama is adamant. The child is too fragile, both for walks and extensive study, and that's that." Hortense addressed David. "Go lie down and rest for a while, sweetheart. Jane and I shall have a little talk."

I must make my stand, thought Jane. She waited until David was out of the room before she drew herself up and said firmly, "I have two things to say to you. First, I am *Lady* Jane. And second, Lord Dashmont has instructed me to teach his son, and so I shall. I let him go today, but in the future, unless he shows valid signs of being ill, he will stay in this classroom and do his studies. As for the walks—"

"Mama won't like this!" An unspoken fear was alive in Hortense's hazel eyes. "I shall report you to Mama immediately."

"Do that," said Jane. *You milk-and-water miss,* she thought, but wisely refrained from saying. She recalled the resolve she had made yesterday when she arrived: *I shall do my best to become friends and always be pleasant, as a guest should be. I shall greet any kind of snub, or slight, with equanimity. I shall be good with David, who's such a fine little boy. My behavior shall be impeccable.*

Ah, how little had she known! But still . . .

What if I had been raised by the dominating Lady Cavendish? Constantly criticized. Constantly told I was too fragile to lead a normal life? Forced to creep around with the vitality of a snail? How dreadful! I, too, would be a quivering, cowardly mess, no doubt worse than Hortense.

The poor girl was so under her mother's thumb she had no friends, and certainly no suitors. In fact, did she have any kind of a social life? Impulsively, Jane asked, "Hortense, have you ever had a Season? I don't recall ever seeing you at any of the events in London."

"With my delicate health?" asked Hortense, not masking her surprise. "Of course not."

But there was nothing wrong with her. This was all the fault of her horrid mother. *Poor Hortense.* Obviously there was no use in being unpleasant to the poor girl, disagreeable though she was.

In fact, what if I tried to help her?

It would not be easy. Jane's impulse was to inform Hortense just what she thought of her hostile attitude. There would be a certain gratification in that, but spiteful words, even though true, would accomplish nothing. The noble course would be to rise above vindictiveness and try—dared she even think it?—to be friends, or at the very least, not enemies. How she could accomplish such a formidable task, she wasn't sure. Hortense was *such* a prig. And yet, wasn't there some good in everybody, even the most heinous of criminals?

There must be something good about Hortense, thought Jane, surreptitiously looking her nemesis up and down. That awful scowl and hostile attitude—that unappealing skin—that too-high forehead—the drabness of her gown—no, there wasn't a thing, unless . . . those eyes! Hortense's eyes were large, of a soft hazel color, flecked with a beautiful emerald green.

"What pretty eyes you have." Jane braced herself, prepared for a rebuke. "Do you know, I have a pair of beautiful emerald earrings that would bring out those little flecks of green just perfectly."

For a fleeting moment Hortense's face relaxed its hostility and gave way to an expression of pleased surprise. A blush crept over her cheeks. "I . . . I . . ." she stumbled, until aware her barriers had relaxed, she whirled around and hurried to the door. Turning back, her hostile expression restored, she snapped, "I cannot be distracted. You can rest assured I shall report all this to Mama."

Silent, Jane watched her take her leave. *How discouraging.* Her meeting with David had been most unsatisfactory, and now this. If she wished to make a friend of Hortense, it would be a most formidable task.

That evening, dressed for dinner, Jane knocked on the door to Lord Harleigh's rooms. James, the valet, opened the door and invited her into a large room in dark shadows where, dominating most of one end, a canopied rococo bed sat upon a raised, carpeted platform. It was hung with gold lace, its posts formed of palm trunks. Near a large marble fireplace Lord Harleigh was sitting at a small table set for two with fine china, silver, and flickering candles casting shadows upon the blue damask walls.

"Well, don't stand there, come in," he called and waved her to sit across from him.

After she had seated herself, she politely inquired, "Are you sure I am not inconveniencing you? Perhaps you prefer to take your meals with Lady Cavendish and her daughter in the dining room."

"Are you daft?" Lord Harleigh's lip lifted disdainfully. "Those bird-witted women keep to their part of the house, and I to mine. Haven't taken a meal with them for years." He regarded her curiously. "Can't understand why you were so dead set on eating with them."

James deftly set a plateful of food in front of her. Just plain food, she noted, as the pungent aroma of roast beef wafted past her nostrils.

"You'll not find fancy food here, missy," warned Lord Harleigh. "If you want fancy food with fancy French names, go downstairs."

She laughed and breathed a contented sigh. "I'm happy with this, sir."

After dinner, Lord Harleigh led the way to his adjoining study lined with deep mahogany shelves full of ancient leather-bound volumes and manuscripts of every description. "So here you have it—the books from Linneshall." Proudly the old man pointed his cane at a stack of manuscripts on a table. "Those are the ones I've translated. The rest, all to be done. You have come along at the right time, my dear."

Jane could see by the eager gleam in his eye that he was indeed glad to have her to help him. She spied a beautifully bound volume, opened it, and traced her fingers over green leaf scrolls intertwined around illuminated letters of purple and gold. "How beautiful . . . in Latin, I see." She glanced about the room. "What treasures you have here."

"More than that, there's real treasure at Linneshall Abbey."

Treasure. The very word held magic. "Real treasure? You must tell me."

"If you insist, but don't think you're going to find it." Lord Harleigh had them both settle into two comfortable elbow chairs facing on either side of the fireplace. Then he began, "When the suppression started in 1535, a brave man named Abbot Wulfric was head of Linneshall Abbey. He was a gentleman by birth and education, but a profound, austere monk—quite obviously a saint, which was most awkward for the king, who, for a time, left Linneshall in peace. But eventually the king ordered Linneshall destroyed like the others, and its treasure turned over to his coffers. Abbot Wulfric refused. As the story goes, he and his monks buried the treasure somewhere in the abbey, but it was never found."

"What sort of treasure was it?" asked Jane.

"There were crosses, of course, some plain gold or silver, others encrusted with precious stones, hanging from heavy gold chains. There were gold plates, silver goblets, and dishes. It is said a solid gold chalice was the pride of the monastery. It was embedded with sapphires, emeralds, and rubies—or so I am told, but it was so long ago that who knows the truth of it?"

"What happened to Abbot Wulfric?"

"He and seven of his monks were taken to London, to the Tower, where they were tried, found guilty, and executed. Thomas More, by the way, watched from his prison window."

"What a fascinating story," Jane declared, "and how sad. Do you think it's true?"

"There's buried treasure out there, I have no doubt, but where to dig? Walls have collapsed, as have roofs. As you saw this morning, much of the abbey grounds are covered with tons of rubble, including huge, unmovable stones."

"Could he have left a map?"

"Perhaps, but where?"

Treasure—so exciting to think about. "I shall keep my eye out while I am here."

"Best forget about it. 'Tis not likely you'd ever find it."

She laughed. "Whether I would or not doesn't matter, but I can dream, can't I? Last night when I arrived, I thought my life was over. Now I have the manuscripts and the treasure to think about." She smiled wryly. "Not much, I know, but it appears your nephew has inadvertently done me a small favor."

"My nephew is careful about whom he does favors for. He must like you a good deal in order to trust his son to you."

"I didn't get far today," Jane answered ruefully. "David would hardly look at me, let alone talk. When I suggested I take the boy for a walk, Hortense said David is not allowed out. It appears Lady Cavendish is concerned about his delicate condition and fears 'bad vapors' in the air."

"Bah!" After a moment, Lord Harleigh shook his head. "Pity about the boy. The shock of his mother's death was bad enough, but then Anthony compounded the problem by putting David in his grandmother's care. That woman"—his face was marked with disgust—"it's painful to see what she's doing to the child. In truth, she's making an invalid of him, as she's done to Hortense, if he isn't one already."

"I'm not sure what to do," said Jane. "I tried to be firm today, but David defied me, supported by Hortense."

From underneath his bushy brows, Lord Harleigh's keen eyes stared directly into hers. "Forget Hortense. You must stand up to Lady Cavendish. If Anthony left his son in your charge, then you must make it clear to her imperious ladyship that you are indeed the one in charge."

When Jane finally left Lord Harleigh's rooms, it was with lifted spirits. Her stomach was full; she had enjoyed an evening of good conversation, despite Lord Harleigh's gruffness; and best of all, she would be helping to translate the Linneshall manuscripts, a task she would hugely enjoy. For the first time in her life she felt a sense of purpose, though it was tempered by today's defeat with David.

And then there was the treasure . . .

How silly of her to think she could actually find it. Yet the fun lay in thinking she might, so she would not forget about it, as Lord Harleigh had advised. Her future wasn't as totally bleak as she had thought last night, and yet . . . *What am I thinking of?* she thought grimly, and her spirits dipped again. She was still removed from friends and family, still penniless, still taking her meals with practically a total stranger, and living in a squalid room on the servants' floor.

Yet another problem bedeviled her. If she was to help David, tomorrow she must confront the formidable Lady Cavendish.

"What do you want?" Lady Cavendish and Hortense were seated in the small salon, both stitching their embroidery. "Can't you see we are busy?" the older woman asked, raising eyes filled with annoyance.

Jane took a deep breath and stepped inside, making sure her misgivings didn't show. "I have come to have a word with you concerning David."

Lady Cavendish eyed her shrewdly. "Only David? So everything else is to your satisfaction then?"

Jane returned an arched glance. "If you are referring to my room, hardly. As for my eating arrangements, as you may have heard, Lord Harleigh has kindly invited me to take my meals with him." She could not prevent herself from adding, "I am delighted. I could not ask for better company."

Jane watched, secretly amused, as Lady Cavendish's eyebrows flew together in a scowl. "Lord Harleigh good company? Bah!"

"He is a bit gruff, but I find him—"

"That man is the bane of my existence." A muscle flicked angrily in her ladyship's jaw. "Heaven only knows the sacrifices I made in order to come here and care for David, not the least of which is having to put up with that rude, uncouth old man."

Hortense chimed, "He does not have good manners," bobbing her head up and down in smug agreement with her mother.

"No, he does not," echoed Lady Cavendish. "And furthermore, he spends his days in unnatural pursuits, such as poring over those filthy old manuscripts from the ruined abbey. They're not even in English—a complete waste of time."

"Perhaps," said Jane. She had not been asked to sit, and thus was anxious to end her ladyship's ranting. "But be that as it may, I have come to discuss David."

"What now?" Lady Cavendish threw her embroidery hoop aside in disgust. "Haven't I done all I can to accommodate Lord Dashmont's wishes? You've seen the classroom. You had all day yesterday to get acquainted with the child, so by now you must be aware of how frail and delicate he is. Surely you realize he must not be burdened by lengthy hours of study." She sniffed and raised one side of her upper lip disagreeably. "If only I'd had the opportunity to discuss this with Anthony before he"—a fleeting look of fury crossed her face—"but never mind. I have done his bidding and that's that. So what more did you want, Jane?"

Jane wanted very much to scream at this strident woman, not Jane, *Lady* Jane, but that was not the purpose of her visit, so she refrained. "Yesterday David was terribly withdrawn and hardly spoke to me, in contrast to that day in the park when I saw him smile and heard him laugh. But no wonder. He's all cooped up most of the time, and according to Hortense, hardly ever goes outside. That's what I'm here about. The child needs fresh air and sunshine."

"Out of the question."

"No, it is not." Here came the hard part, not unexpected by any means. She had known she would have a difficult time with Dashmont's mother-in-law. Jane forced herself to smile pleasantly. "I see no reason why David cannot be allowed outside for at least a stroll. Rest assured, I shall be right there with him." Firmly, she added, "Lord Dashmont did say I was to do what I think best for the boy." She gathered up all her courage and took a deep breath. "And what I think best is for David to spend some time outside in the sunshine."

Jane stood silently and watched the expression on Lady Cavendish's face change from shock, to incredulity, to a kind of reddening fury. "You . . . you dare question my authority?"

Jane kept her polite smile. "Not at all, m'lady. I am simply carrying out Lord Dashmont's wishes, as I am sure he, and you, would wish me to do."

"Why . . . why . . ." Lady Cavendish, her cheeks flushed red, could do nothing but sputter.

"So starting today David and I will go for a short stroll." Jane moved quickly toward the door. She must be quick before this rigid, intolerant woman got control of herself and started issuing orders. "Good afternoon, m'ladies." Jane performed a quick curtsy and was out the door.

Returning to her room, Jane felt flushed with triumph—far more, she realized, than the occasion called for. But after that ignominious defeat in the dining room two nights ago, she was proud of herself for standing up to Lady Cavendish, if only in a minor way. But far more important, that poor, pale little boy was going to get some sunshine. It mattered. *He's Lord Dashmont's son.*

Now why should that matter? she wondered on her climb up the steep servants' staircase to her room. Dashmont was one of the most detestable men she had ever known. She would never dream of trying to impress him by any sort of success she might have with his son. *So why should that matter?* she asked herself again.

At the end of her climb, as she arrived breathless at the landing on the third floor, she still had no answer.

"I'm tired," complained David. "I want to go back."

They had reached the end of the rose garden. "But we've

only just begun our walk, David," Jane gently protested. She waved toward the wooded hills ahead of her. "I thought we could follow this path clear to the hill, and perhaps even to the top."

"Want to go back."

Jane knelt in front of the pale little boy and gently gripped his arms. "But the sunshine is so good for you. You don't get nearly enough."

"No."

Jane detected a spark of rebellion in the boy's blue eyes, so different from his father's dark ones, and yet, in shape and something intangible so much alike. She was suddenly struck by the resemblance David bore his father. It was something about his mouth . . . the structure of his cheekbones . . . the way he held his head. *Anthony.* As if from nowhere, the memory of Lord Dashmont's embrace in the hallway came hurtling back. She felt a tingling in the pit of her stomach as she remembered how his powerful arms had drawn her closer, how the feel of his fingers in her hair had sent little shivers of excitement dancing through her, and . . .

She was shocked at herself. How could she daydream of an embrace in the midst of the day, especially while taking care of this sad little boy? And worse, why had she not erased every memory of his father totally from her mind?

"Are we going back now?"

"Of course, if that's what you want." No sense forcing the child. With no further argument she turned on the path and started back. "But we shall walk tomorrow, David, and every day," she told him brightly. A thought struck her. "Where is your hoop—the one you had in London?"

"I left it there. Grandmama says I must rest a lot, so I have no need for toys."

We shall see about that, thought Jane. She must get him another hoop, and other toys, too. *And I must stop thinking of Lord Dashmont.* Easy to do, she was sure. It was simply that she had been startled by the resemblance she had detected between David and his father. Now that she was aware of it, her sudden . . . warm enthusiasm was the best way she could put it . . . would not return again.

Lord Dashmont, indeed. Horrible man. But though she had no use for him, she would do her utmost to bring a smile to the sad, woebegone face of his little son.

Back inside, Jane sent David to his nanny for a nap. She climbed the stairs, thinking she, too, might lie down for a while. Opening the door of her room, she gasped in surprise when she saw Hortense standing in front of the small mirror, holding Jane's emerald earrings up to her ears. "Hortense! Whatever are you doing here?"

"Oh!" The unlikeable girl drew in a horrified breath and jumped back. "I thought you were out walking with David."

"Obviously I'm not. What are you doing in my room?"

"I . . . I . . . was not stealing anything. It's just . . ." Hortense seemed to crumple before Jane's eyes.

Jane could see that she was trembling. "It's just what?" she asked more gently.

"I'm so terribly sorry." Hortense held up the earrings. "You had said you owned some earrings that would bring out the color of my eyes. I just wanted to see . . ." Tears welled. She sank to the bed, her hands to her face and in anguish cried, "Please don't tell Mama!"

Any anger Jane might have felt fast disappeared. She sank down on the bed next to Hortense. "Of course I won't." She waited until Hortense's tears subsided. "You could have asked. I would have been happy to loan you the earrings."

Hortense emitted a bitter laugh. "'Tis more than borrowed earrings I need. Look at me!" She made a derisive gesture at herself. "I have no style, no grace, no pretty clothes. I don't know how to dress, how to wear my hair."

"But—"

"You don't understand, and how could you?" Tears streaming, Hortense leaped off the bed and faced Jane. "You, with your beauty, your charm, your beautiful clothes—how could you know! Do you remember that day in the park when you rolled the hoop with David? I sat in the carriage and watched you, sick with envy. How pretty you looked—how graceful! Even your laugh was carefree and delightful. I saw how Lord Dashmont looked at you that day. He wanted you. I could see it in his eyes. Just like every man who ever sees you wants you, whereas I . . ." She closed her eyes as anguish struck her. "I've never even had a beau! I've never had a Season, or even a dance, or a kiss or a flirtation, and why? Because I'm ugly. And I shall spend the rest of my life all lonely and alone, with only Mama to love me, and even then, I'm not so sure she does."

Hortense collapsed in tears on the bed again. Jane, stunned at her outburst, took a moment to collect her thoughts. *Where to begin?* How could she find adequate words? "You are most definitely not ugly," she began, aware how inadequate that sounded.

Hortense raised her head long enough to protest, "How can you say that? You, who have everything."

"Do I?" Jane asked with an ironic lift of her brow. "If that is true, then why have I no dowry? Why am I living on the servants' floor? Why am I far away from my dear family?"

"You know what I mean." Hortense's tears were subsiding. She faced Jane again. "You still have your charm, your beauty. Mark you, Lord Dashmont will seek you out—I know he will."

"Oh, but I'm sure he finds you most attractive—"

"He's never even looked sideways at me!" Hortense protested vehemently. "Not that I care. I've been told all my life how plain I am, and how sickly and delicate. Then Georgiana died, and Mama let me know I must always stay by her side, that I could never have a Season, let alone marry."

"You look perfectly healthy to me." *How monstrous!* Jane tried to think of comforting words, but none came to mind. However, there was something she could do. "Where is your mother right now?"

"Out on a round of visiting. But why—?"

"Good. Come with me."

"Where are we going?"

Jane bent over the open bottom drawer of her battered bureau. On top, where Hortense had obviously pulled them from their inadequate hiding place, lay the emerald necklace that matched the earrings and a green-jeweled comb. Jane scooped them up, then took her favorite ball gown from a peg. "We need a dressing table and a great big mirror, which we most certainly won't find here. Come, Hortense, bring those earrings and lead the way to your dressing room."

"Fantastic! Go look."

Jane, who for minutes had been fiddling with the placement of one small curl, stood back to admire her work. She had not allowed Hortense, seated in a gilded chair, to see either the dress or the elaborate coiffure she had been slaving over for at least an hour. Considering her lack of skill at hair-dressing, she was amazed at how well it turned out. Much easier to do someone else.

With an expression of trepidation, Hortense stood up and walked to her tall gilt mirror. After one glance, she gasped and cried, "What a difference!"

Jane agreed. Hortense's hair, which she had always worn pulled back flat and unadorned, was arranged in wispy ringlets around her face, hiding her high forehead and giving her face a softness it lacked before. The rest of her hair was piled in a comely bun atop her head, pierced with the green-jeweled comb. Luckily, although Jane was taller, she and Hortense were the same size, so the dress of lace sheer layered over water green sarcenet, with its double-tiered puffed sleeves and daringly low-cut neckline, fit perfectly. "Is it me?" cried Hortense.

Jane laughed and nodded. "It's you all right, and just look at how pretty you are." To herself she marveled at the change. The green of the dress and earrings had indeed brought out the sparkling emerald flecks in Hortense's eyes. There was a glow about the girl that had not been there before, all because a look in the mirror had told her she wasn't ugly after all. She was standing straighter, not slumping her shoulders, which was her usual mode, and holding her head higher, which brought out the delightful curve of her neck and the saucy tilt of her small nose.

Jane stepped up to smooth Hortense's hair. "I'm such an amateur. Sarah, my lady's maid—my *former* lady's maid—could have done much better. Ah, well, now we need a finishing touch."

She hurried to her room and quickly returned with her elegant swansdown fan and her lavender paisley shawl edged with green ribbon. Hortense tossed the shawl about her shoulders, then posed provocatively, holding the fan at a jaunty angle. Jane was amazed. The timid, colorless mouse was gone, replaced by a full-bosomed beauty with a come-hither gleam in her eye. Hortense may not be called truly beautiful, but she was close to it, especially when she smiled, which she was doing now, the first smile Jane had seen on that usually dour face. "You're the belle of the ball," she said softly.

"I have you to thank, Jane," Hortense answered gratefully. "I was horrid to you, and I'm so terribly sorry. Will you be my friend? I promise, I'll never be nasty again."

"Of course I'll be your friend. I would adore helping you with your hair, your clothes—"

"Oh, no!" A stricken look crossed Hortense's face. "Mama would never permit it. Mama must never know."

"But why?" asked Jane, thoroughly perplexed. "I should think she would be delighted if you married well. Perhaps even Lord Dashmont—?"

"Indeed not!" Hortense cried, sadly shaking her head. " 'Tis Mama's devout wish that Anthony remain single. She adores being mistress of Fairfield, but if Anthony should marry again, even me, she would have to step down. You should see our wretched estate in Cornwall—it's damp and chilly, and the roof leaks. Mama would *die* if she had to move back there."

"Well, then, you at least should think of marrying well."

"I fear not. My father died when I was two. Ever since, Mama has kept me close by her side. I was a sickly child, so she had good reason, or claimed she did. Since Georgiana died, she's been even worse."

Jane was appalled that this poor young woman was doomed to spinsterhood. "But isn't there someone you care about?"

Hortense bit her lip, appearing to debate whether or not to reveal a confidence. Finally, in a breathless voice, she admitted, "This may surprise you, but 'tis not Lord Dashmont I dream about."

Indeed, Jane was surprised. "It's not?"

"No, although I do find him most attractive."

"Then who—?"

"Tatton Fulwood." Hortense clapped her hands to her heart.

"Oh, Jane, I know his reputation, but I find him devastatingly attractive, as well as intelligent and entertaining."

"I am thunderstruck!"

"But 'tis true!" A blush spread over Hortense's cheeks. Her eyes brightened. "When he comes visiting with Anthony, I find my heart starts pounding the minute he steps into the room."

Jane felt a rush of pity. Hortense hadn't a chance with the honorable Mister Fulwood, for many reasons. She should be dissuaded from her unlikely fantasy. "But he's awfully short," she said, reminding herself of the old days when such things mattered.

"I'm shorter," Hortense replied.

"He's a confirmed bachelor."

Hortense came close to a smile. "Aren't they all?"

"Don't forget he's a second son," Jane persisted. "I understand he has a fair income, but he'll never—"

"You think I care what he'll inherit? I have money enough for two."

"But—" Jane stopped short. She could hardly mention the real reason Hortense hadn't a chance.

"Oh, I know what you're thinking," Hortense went on. "Tatton Fulwood surrounds himself with beautiful women. What could he possibly see in a dowdy girl like me?" Jane started to protest, but Hortense continued, "You're right. I know I shall never marry, and I shall be under Mama's thumb for the rest of my life, doomed to frumpy hair and black bombazine."

"But perhaps not—" Jane began, but Hortense, sighing, raised a restraining hand.

"Mama will live to be a hundred, at the very least. So I shall spend every night of my life dreaming of Tatton Fulwood when the lamp is out."

"We never know what the future holds," Jane said wistfully.

"Who would know that better than you?" Hortense asked gently. "Spare your pity. I'm resigned to my fate."

"But—" Jane began, then stopped abruptly. Up to now, she had been so engrossed in helping Hortense she had forgotten all her own problems. Now her euphoria slipped swiftly away. What was the use? Nothing would change for poor Hortense.

Lady Cavendish would continue to rule her every move, and there was nothing anyone could do.

As for her own situation, and her family's . . . a lump grew in her throat. There was no hope. Jane felt a sudden, sinking despair.

Chapter 10

Riding easily astride his horse, Anthony approached the slight rise at which he always stopped when returning home from his fields at the end of the day. When he reached the top, he pushed back the broad brim of his planter's straw hat and leaned back in the saddle. Before him lay the finest sight in Jamaica: to the south, the green, rolling fields of Montclaire; to the west the sun, a massive, orange ball now, fast slipping behind the glittering sea. To the northeast . . .

With a faraway look in his eye, Anthony gazed beyond the heavy growth of palm trees, beyond that great expanse of blue ocean, to where lay England.

He recalled his return to England only months ago, after the two-and-a-half-year exile he had imposed upon himself. He had arrived with high hopes of resuming his old, carefree life and—his lower lip twisted wryly down—being once again the rake of London. Brooks—the soft, scented arms of Brilliana—ah, how eager he had been. But within days he had found himself with a feeling of discontent, yearning for Jamaica again. Or was it really Jamaica he was yearning for . . . ?

A vision of a tall, slender girl in a swirling blue dress danced before his eyes. How pretty she looked that night, so confident in herself, so graceful, with an indefinable charm that made her stand out from that bevy of witless beauties at the ball. What a terrible calamity she'd suffered because of her father. At the very least, the cad deserved a good thrashing, which Anthony would have been glad to administer, had not the poor wretch tried to kill himself. Probably should have let him.

But at least she was safe. Anthony still gazed northeast. *It's dinnertime in England. Doubtless she's seated in the dining room with Lady Cavendish and Hortense, bringing some much needed life into the conversation. What kind of a day did she have? Has David taken to her as I predicted? Is she comfortable and happy? Does she think of me? Does she—?*

Anthony caught himself and laughed. Why was he daydreaming of a haughty chit who had but for a brief moment caught his eye? Out of the kindness of his heart he had done her and her family a favor—not easy, considering the derision he had received from those close friends who knew. Sometimes the hardest thing to do was an act of kindness, but he had not hesitated—had, in fact, been all eagerness to offer his assistance.

He must will himself to stop thinking of her. Resolutely, he picked up the reins and headed back down the slope toward home. He must have a dinner party soon, he advised himself, and invite close neighbors, including that paragon of virtue, Miss Isabella Wentworth. What would it be like to kiss her? He tried to envision his arms encircling that solid waistline, his lips passionately pressing those thin, cool lips of hers. But to no avail. The cherry lips of a laughing girl in a pretty blue dress kept getting in the way.

It was after dinner. Black shadows were filling the corners of Lord Harleigh's paneled study. Jane, sitting at the massive, dark mahogany table, lit a candle and set it next to the thirteenth-century Cistercian manuscript she had been translating. "What do you think, sir?" she asked of the old man, who was sitting across. She turned the manuscript around so he could see her translation. "Have I done it right?"

She knew she had. The truth was, as much as Lord Harleigh annoyed her, she could not help seeking his approval.

"Hrrumph!" With a shaky finger, Lord Harleigh traced the illuminated original manuscript, then her translation. "How long have you been here?" he asked.

"Nearly three months, sir." As if he didn't know.

"I see nothing wrong with it, considering you are still a novice."

Which meant she was doing very well. Actually, now that she was growing more accustomed to the old man's irascible manners, she was liking him more. She was beginning to perceive that beneath all that grouchiness lay a man of strong character whose heart wasn't as cold as he would like her to believe. "You have taught me well," she conceded.

"You've a kind word to say?" The old man feigned astonishment. "A far cry from when we met and you took offense at my every word."

"Did I not agree to take my meals with you?" Jane countered.

He sniffed scornfully. "Either that or starve to death."

Smiling, Jane tilted her head and fluttered her eyelashes at him, as she had done in London with her beaux. "I feel different now. You grow more handsome every day."

"Don't play the coy hoyden with me," he replied, though not unkindly. After a thoughtful gaze, he continued, "It appears you find it tolerable here."

Tolerable? How could she begin to describe the great weight that rested upon her heart? How could she tell him how she anguished whenever she received a letter from her mother saying everything was fine when she could read between the lines that it was not? How could she describe the continuing rudeness with which Lady Cavendish treated her? Worse then ever, if that was possible. She was more civil to the servants than she was to her and seemed to take delight in bedeviling her with her cutting remarks.

At least Hortense now refrained from sharing her mother's hostility, and had tried, as much as she was able, to be a friend. Sadly, though, thanks to her mother, she was just as mousy as ever. It was as if that golden moment when Jane had turned her into a beauty had never been.

Jane had grown accustomed to her tiny room on the servants' floor, but still, it was a source of constant humiliation. Not that she would tell Lord Harleigh any of these things. He would not tolerate her complaints, however well they might be justified. Besides, she could always find some good things about Fairfield Manor. She loved working with David and seeing his improvement. But most of all . . .

"I find it tolerable here," she answered honestly. "All this"—she waved her hand around the room, indicating all the monastery manuscripts—"I cannot tell you how much I have enjoyed being a part of preserving them. It's like a dream come true, living next to a real thirteenth-century Cistercian abbey, being able to visit nearly every day."

"So you're not as bad off as you thought."

"All right, so I am not," Jane laughingly conceded, "and I do have David." The thought of the little boy made her smile. "He's picking up on his Greek and Latin quite nicely. Not only that, you should have seen us when we went outside today. We walked clear to the top of the hill. He kept running ahead, laughing, and it was all I could do to keep up with him. You should have seen his rosy cheeks. David does not look at all like the poor, pale little boy he was when I arrived."

"Anthony will be pleased," said Lord Harleigh.

Anthony. The sudden sound of his name ended the pleasant interlude. "Yes, I suppose he will be pleased," she answered reluctantly, "although I hardly think he—" She halted abruptly. Her opinion would be out of place.

"You think he hardly cares about his son, is that it?" shrewdly asked Lord Harleigh.

She would be nothing less than honest. "No, I don't believe he does care. But even if he did, how could I possibly think highly of a man who has the reputation as the biggest rake in London?"

"He cares. Let me tell you . . ." Lord Harleigh stopped to summon James to pour him a brandy, then proceeded. "Georgiana, David's mother, was the most empty-headed woman I have ever known in my life. Anthony never loved her. Married her because his parents wanted him to. Damned if I know how he put up with her silliness and giggles all those years, but he did, and not only that, he was faithful." Lord Harleigh gave her a piercing look over the top of his glasses. "You know what I mean by faithful?"

"Of course, m'lord," Jane answered swiftly. It was important that he know she wasn't born yesterday and knew what went on in the world and the ways of men.

"But when she died, Anthony was devastated, doubly, it would seem. First, because he had given permission for her to drive the phaeton, albeit reluctantly. Second, because he had not loved her and could not grieve."

"But he did," said Jane. "I heard him say once, 'I grieve because I don't grieve.'"

"Exactly. Now if'd been me, I'd have been glad to get rid of the ninny, but Anthony, though he may not look it, has a soft heart and was stricken with guilt."

"So drinking, gambling, and consorting with women was the answer?"

Lord Harleigh shrugged and did not reply. Instead, he reached into the pocket of his dressing gown and pulled out a letter. "He writes about you."

"Really?" Feeling the need for something in her hands, Jane reached for her sewing basket and pulled out a hoop of embroidery. Feigning intense interest in the colorful threads, she continued, "I have no interest in anything Lord Dashmont has to say."

Ignoring her, Lord Harleigh started to unfold the heavy parchment. "I just received this letter from him, written in Jamaica six weeks ago. Here's the part that would interest you." He adjusted his glasses and began to read. "And how is Lady Jane? I trust she has settled in by now and, despite her recent family catastrophe, is enjoying the hospitality of Fairfield Manor."

"Ha!" said Jane.

Lord Harleigh ignored her and continued. "I think of her often and fancy she has done wonders for David. Though she may not appreciate it, kindly extend to her my deepest regards." The old man lowered the letter. "It would appear he likes you."

Jane wrinkled her nose. "That's his misfortune. I do not want his regards."

"Ah, well." Lord Harleigh pushed himself painfully to his feet. "I'm off to bed."

"But it's early yet."

He pressed his hand to his heart. "Not feeling well. Must be something I ate." Leaning heavily on his cane, he hobbled to the door. "Take a look," he said, jabbing his cane at one of his most priceless manuscripts, *The Gospel Book of Saint Bertin*, which he had left lying open on the table. "The Q of Saint Luke can be compared both with the Q of the Carolingian *Harley Gospels* and with the D of the Anglo-Saxon *Arundel Psalter*.

Note that the scroll in the border is clearly Anglo-Saxon in origin."

After he left, Jane pondered with pleasure how much she had learned about illuminated manuscripts from Lord Harleigh. How little she had known before. But now she was beginning to feel like an expert, thanks to that crotchety old man. It was not like him to complain of not feeling well. She felt a tinge of concern and hoped he would be all right.

An hour later, Jane came out of her deep concentration to see that the candle was flickering and burning low. She knew she should retire, but the precious manuscript Lord Harleigh had recommended was fascinating.

But she must get to bed. Tomorrow she had promised David a picnic, an early one, and it would not be wise to stay up half the night. She stood, and in her haste to return *The Gospel Book of Saint Bertin* to its shelf, accidentally knocked it against the back of her chair. The book flew from her fingers and fell to the floor. She gasped in dismay. What if she had damaged this fragile volume? Stooping swiftly, she picked it up and laid it gently back on the table. "It looks all right," she whispered to herself, vastly relieved. She replaced the book on the shelf and was about to turn away when she noticed something different about the binding. Oh, no. Had the fall jarred the binding loose after all? Peering closer, she saw that the binding was fine, but a piece of thin paper was poking out. Carefully, slowly, she pulled it from the binding. It was a separate piece of paper—parchment, actually—and there was something written on it. She sank into her chair again and held the parchment close to the candle. This wasn't part of the book. This was a note of some kind that someone had slipped into the back binding. She unfolded it and began to read:

> *Hark ye to where our hearts are buried*
> *Go ye forthe through the nave, to the east transept.*
> *From the northe side of Brother Osbert de Guees*
> *Looke ye IV foote to the cross and fleur-de-lis.*
> *Thence VI foote east to the priest's grave marked with a*
> *chalice, thence southe to the knight's marker.*

> *In the middle of these, search ye the chambre beneathe*
> *that conteyneth the treasure of Linneshall.*
> *All is loste in this year of our Lorde, 1536.*
> *Abbot Wulfric*

What on earth? Could this be—?

An urgent knocking on the door interrupted her thoughts. James burst in, eyes wide with alarm. "His lordship has fallen ill!"

Without thinking, Jane hastily stuffed the piece of parchment into her sewing basket and rushed into Lord Harleigh's bedchamber. White as a sheet, he was lying in his rococo bed, his hand resting over his heart.

"Oh, m'lord, are you all right?" she asked, sinking by his bedside.

"Of course I'm all right," he snapped feebly, obviously in pain. " 'Twouldn't be the first time. James has summoned the doctor. When the ninny arrives, he will no doubt let some blood out and I'll be as good as new."

"You have given me a scare."

With a gentleness she had never seen in him before, Lord Harleigh clasped her hand. "Never be scared, my dear. I'm not. When my time comes, I'll thank God for the good years I had on this earth and slip away, meek as a lamb."

In the days that followed, Jane spent every moment possible by Lord Harleigh's bedside. "He has a bad humor," said the doctor, shaking his head, not sure his ancient patient would survive. But to Jane's vast relief, gradually the old man started to improve.

"Thought you'd be rid of me," said Lord Harleigh, his voice quaking more than usual, on the first day he was allowed out and James had carried him to a bench in the formal garden.

Jane tenderly tucked a blanket closer around him, finding that for once she could not be lighthearted in return. She had discovered a few truths about herself these last few days, the most astounding of which was that she cared deeply for this dear old man and would have mourned him deeply had he died. "Rid of you? I don't know what I would have done without you"—she managed a wry smile—"died of starvation, I suppose."

He shook his head. "You have a will to survive, my dear. If you'd had to lower your pride and eat with the servants, you'd have done so."

She thought a moment. "Yes, I suppose I would. I do want to live, despite . . . you know." Never would she recite her litany of troubles.

"You're sturdy as an oak, my girl. By gad, you're not one of those silly London chits, and I regret I said so."

"What?" She feigned astonishment. "You are actually apologizing?"

"Yes, and furthermore . . ." Lord Harleigh paused. A crafty expression came over his face, which told her he was up to no good. "Wrote to Anthony. Told him he ought to come home."

"You didn't."

"Didn't mention your name, so don't get all in a dither. 'T'was David I wrote about. The boy has improved, to the point where Anthony should at least come home and see for himself."

"I shall hide the whole time he is here," said Jane, realizing how childish that sounded, but she meant it.

"Do as you please, though if 't'were me, I would think twice before I acted like a five-year-old."

"Whatever do you mean?" she asked, although she was sure she did know.

"Anthony is rich." He gave her a piercing gaze. "Do you have any idea how rich?" She shook her head, and he continued, "Not only has he inherited a vast estate, but he makes a fortune from the rum he ships to the Americans."

"Money is not everything," she said with a smile, knowing full well how ridiculous that sounded.

He ignored her. "Not only that, Anthony is a bachelor, handsome—some would say charming—who obviously has an interest in you."

She grew serious. "Lord Harleigh, I appreciate your interest and concern. You know I never speak of personal things because . . . well, you really don't want me to. But your nephew offended me deeply before he went away. In the months I have been here, I have changed in many ways, but never, never shall I forgive him, much as you might wish me to."

"Stubborn chit," the old man muttered, but said no more. Instead, he asked, "Well, have you been working on *The Gospel Book of Saint Bertin*?"

"Not since your illness, sir. I—" Suddenly she remembered the piece of parchment that had fallen from the back of the binding. "I meant to tell you—the night you became ill, I found a message of some sort in the binding, written on parchment. I had no chance to read it thoroughly, but as I recall, it was signed by Abbot Wulfric himself."

Lord Harleigh was momentarily speechless with surprise. His eyes lit with interest. Eagerly, he gripped her hand. "What do you recall, girl?"

"I . . . I cannot remember. Something about fleur-de-lis . . . a knight's marker . . . treasure."

"Well, where is it?"

"I . . . cannot remember. Perhaps I put it back in the binding. When we go back in, I'll search."

It was hopeless. Jane examined the bindings of countless books, but could not find the piece of parchment. She knew that in the excitement of the moment, she had stuck it somewhere, but where? Even though she racked her brain, she could not remember.

Chapter 11

"The weather was rather warm today, was it not?" inquired Miss Isabella Wentworth.

"Indeed," replied Anthony, only half listening. With bored indifference he glanced around the elaborate ballroom of the Wentworth Plantation, where the cream of Jamaica's high society, dressed to the glittering nines, were waltzing around the dance floor. He was growing too old for this, he told himself, at the same time aware thirty-two was not old, and it wasn't age that was causing his jaded attitude. More than one pair of eyes were upon him, he noted glumly. All belonging to the young chits of marriageable age and their mothers, who assumed that he, the so-called dashing widower and rich plantation owner, would make a fine catch. *What a travesty.* They were wasting their time. When he married again, and he knew he must, then Isabella Wentworth would be as suitable as any. Suddenly a tall, willowy girl in a blue dress came twirling by. *Jane.* His heart leaped. But it wasn't Jane. How could he think it was? This girl wasn't half as pretty, half as graceful. Few girls could be . . .

"Your thoughts seem far away this evening, Lord Dashmont."

"Hmm? Oh, no." Anthony forced himself to return his attention to Miss Wentworth. "Would you care to dance?"

"I think not. I really do not care for dancing."

No surprise. Anthony gazed down at Miss Wentworth, who was modestly attired in an uninspired dun-colored gown. A frown creased her brow.

"Observe the low cut of that bodice," she remarked of a blond, full-chested girl across the floor. "Such a brazen display should be outlawed."

Pray that it may not. He must keep reminding himself to look beyond those prim, tight lips and perpetual scowl and remember that Miss Isabella Wentworth would make the perfect wife. Grace and beauty, of which she had none, were not required, nor was a sense of humor. What mattered was that through her diligence and admirable self-discipline she ran her father's great plantation house with iron-handed control. The Wentworth plantation lay next to his own. Someday the two would be joined . . . *if I marry this marvel of efficiency.*

His rather sneering thought surprised him. Of course he was going to marry her. What idiocy possessed him to think otherwise? During these past few months he'd had time to reflect that during those few weeks he spent in London a kind of metamorphosis had overcome him, so much so that his sinful pursuits of the past had faded in their appeal. The reason for this change escaped him, unless . . . had Lady Jane's sharp comments been of any influence? If so, it was only because he was deucedly attracted to her—yes, he would admit that, but he must be practical. She was far from the competent wife he needed to run Montclaire. Furthermore, love was of no import, no matter what Tatton said. Without doubt, Miss Wentworth was by far the better choice.

As for anything else . . . he let his eyes wander idly over Isabella Wentworth's rigid face and lumpy figure and tried to picture her in his bed. Would she lose that drawn-up-tight expression? Would she laugh? Could she possibly produce a playful giggle?

Not likely. Not the way he imagined Jane . . .

Unbidden, a tantalizing picture filled his mind. It was Jane who was lying in his bed, her fine, long chestnut hair fanned out over her bare white shoulders. Savage passion flared in the velvet softness of her blue-gray eyes as he, afire for her, ran his hands freely down the smooth, warm skin of her cheeks, neck, soft breasts, about to—

"I find I am quite thirsty, Lord Dashmont. Might I trouble you to get us some punch?"

"Of course, Miss Wentworth. I was just thinking the same."

At the punch bowl, while he watched a servant ladle the pink liquid into crystal cups, Anthony's thoughts ran wild again.

Jane . . . Jane . . . I think of you constantly. I command myself to put you out of my mind, but you won't go away.

Six months more and he would return to England. But why not sooner? After all, he had found a fine overseer to run his plantation. The truth was, he had been feeling somewhat unsettled lately, as if there was something unfinished in his life. Surely he could put off his proposal to Miss Wentworth. Meanwhile, if he returned now, not only could he check on David's progress, he could see Jane again. Once and for all he could satisfy himself that it was pity he felt for her, more so than affection, and most certainly not love. Perhaps, too, he could ease her hostility toward him. Not that it mattered one wit, but she did most definitely despise him, and that made him feel, at the least, uncomfortable.

Of course, there was Tatton to reckon with. He could easily picture his best friend's inevitable smirk, accompanied by "What's this, Anthony? Back so soon? Good grief, man, cannot you make up your mind?"

There would be no sense lying, of course. Tatton could always ferret out the truth.

But what is the truth? Am I falling in love with Lady Jane, or is it only pity I feel for her?

Whatever it was, he had made up his mind. Visions of Lady Jane were haunting him, taunting him, driving him mad. He would take the next ship back to England.

In the tangled garden of Linneshall Abbey, under a weak autumn sun, Jane, David, and Lord Harleigh had just finished their picnic lunch, and David, bright-eyed and eager, had wandered off to play in the ruins.

"You have done wonders for the lad," said Lord Harleigh. Although still weak, he had lately been able, with James's help, to make his way to the ruins and take up his painting once again. "Not the dull boy he was before you arrived here." He picked up a brush and started daubing on his latest portrayal of the ancient stone walls of Linneshall. "Wait till his father sees him."

"I can wait," Jane replied succinctly. Seated on a bench near the sundial, she opened a book she had brought along.

"Anthony was supposed to be gone at least a year, but—" Lord Harleigh paused, seemingly intent upon mixing white with his azure blue.

"But what?" Instantly, Jane was annoyed with herself. She didn't care one whit when Lord Dashmont would be back.

"But he might return sooner," Lord Harleigh replied with a casual shrug.

Silly old man, why would he think she would be interested in anything Lord Dashmont might do? She would like to resume reading, yet curiosity got the better of her. "Why do you say he'll soon be back?"

"Because of his letters." The old man slanted a sly gaze at her. "The man wants to see you again. Doesn't came out and say so, but I can read between the lines."

Despite herself, Jane felt a warm glow course through her at Lord Harleigh's words. Quickly, she quelled it. "I haven't the slightest wish to see him again. If I did, I could only inform him of my additions to the list of reasons why I find him detestable."

"Really, now. What have you to add?"

"How can you even ask?" Jane inquired incredulously. "Have you forgotten what he promised me? I was to be an honored guest and dine with the family. Oh, how those smooth words rolled off his tongue! Instead, I'm treated like a servant, and if it hadn't been for you . . ." She fell silent and cast an affectionate smile at her benefactor. No need to recount the abominable way Lady Cavendish treated her. No need to reveal the continued heartache she felt being so far from her family, a fear compounded whenever she received a letter from Mama or Christabell. The drafty cottage was never warm enough, thus causing the children to suffer from earaches and fever; Christabell was listless and cried more than ever; Aunt Eugenia's mind had most definitely clouded; Mama wasn't well, and the baby was due any day now. They were desperate for money, with hardly enough food in the house, no horse and carriage, no new clothes. Jane was sick with worry. If only she had the means to provide more for them. But short of marrying the detestable Lord Bradbourne, she was doing all she possibly could.

David appeared, his cheeks rosy, his eyes bright. "You're it," he called. He tagged her shoulder and raced away.

Jane dropped her book and took off after him, lifting the skirts of her blue muslin gown as she darted lightly about the huge piles of rough stones that covered the floor of the nave. "There's no escape, I'll catch you," she called merrily as the boy leaped away. From the direction of the wooded hill she heard male laugher and looked around . . .

Lord Dashmont.

With his smooth, swift grace he was striding down the wooded path, looking even more handsome, if that were possible, in his simple gray frock coat worn over a waistcoat and nankeen breeches. "Good afternoon, Uncle, Lady Jane," he called. His eyes locked on David. "Hello, son."

David took one look and cried, "Papa!" then came running and threw himself into his father's arms. With a look of complete astonishment Lord Dashmont knelt and wrapped his arms around his son.

"Papa, I'm learning Greek and Latin," the slender, sandy-haired boy announced excitedly. "And we go on picnics every day and Jane lets me play in the ruins."

"Ah, David, you're back," his father murmured in a joyous voice, his face alight with pleasure. Jane thought she caught a glint of moisture in his eye. He drew his son closer, buried his face against the boy's fair hair, and for a long moment held him tight. Finally he looked over the top of David's head at Jane and inquired softly, "However did you do it?"

A flood of feelings engulfed her. She was moved nearly to tears by the poignant tableau of father and son reunited, proud of her part in David's improvement. Why, she wondered, was Lord Dashmont here instead of Jamaica, where he had said he would stay for at least a year? But why should she care? Here was a man she detested, and with good reason, but she was hard pressed to think of that right now. His handsome face, his knowing eyes, that tanned lean body—his very nearness had caused something so intense to flare within her that she could only stare at him, unable to speak. But he had asked a question, and she must answer. *How did I do it?* To give herself time to regain her composure, she plucked a purple violet that grew from beneath a rock and twirled it between her fingers. "It was not difficult, sir. Fresh air, sunshine, love, and a lot of attention." If she thus implied David had received little love or attention from Lady Cavendish, so be it.

At least she didn't snap my head off, thought Anthony. What a beguiling picture she made. The delicate skin of her face flushed with a rosy glow—silky, long hair flowing—and underneath the bodice of her modest blue gown he could make out the tempting shape of her bosom, quieting now, after heaving up and down so very enticingly chasing after David. What marvelous eyes she had—large, intelligent, sparkling. And the way she was looking at him—in wonderment, as if possibly she might have forgotten for a moment how much she detested him. *I could take her in my arms right now . . .*

This was nonsense. Anthony willed himself not to allow Jane to distract him, especially after the marvelous discovery that his son was actually speaking and laughing again. Still holding David's hand, he stood and looked over at his uncle who, despite his arrival, had not deigned to show the slightest interest and was still busily painting his latest landscape. "Greetings, Uncle. You look fit."

"Hrrumph! Of course I look fit. I *am* fit." The old man eyed him shrewdly. "Back so soon? Jamaica didn't suit you?"

"Jamaica suits me fine." Anthony considered adding some excuse for his quick return, but knew he could never fool his wise old uncle. He turned to Jane. "I trust you are well?"

"Quite well, m'lord."

"Of course she's fine," Lord Harleigh broke in with a sniff. "She's young—healthy—why would she not be fine?"

Anthony laughed. "Uncle, I see you haven't changed, not that I would wish you to." He smiled at Jane. "I trust your accommodations at Fairfield Manor are to your satisfaction?"

"Of course," she answered. Lord Harleigh let out a snort and was about to speak, but she shot him a warning glance that silenced him. With an odd smile she continued, "I cannot tell you what a lovely room I have, or how I have enjoyed dining with your lovely family."

She seemed sincere, yet Anthony found something amiss in the way she said it, but he could not discern what it was. This was hardly the time to find out, though. Instead, he looked around at the remains of Linneshall Abbey. "I see you have discovered our local ruin."

She frowned and answered, "It's more than a local ruin—it's precious history."

Lord Harleigh chuckled. "You must excuse my nephew. He does not hold the same love for Linneshall Abbey that we do. To him it's an ugly pile of stones. If 'twere up to him, he'd tear the place down, sell off all the stones to the nearest quarry, and build a guest house."

She gasped in near horror. "Why, that's . . . that's sacrilege." She gave Dashmont a compelling glance. "Say it's not true."

Anthony laughed indulgently. "My uncle is correct, in part. I confess, I've no great interest in ancient ruined monasteries. On the other hand, he has me thoroughly convinced I would suffer the tortures of the damned if ever I destroyed what remains of the abbey, so I can assure you I would not."

"An admirable decision, sir," Jane said dryly. Within, she was vastly relieved. The idea that someone might wish to destroy what remained of the abbey had never occurred to her. How monstrous if they did.

Lord Dashmont spoke again. "I shall return to the house now and clean up from my journey. Tatton Fulwood accompanied me, by the way." He addressed his uncle. "I know you prefer taking meals in your rooms, but might we not see you at dinner tonight?"

"Dine with those two ninnies? Hrrumph!"

"As a special favor?" Anthony flashed one of his charming, disarming smiles. With a meaningful look down at David, he tousled the boy's hair. "We have much to celebrate."

"If I must, I must," grumbled Lord Harleigh, "if only to keep peace in the house."

Anthony turned to Jane. "Of course I shall see you at dinner tonight."

If only he knew. So many feelings vied for her attention that her throat tightened and she could hardly speak. "But of course," she finally managed, proud of herself for sounding perfectly calm and keeping a straight face.

When Anthony left, taking a delighted David with him, Lord

Harleigh cast her an inquisitive look. "Why didn't you tell him?"

"Tell him what?" she asked, feigning ignorance.

"God's blood! You know very well what."

She thought a moment. "You think I should complain to Lord Dashmont about how badly Lady Cavendish has treated me. Well, I won't. In the first place, how do I know this wasn't his idea? That he lied when he made me those so-called promises? But more important, I could never lower myself to go begging to him."

"So you will cut off your nose to spite your face."

She raised her chin proudly. "I would rather die than reveal the insults and injustices I have suffered at the hands of Lady Cavendish."

To her chagrin, the old man started applauding. "Well done! You have let your pride and stubbornness rule over your good sense."

She frowned in puzzlement. "You think I'm right?"

"Not at all. But there is nothing in this world more boring than a woman with good sense." Lord Harleigh gave her a wicked grin. "You were glad to see him. Don't deny it. I saw it in your eyes."

His remark caught her short. He was right. Upon seeing the handsome Lord Dashmont, her first reaction had been beyond delight, so much so that she had come close to throwing her arms around him, thus making a complete fool of herself.

"This has the makings of a most entertaining evening," Lord Harleigh continued. "It'll be worth coming down to dinner tonight, just to see the look on her fine ladyship's face when she sees you. 'Twill all be compounded, of course, by Anthony's not knowing how you've been mistreated, and you, miss, too high and mighty to inform him."

"Then perhaps I shall not attend," she said loftily.

The old man chuckled. "Wild horses could not keep you away."

She placed her hand on her hip. "And why do you say that?"

"Because . . ." Lord Harleigh finished one final daub and put his brush down. He regarded Jane with a barely concealed twinkle in his eye. "Think of it. You'll be at the same table with that old harpy, and she'll have to pretend she likes you." Suddenly filled with mirth, he started laughing, clapping his hand to his knee. "By gad, it'll be worth it. The old hen's likely to explode."

Jane pictured Lady Cavendish exploding from rage and joined in the laughter. "You have convinced me. If you give me your word you won't tell Lord Dashmont how I've been treated, I shall attend."

"Fine, especially since you're more fond of Anthony than you think. I'm no bearer of tales, missy, but it doesn't matter. Anthony's no fool. I warrant you, he'll find out."

"Oh, Jane, you look magnificent," cried Mary, whose room was next to Jane's. The little maid had volunteered to help Jane dress for dinner. She had even ironed the one decent dinner gown Jane had brought, a long-sleeved white chemise, trimmed with a gathered lavender lace flounce at the wrists, and with a low-cut neckline. Mary proceeded to coif Jane's hair in a braided Grecian bun, with a lavender feather tucked in one side. When she was done, Jane grabbed her small sliver of mirror and tried to see her whole self, but to no avail. "I shall have to take your word for it that I look all right."

Mary beamed. "The truth of it is you look gorgeous in that dress—and your hair looks perfect, if I do say so. Lord Dashmont will love it. Lord Dashmont—"

"I do not give a fig for Lord Dashmont's opinion."

Mary's eyes flew wide with surprise. "Really now? Then why did you say you wanted to look more beautiful tonight than you'd ever looked before? And why did you say—?"

"I believe that will be enough, Mary," Jane spoke up again, careful to remember this was not a servant she was speaking to, but a friend. After throwing a Persian pomegranate shawl of lavender, edged with silk embroidery, over her shoulders, she pulled on her long white gloves, picked up a white lace-and-ivory fan, and snapped it open. A flood of nostalgia swept over her, for she had not been dressed like this since the ball at Lady Ponsonby's, that terrible evening when she first had an inkling something was wrong. How wonderful to feel the touch of satin against her skin again. It brought back with vivid clarity her life as a rich, idle young lady of the *ton*. Would she wish to go back to it? she suddenly wondered. Oddly, she wasn't sure, but this was no time to think of it. Peeking playfully over the top of her fan, she exclaimed, "You see, I'm the coquette again."

"Would 'twas so, Jane," Mary commented mournfully. "You bein' so refined and all, 'n comin' from the Polite World." She immediately brightened. "But the answer is so simple. All you have to do is marry Lord Dashmont."

Jane smiled indulgently. "If only it were that simple."

There was a knock on the door. "Hortense, what a surprise," Jane said when Mary opened it. "Do come in."

Hortense stepped in, gazing at Jane with admiring eyes. "I just wanted to see what you were wearing tonight," she said. "You look beautiful."

Jane replied, "Why thank you, Hortense, and you . . ." What could she say? The girl was dressed in a black, highly unbecoming bombazine gown, and her hair was the usual disaster. How could she not hurt her feelings, yet not tell a lie?

Hortense saved her. "Yes, I know," she said grimly. "I have asked Mama time and again for a pretty dinner gown, but . . ." She bit her lip and cried, "You see, I'm just not worthy."

Exasperated, Jane cried, "You're as worthy as anybody. I shall hear no more of such nonsense!" How neglectful she had been. What with her own troubles, she had hardly given a thought to Hortense these past weeks, but that would change. Somehow Lady Cavendish must be convinced that what her daughter needed was a London Season, along with a new wardrobe and a knowledgeable, preferably French, lady's maid who could turn Hortense out in the style she deserved.

She hugged Hortense warmly. "It's not over yet. We'll think of something. Don't despair. Now let's go down to dinner."

Hortense shook her head. "No. I am pleading a headache tonight and shall have dinner in my room."

"But why?" asked Jane, then realized she knew the answer. "Is it because Tatton Fulwood is here?"

Hortense gave her a bleak smile. "It would hurt too much, seeing him ignore me, and you know he would."

Yes, he would, Jane thought sorrowfully. She pondered a moment, wishing somehow she could help. *But of course—the perfect solution!* "Hortense, do you remember that time I did your coiffure and loaned you the ball dress and you looked so pretty?"

"I shall never forget."

"Let's do it again."

Hortense brought her clasped hands to her heart. Her eyes glittered with sudden excitement. "Oh, Jane, are you saying you would loan me that same dress and fix the same coiffure?"

Jane turned to Mary. "Can you help Lady Hortense with her hair? I daresay you can do a much better job than I. Hortense, of course you can have the dress, although . . ." she paused, frowning slightly.

"Although what?"

"That dress is a ball gown, extremely low-cut, and I don't think your mother would approve."

Hortense's face fell, but only for a moment. "Do you not recall what I told you about Tatton? I adore him! I want him!"

"Enough to risk your mother's ire?"

"Yes!" Hortense resolutely responded with no hesitation.

Jane laughed and answered, "Well, there's no use arguing with a girl who thinks she's in love." She reached to the peg that held the green sarcenet ball gown.

After diligent effort by both Jane and Mary, Hortense soon looked the belle of the ball again, with a coiffure of delicate curls, the daring ball gown, long white kid gloves, emerald earrings and necklace, swansdown fan, and beautifully draped paisley shawl.

"Tatton will be dazzled," said Jane, stepping back to admire her work.

"I shan't appear until right before dinner," Hortense announced, confidence brimming in her eyes.

"Too late for Mama to object?" Jane asked shrewdly.

"Even if she does, I'll have you as an example of courage," replied Hortense, her voice full of admiration. "I shall never forget that day you told Mama David needed fresh air and sunshine. I thought surely she would stop you."

"It was a miracle she didn't."

"She didn't because she was so shocked anyone would actually stand up to her. You were so brave that day. In my heart, I so admired you, and envied you, too."

Jane protested, "But my palms were sweaty and my knees shaking."

"All the more reason why I envied you your bravery." With a laugh Hortense continued, "At least I have one thing in my favor. Mama probably won't even notice me tonight. She'll be in a state of shock when she finds out Lady Jane Sperling is coming for dinner."

I would be thrilled if Hortense should capture Tatton's heart, Jane thought as she headed for the servants' staircase. Then her own problems filled her mind, and she brooded over the many sins of Lord Dashmont all the way down three flights of stairs. His charm and good looks had put her off this afternoon, but she had now regained her senses. During the remainder of his visit, she would act polite but make it clear where he stood in her opinion. She would remember, too, to act her proudest. He would never know how she had suffered these past months at the hands of Lady Cavendish.

At the entrance to the grand salon, Jane paused a moment in awe. Living as she did in the servants' quarters, she had seen this majestic room only briefly, on the day she arrived. "What a gorgeous room," she remarked, noting its high-doomed, painted sky ceiling and magnificent furnishings. Everyone else but Hortense had arrived and were seated: Lady Cavendish dressed in her usual dull black; Lord Harleigh resplendent in the fashion of twenty years ago with knee britches, satin pumps, and a satin frock coat edged with metallic gold embroidery. Both Tatton Fulwood and Lord Dashmont were wearing long trousers, Tatton the height of fashion in a short frock coat with brass buttons; Dashmont looking his most handsome in a double-breasted wool frock coat with claw-hammer tails.

When Dashmont saw her, he arose, came to her, and bowed solemnly. "Lady Jane, how charming you look this evening."

"You are too kind, sir," Jane replied with the utmost coolness and swept right by. That she had given him a slight he could have no doubt. She knew she had wounded him, for she had caught a fleeting glimpse of chagrin deep in his eyes. With unfaltering steps she approached Lady Cavendish, who was seated in solitary splendor on a giltwood couch shaped in the form of an Egyptian riverboat on crocodile feet. "I trust you are well this evening, m'lady," she said with chin tilted high and a confident smile. Fluttering her fan, she stood easily, as if this were her routine every night, and watched closely as the expression on the older woman's face went from distaste to ill-concealed anger, to looking as if she were about to choke. "Have you been taken ill?" Jane asked innocently.

"Should I slap you on the back, madame?" inquired Lord Harleigh with ill-concealed mirth.

"Absolutely not," snapped Lady Cavendish. "I am quite well." Jane watched with immense satisfaction as the older woman struggled with the awful realization that Jane was joining them for dinner and there was nothing she could do about it. Finally her face became a mask again, albeit she appeared a bit more tight-lipped than usual. Jane caught Lord Harleigh's eye. A look of amusement passed between them. *But 'tis small consolation*, thought Jane. Though her pride might be bolstered by her stoic silence, she knew full well that she was dooming herself to endure even more mistreatment at the hands of that contemptible woman after Lord Dashmont left again.

They chatted small talk until, just as dinner was announced, Hortense swept in, looking radiant in the low-cut ball gown.

"Sorry I'm late, everyone," she said with high confidence. She gazed at Tatton and extended her hand. "Why, Tatton Fulwood, I had no idea! I am enchanted to see you again!"

A strange expression crossed Tatton's face as he took her hand. "Lady Hortense . . . I had heard you were unwell, but obviously I was wrong." He bent eagerly over her hand. "What a delightful surprise!"

"Hortense! Go change immediately!" Lady Cavendish's sharp words cracked like a whip around the room. Remembering herself, she softened her voice and added, "I do apologize, gentlemen. My daughter sometimes forgets the delicacy of her health." In a syrupy tone she continued, "Go along, dear. You must find something more suitable"—she gazed pointedly at her daughter's exposed bosom—"something warm that will cover both your shoulders and chest, lest you come down with a chill."

The room fell deadly quiet. Feeling the acute embarrassment of everyone, Jane watched in dismay as Hortense seemed to crumple before her eyes. Her shoulders slumped. The swans-down fan that she had held high now dragged nearly to the floor. *Stand up to her*, Jane silently called. Oh, this was so painful! *Hortense, do not give in.*

As if Hortense had heard her, she looked Jane's way with a questioning gaze that asked clearly, *can I do it? Do I have the nerve?*

Yes you do, Jane signaled with her eyes and a faint nod. Hortense pulled her shoulders back, raised the fan again, and took a deep breath. Tilting up her chin, she gave her mother a conde-scending smile. "Oh, Mama, you worry too much," she said with a light-hearted laugh, as if such a scene happened every day. "I shall be fine." She directed a flirtatious gaze at Tatton and moved toward him, totally ignoring her mother's stunned gaze. "Mister Fulwood, how handsome you look tonight!" She batted her eyelids at him and gave a little pout. "Oh, dear, it ap-pears I have no one to escort me in to dinner."

"I would be delighted if you would do me that honor," Tat-ton replied. It was easy to see the gleam of interest in his eyes.

In the satin-paneled dining room, resplendent with its twelve-branch ormolu-and-rock-crystal chandelier, Anthony finished the last of his pork cutlets with *sauce Robert* and glanced around the table. *I am missing something*, he thought. *There is a puzzle here that I have perceived all evening.* He peered carefully around the table. His uncle was the same old obdurate fellow, of course, no mystery there. Hortense and Tat-ton were hitting it off surprisingly well. That left his mother-in-law and Lady Jane. *The chit still despises me*, he thought matter-of-factly. No mystery there, either. He would have been a fool not to notice her enmity when she entered the salon this evening, every curve of her body bespeaking her dislike.

So the mystery lay with his mother-in-law, who for some un-known reason had appeared all evening to be smoldering be-neath the surface—much, he fancied, like Mount Vesuvius before it finally erupted to destroy Pompeii. He recalled her agitation earlier when Lady Jane had entered the grand salon, revealing a coldness that she could but barely control. Then, too, he had caught the look of amusement that had passed between his uncle and Lady Jane. But what was so amusing? Since then, the evening had been congenial, yet he could not escape the feeling of tension in the air. Well, no sense fretting. Lady Cavendish was talking about Hortense and her piano. He had better get back to the conversation.

"After dinner you must hear her play, Anthony. Hortense has been practicing assiduously. She plays divinely, every bit as good as dear Georgiana."

Which is saying little. He looked at Jane across the table. "Do you play, Lady Jane?"

"A little," she replied frostily.

A pox on you. I don't deserve that. He smiled. "Then you, too, must play tonight."

"I would do naught but hurt your eardrums, it has been so long since I have touched the keys."

"Come now, Lady Jane," he chided, "with that fine piano in the salon? Surely you have tried it."

The awkward silence that followed his simple remark had Anthony puzzled. Again he thought, *there is something wrong tonight. Think, Anthony. There must be something . . .*

"That was wonderful, and such a treat," Lady Jane was saying, putting down her spoon after her last bite of apple tart and sitting back content in her chair. "So many courses I couldn't count, not like . . ." She stopped abruptly, with a sudden frown of chagrin that must be directed at herself.

Anthony suddenly felt a jolt. Something was coming clear. He remembered when she walked into the grand salon and had remarked how gorgeous it was, as if she had never seen it before. Then Lady Cavendish's obvious enmity. Then the piano. And now this obvious enjoyment of the dinner when she should be thoroughly accustomed to fancy food by now and not be making such a to-do over a simple apple tart . . .

Of course.

"Lady Jane," he said forcefully, turning a sharp, assessing gaze full upon her. "Do you find your room comfortable?"

She appeared startled. "Why, I . . . I . . . it's fine."

"And where is your room?"

She laughed awkwardly. "Upstairs, of course."

Lady Cavendish began, "Anthony, really—" but he waved her silent.

"Where upstairs?" he demanded in a low but demanding voice, "which floor?"

He watched with keen eyes as Lady Jane glanced at Lord Harleigh, who gave her an encouraging nod. She then glanced at Lady Cavendish, who returned a hateful glare. Finally she looked Anthony square in the eye. "The third floor, m'lord."

"The servants' floor," he stated coolly. "And where, Lady Jane, do you usually take your meals?"

"Since you ask, I was to take them in the kitchen with the servants, sir. However, Lord Harleigh kindly allows me to dine with him."

It all came clear. Huge anger arose within him. He let his face become expressionless, his shield against displaying personal feelings. The silence that had fallen over the table was awkward and frightful, but he took his time thinking through what he was about to do. Finally, with all eyes glued upon him, he arose, carefully laid his napkin on the table, and turned to his mother-in-law. "May I see you alone, madame?"

There was defiance, mixed with fear, in her eyes as Lady Cavendish gave a tight nod, arose, and the two left the room.

"Oh, dear," exclaimed Hortense.

"Oh, dear indeed," heartily echoed Lord Harleigh. "Jane, what'd I tell you? Anthony's no dummy. He figured it out."

Was it true? She could hardly dare hope. But this would be marvelous if he had found out without her saying anything. She waited anxiously, and after ten minutes, Barkley entered and summoned her to the music room.

The air was tight with tension as Jane stepped inside and saw that both Lord Dashmont and Lady Cavendish were standing, he with dark eyes snapping with anger, she shockingly white-faced.

Dashmont spoke first. "Ah, come in, Lady Jane. Her lady-ship has something to say to you."

"Indeed?" Jane was hard put to know what to do. Would this

be an apology? If so, what was the correct protocol for accepting an apology? Did one stand or sit? Stand, she decided, considering the momentous nature of the occasion. Heart pounding, she stood and waited, watching closely as the older woman started to speak, then changed her mind, as if the words were stuck in her throat and could not possibly come out. How awkward this was. In the heavy silence Jane felt her palms grow damp and grew increasingly aware of her heartbeat.

"Well?" demanded Lord Dashmont, folding his arms across his chest, leaning lightly against the piano. "Of course, you need not say a word if you do not wish to, madame. In which case, at dawn tomorrow my coach will be carrying you back to your drafty excuse for a mansion in Cornwall. From whence, I might add, you shall never return."

"I . . . I . . ." Lady Cavendish began, licking her thin lips, "it appears, Jane—"

"Lady Jane!" he thundered.

"Lady Jane," she shakily repeated, "it appears there has been some sort of misunderstanding."

"There was no misunderstanding," he uttered in a hard, cold voice. "The truth!"

Lady Cavendish actually cringed. Jane could well understand why. This was a part of Anthony she had never witnessed before. So cold, so unyielding—no doubt the way he acted when master of his plantation.

"What I meant to say was . . ." The older woman nervously clenched and unclenched her fists, then finally, as if she were about to jump from a cliff from which there would be no recovery, took the plunge. "I should not have put you on the servants' floor."

"Had I directed you to do so?" asked Anthony.

"No, indeed, sir, you had not. Nor had you directed me to tell Jane to eat with the servants, and—" She stopped abruptly, as if exhausted after each word had been wrung from her mouth.

Dashmont showed no pity. "And?" he prompted.

The words tumbled out. "And in future I shall make sure you are treated as an honored guest."

"She shall be given our finest guest room, is that not right, madame? And she shall dine with you and Hortense every night."

"Oh, no," hastily cried Jane, "I much prefer dining with Lord Harleigh."

"As you will." Anthony turned wintry eyes to his mother-in-law. "Agreed?"

Lady Cavendish bowed her head and whispered, "Agreed." She had begun to shake, doubtless from pure humiliation. Jane felt the beginnings of pity for the woman, until she reminded herself of all her nasty words and petty cruelties. She felt no triumph though, and wanted nothing but an end to this mortifying scene.

Lord Dashmont turned to Jane. "Is there anything else?"

Jane was about to shake her head no when she remembered Hortense. "Hortense has been horribly neglected. She needs some new clothes, and a lady's maid, and . . ." Was she going too far? Well, why not ask for the moon? She just might get it. "Hortense needs a London Season."

Anthony nodded equitably and turned to Lady Cavendish. "Well?"

"Yes, yes, of course," the trembling woman answered. "Hortense shall have clothes, the maid, a Season."

"How kind of you, Lady Cavendish," Jane said politely, thinking, *at this point the woman would agree to walk naked down St. James's Street at high noon.*

Lord Dashmont nodded in agreement. "Then you may take your leave, madame. And remember, no more lies."

Lady Cavendish scurried from the room as fast as she was able, eyes down, shoulders slumping.

Muttering a curse, Lord Dashmont moved to the door and closed it firmly. When he turned to face Jane, she could tell from his smoldering eyes that his carefully controlled anger had turned to near-scalding fury. A foreboding silence filled the air until, his face a glowering mask of rage, he demanded, "Why the deuce didn't you tell me?"

Chapter 12

Lady Jane looked shaken, but her cool blue eyes looked squarely into his. "I am not a teller of tales, m'lord, so why should I have told you?"

Now Anthony understood how a man could thrust a fist through the wall. "All these months, and I never knew," he exclaimed. "Devil take it, I had pictured you living warm and protected—sheltered within these walls. Given your present circumstances, I had no thought you would be deliriously happy, yet I hardly expected you would be treated like a servant."

"I managed."

"Managed? *You?* Living on the servants' floor?" His anger surged at the thought of this genteel girl, whose family had been torn asunder, living in one of those tiny, wretched rooms. *Intolerable!* "I accept full responsibility, of course, but why did not you write me? Or have my uncle write. Or, at the very least, have the courtesy to inform me of your plight this afternoon when I returned home?"

"Because, sir, I did not wish to." She glared defiantly as she threw the words at him like stones. "Besides, for all I knew it was your wish I be so treated."

"You realize now that it was not?"

"I . . . suppose so. Lady Cavendish has made that clear. I never saw your letter. She gave me her version of what it contained, then discarded it."

Anthony pictured his hands around the scrawny throat of his mother-in-law. What a pity he could only imagine such a fate for that intolerable woman. But at least he could provide Jane a further explanation. "Lady Cavendish—" He stopped abruptly.

What was he thinking of? He had apologized, and that was enough. Why on God's green earth should he now find it necessary to explain himself?

She stood waiting, maddeningly composed, regarding him with those big, innocent blue-gray eyes. "Lady Cavendish?" she prompted.

"Confound it!" He hardly knew what to think, his frustration such that he could not stand still and had to pace. "How old are you?" he asked as he circled the room.

"Nineteen."

"Well, with all the great wisdom you have accumulated in your nineteen years, you should realize things are not always what they seem."

"Whatever do you mean?" she asked.

He had said too much. He, from the maturity of this thirty-two years should know better than to expect brilliant logic and perception from a girl not yet twenty. And yet . . .

Why could she not understand he was only trying to help her? He wished he could look into the mind and soul of this exquisite young creature standing proudly, so poised and composed, looking both an angel and a temptress in that enticing low-cut white gown. He stopped his pacing, stood before her, shoved his fists to his hips, and asked, "Has your life here been completely miserable?"

"Of course not." The tension in her face eased slightly. "Who would not enjoy the beauty of Fairfield Manor? And, of course, there's David. I cannot tell you what a pleasure it has been to know the child and to think I played a part in bringing him out of his shell. Then, too, there's Linneshall"—her eyes lit with pleasure—"it's like a dream come true, living next to the ruins of that beautiful old monastery, having access to those ancient books. Helping your uncle with the translations helped ease the pain of . . . the other things."

Perhaps she didn't despise him after all. "Then I am pleased you have found some pleasure in your stay here." He could hardly believe the next words forming in his head would actually pop out, but he had no way of stopping them. "So am I to assume you no longer harbor ill feeling towards me?"

Swift as clouds in an April sky, her manner changed. With a

hostile gaze she lifted her chin. "You are a blackguard and a devil. I can assure you, hell would have frozen over before I came crawling to you to complain about Lady Cavendish."

He was stunned. He had blundered again. Somehow he had thought . . . but no, it was obvious he had misread her and she hated him still. "How absolutely witless," he lashed back, his voice cutting. "You were only hurting yourself."

"If so, that is my concern. I only know it was you who encouraged my father and my brother to flee to America. Papa should be here"—her voice trembled, and she had to stop a moment to collect herself—"ruined or not, helping my family who are still destitute, and Mama not well." Her eyes appeared to moisten. "Not well at all, sir, and I blame it all on *you*."

Ah, so things were not so good with her family. That explained a lot. He was mortified, seeing her standing there, so brave, so defiant, and felt an almost irresistible urge to draw her into his arms. Most definitely not a brilliant idea, though. If he gave the least appearance of weakness, her contempt would grow. "I shall add to your stipend," he informed her coolly. "Fifty pounds more should be of great comfort to your family."

"Fifty pounds? That's an insult. I shall not take your charity."

Damn her pride. "Twenty pounds, then. You've earned it for what you've done with David."

She opened her mouth for what was obviously going to be a nasty reply, but apparently thought better of it. Doubtless because she decided he was right, she had earned the money, and it most certainly could be put to good use.

So what now? He felt drained, a heaviness pressing on his chest. He could continue on, he supposed, trying to explain himself, but aside from his pride preventing him, he might just as well be arguing with the cold, stone walls of Linneshall. Never had he felt so frustrated. There was nothing else to do but leave. "I shall depart for London tomorrow," he said.

"So soon?"

Damme. How dare she regard him with such blatant contempt. "I have urgent business in London."

"When shall I tell David you'll be back?"

He awarded her the iciest of stares. "I shall be taking David with me, at least for a time. Meanwhile, my uncle informs me you've been of some help in cataloging the Linneshall manuscripts. So stay. 'Tis a good way for you to earn your keep." He stalked to the door and turned. "Have no fear I shall further annoy you. I cannot imagine any circumstance under which I would return to Fairfield Manor any time in the near future— or distant future," he snapped, and left, emphasizing his hostile message with a sharp slam of the door.

What have I done? Jane stood in a daze, her senses so numb she felt dizzy and had to grip the back of a chair for support. She had meant every word she'd flung at him, yet her legs turned weak when he lashed back at her, and she felt bereft. All because of her shock and surprise at his stunning vehemence, she told herself. *How he must despise me.* She had no idea he harbored such enmity. *But remember, you called him a blackguard and a devil*, she reminded herself with full candor, and knew that despite her unease, she did not regret standing up to him. She would have been ashamed had she done otherwise.

She fled the music room and was headed up the main staircase when she met Barkley halfway. The butler, face blank as usual, announced, "Your belongings have been moved to the room next to Lord Harleigh's, Lady Jane." The emphasis on "Lady Jane" assured her Barkley had already received his new instructions.

At last she was rid of the servants' floor. She should be feeling giddy with delight. Instead, she felt miserable. All she could see was the anger in Lord Dashmont's eyes. But she would soon forget that ugly scene, she told herself. By tomorrow she would feel better.

"I have come to say good-bye, Uncle. Tatton and I are leaving first thing in the morning."

"God's blood, Anthony, you just arrived."

"I have urgent business in the city."

"The devil you have. It's that little chit, and don't tell me otherwise."

"The walls still have ears, it seems."

"Of course they have. Called you a blackguard and a devil, didn't she?"

"What Lady Jane chooses to call me matters not one whit. In

any event, I shall be returning to Jamaica soon, where I plan to propose to Miss Isabella Wentworth."

"Do you love her?"

"Of course not."

"You're a fool, Anthony. You married once to please your parents. Now you choose to marry for convenience. Did you ever consider marrying for love?"

"Ha! If ever I were tempted, I need only recall that disastrous year I took Georgiana to Jamaica. Not only did she take to her bed shortly after we arrived, she then proceeded to tax my patience to the limits with her whining and constant complaints. The food was abominable—the climate too hot—my friends and neighbors much too low-class for a lady of her quality. What a travesty! Do you honestly believe I would be so stupid as to repeat the past with another London belle?"

"Lady Jane has twice . . . three . . . a hundred times the character and brains as your first wife. Besides, she has changed considerably since she's been here."

"One thing you left out, Uncle—she loathes the sight of me."

"I remember that letter you wrote wherein you told me you had prevented her father from doing away with himself. Why not tell her? She's no fragile flower. I warrant her loathing would fast disappear if she knew the truth."

"Never. 'Tis true, I do have certain feelings for her, but I can assure you, after that unfortunate scene in the music room, I vow to forget her—a vow I shall honor, my dear uncle, if it takes me the rest of my life."

The next morning, a puzzled Hortense visited Jane in her spacious new bed chamber. "I don't know whether to laugh or cry," she declared.

"What's this?" Jane asked, surprised. "After you have just been promised a Season, and beautiful new clothes, and jewels, and a lady's maid? I should think you'd be floating on air this morning."

"Oh, I am, and so grateful to you, Jane. It's a miracle how Mama suddenly changed her mind. I don't know exactly what happened in the music room, but you obviously had a part in this. But"—Hortense's face fell—"last night I could have sworn Tatton found me to his liking."

"He did. I am sure of it."

Hortense spread her palms. "Then why did he and Lord Dashmont leave for London this morning without a single good-bye?"

Jane felt a sinking feeling in her stomach. "Are you sure?"

"His coach left by dawn's first light," Hortense replied. Her voice broke miserably. "I am so disappointed!"

So he did leave, just as he said he would. Feeling an acute sense of loss, Jane forced herself to smile brightly. "Tatton was indeed attentive to you last night—everyone could see that. No doubt Lord Dashmont was in a hurry, so Tatton didn't have a chance to say good-bye."

Hortense's face brightened. "Do you think so?"

"I know so. And just think—now you'll have all the more reason to collect a beautiful new wardrobe and make your plans for London in the spring. Tatton will be there—just ripe for marriage, I'll wager, waiting for you to dazzle him."

"And I'll do it, too," said Hortense, a pleased smile lighting her face. She clasped her hands together. "Oh, I have much to look forward to!"

I wish I did, thought Jane, but she kept her sad thought to herself.

Two weeks went by. Jane had assumed she would soon forget that terrible scene with Lord Dashmont, but she could not. Every day she was haunted by thoughts of him. Every day she reminded herself that he was a terrible man whose very existence she should forget. But at night, when she lay in her bed and gazed into the darkness, she could not prevent her thoughts from returning to that dreadful night. She pictured his lithe, hard body as he paced the music room. He'd reminded her of a panther, with the same kind of natural grace. Then, when he had stopped his pacing, he had stood and rocked back on his heels, thrusting his fists to his hips, thus pulling his jacket back, revealing not a little paunch, like so many men, but a flat, hard stomach that bespoke of hours of hard riding in the saddle, not card playing in the drawing room. How utterly masculine he'd looked in that sure, defiant stance of his, his wounded male ego visible in his blazing eyes and that little muscle in his jaw that flicked angrily. Indeed, she had brought him down. Instinctively, she knew she had the power to perturb him. He was only angry because he cared, but how much?

Some nights her imagination would take flight. She would take a pillow in her arms and imagine it was Dashmont lying close beside her, his strong arms around her, regarding her hungrily with those dark, shrewd eyes. "I want you," he would whisper, that one lock of his dark hair falling a little forward on his forehead. Then he would kiss her, long, with a passion that made his breathing come hard, and she, all prudishness cast aside, would press her whole self against his warm, taut body and kiss him back.

There were times when she lay wide awake half the night, staring into the darkness, thinking of Dashmont. Those were the times she had to remind herself of how much she despised the man.

"You're not yourself, missy," Lord Harleigh observed one evening. They were in his study, poring over manuscripts. "You should be in fine fettle, now you've escaped the servants' quarters. Instead, you've been dragging around as gloomy as a graveyard at midnight."

"Truly, I'm fine, sir." She had been given the finest guest room, spacious and lavishly furnished. "I adore my new room. It's just that Lord Dashmont . . ." She paused, aware she should not reveal any of her enmity to Lord Harleigh, who was exceedingly fond of his nephew.

"Oh, I know all about your quarrel," said the old man, seeming to read her mind.

She smiled wryly. "I should have known."

Lord Harleigh chuckled and slapped his knee. "On my soul, you made him mad as a wet cat. He's not coming back, or so he says."

"All to the good. I don't wish to hurt your feelings, m'lord, but I despise the man."

"You only think you despise him." He waggled a finger at her. "You would think differently if you knew the truth."

"Indeed?" Jane put down the quilled pen with which she'd been transcribing and regarded him with somber curiosity. "Pray, what is the truth?" She had asked the question lightly, but found herself holding her breath as she waited for a reply.

Hunched over in his chair, the old man was silent for a time, seeming to mull the matter. "You are greatly changed," he said finally. "Months ago when you arrived, you were young and shallow, with naught but your frivolous lost life on your mind."

"And my empty stomach," she quickly added, and they both laughed. She asked, "Why do you think I have changed?"

The old man pondered, tapping his finger to his lip. Finally he asked, "What if a miracle occurred and your father came back with his fortune restored? Would you then rejoice that you could return to your old life?"

It was her turn to ponder. "My family is in such dire straits that at first thought, my answer would be yes."

"So you would thrill to be the belle of London once again."

"I would be a liar if I said I didn't miss the London Season. But go back to my old life?" She pondered again, frowning, until she quietly said, "Never. To think, I never lifted a finger to accomplish anything, not like now. I have so enjoyed working with you. At the end of the day, when I've taught David something new and seen his smile—when I've heard you praise me for my translation of a manuscript, I have the most satisfying feeling that I've done something useful today. I was such a vain creature. I still am. But before, I was vain because of my looks and the beaux I captured. Now"—she made a sweeping gesture around the book-lined room—"it's not vanity I possess, but pride. Pride because I've had a part in restoring the priceless manuscripts of Linneshall."

The old man grunted his approval. "Society's notion that a lady must never lift a finger for any kind of work is preposterous."

"I led a shallow, useless life with nothing to recommend it, although . . ." Jane smiled ruefully and added, "I do miss the balls . . . the jewels and beautiful clothes, but I could never go back to being what I was. Even at the time, I was getting awfully bored with the endless parties, and so tired of flirting with those swell-headed dandies."

Lord Harleigh shifted in his chair. There appeared to be something weighty on his mind. "By God, I'll tell you. Anthony would have my head if he knew. Not that it matters. I'm too old and obstinate to care."

"But what—?"

"Shush!" Lord Harleigh's shaky, gnarled fingers fumbled in the pocket of his dressing gown. He pulled out a letter. "This nonsense has gone on long enough. I want you to listen. This is from Anthony, written from Jamaica soon after you arrived here." He adjusted his glasses and began to read:

> *Uncle, I was in a quandary. Lady Jane thought that I, heedless of her family's feelings, had urged her father to flee to America out of some reckless whim. She made it abundantly clear that she would never forgive me. I can hardly blame her, though I was surprised by her vehemence, and would have wanted to allay it, but how could I tell her the truth?*

Lord Harleigh lowered the letter and peered at her over the top of his spectacles. "I would not have read this to that shallow girl who arrived here a few months ago. Now I know you can handle this." He began to read again:

> *The night that Sperling lost his fortune, I found him in an anteroom at Brooks, a gun to his head. Clearly he was intent upon killing himself and would have, within seconds, had I not walked in. Even then, I was compelled to use all my powers of persuasion to induce him to put the gun down, as he was bound and determined to finish the deed. It was only when I, in desperation, mentioned his finding a new start in America that I saw in his eyes a faint glimmer of hope.*

Lord Harleigh lowered the letter again. "Shall I go on?"

"No." Jane threw her head back and shut her eyes, the shock of discovery hitting her full force. Her strong, brave papa had tried to kill himself? *Oh, how could that be? Anthony was lying.*

But no. A wave of anguish struck her as she recognized the truth. "So that's the reason—"

"That's the reason Anthony deigned not to tell you. He knew how hurt you'd be. He wanted all those fine memories of your father to remain intact."

"You were right to tell me," Jane said over the lump that had arisen in her throat. "Papa was not himself that night. Had he been in his right mind, he would never have contemplated such a horrible deed."

"Stop making excuses for him," Lord Harleigh snapped. "If you're adult enough to hear the truth, you're adult enough to remove your father from that pedestal you've had him on all your life. You must recognize his weaknesses."

She started to protest, but thought better of it, aware she could no longer deny herself the truth. "I still deeply love my father."

"Of course you do, but don't think he's God. Keep your eyes open and love him for what he is, with all his faults."

Jane thought of Lord Dashmont. In light of this new revelation she wanted to cringe. "Your nephew . . . I've been horrid to him."

"Words won't crush him. Anthony's tough as bull beef beneath all that charm."

Jane groaned and put her palm to her forehead. "But I said some terrible things."

"Yes, you did."

"He will never forgive me."

"My nephew is another man who doesn't deserve to be put on a pedestal," Lord Harleigh answered with a disdainful sniff. "He was the rake of London, don't forget, although I always felt he was uncomfortable in that role."

"Then why did he do all those wild things?"

"Guilt. When Georgiana died, he suffered a double dose of guilt. He let her have the phaeton—he never loved her"—Lord Harleigh made a wry face—"no surprise, considering what an empty-headed twit she was. But Anthony's feelings run deep. Though he hid it well, her death devastated him. I tried to reason with him, but to no avail. He was appalled at himself. Not only had he ceased to love her, but those last years of the marriage he'd stayed away from home most of the time, hardly able to stand the sight of her. Then, when she died in that sudden, horrible way, he was tortured to think how he'd neglected her, and how, perhaps if he'd tried harder, the marriage might have worked. That led to all that tomfoolery that made him the talk of London. That's in the past, though. Lately he's had a change of heart. For reasons I cannot fathom, the man's apparently decided to settle down, put his wild ways behind him. Matter of fact"—Lord Harleigh slanted an odd glance at her—"he confided in me he plans to marry soon."

Jane felt a wrench of disappointment. "Married? To whom?"

"To Miss Isabella Wentworth of Jamaica, a plantation owner's daughter. It should be a fine match, although there's no love lost there. It appears Anthony never marries for love."

"Perhaps he's never been in love."

"Don't be so sure. I have seen how he looks at you."

Despite herself, Jane's heart gave a leap, but she disguised her reaction with a wry laugh. "You were not privileged to see the last look Lord Dashmont bestowed upon me that night he stormed out of the music room. It was full of anger and contempt and hate."

"What did you expect after what you said to him?"

She felt like clapping her hands over her ears. "Must you be so honest?"

"Don't you see what I'm doing, child?" Lord Harleigh's usual scoffing demeanor had disappeared, replaced by an expression of deep concern.

"No, I don't see."

"Anthony is in love with you."

"*What?*" She regarded him as if he had just lost his sanity.

"I shan't be around much longer," continued Lord Harleigh, oblivious to her chagrin. "You're young yet, but you've the makings of a fine woman. Before I go, nothing would please me more than to attend yours and Anthony's wedding."

Wedding. Her heart swelled at the thought, but she warned herself she must keep her senses. "My feelings regarding Lord Dashmont are different now, after what you've told me. I would like to tell him so, but"—she shook her head sadly—"I cannot."

"And why not?"

"He has made it exceedingly clear he's not coming back to Fairfield Manor, so I shan't be seeing him anytime soon."

"Then for God's sake, write. Tell him your feelings have changed because you now know the truth about your father."

"You don't understand, sir," she said, clearly surprised that he had suggested such a thing. "A lady could never write such a letter. It would be considered forward, and . . . and well, quite unladylike."

"That's addle-brained."

"Oh, I know what you're thinking, and you're right. I'm trapped by society's stuffy rules, and if I had a bit of sense, I would defy those rules and write to Anthony."

"Ay, girl, there's the sensible thing to do."

"Well, I won't." Jane smiled sadly. "I cannot help how I was raised. I would rather die than ever have a man think I was chasing after him." She aimed a warning glance at Lord Harleigh. "And don't you tell, either. Promise?"

"Hrrumph! What utter foolishness. Women!" Lord Harleigh regarded her with disgust. "All right, I promise, though I think you're being a ninny."

"I know I'm being a ninny, but it's how I was raised and I cannot help it. Anthony must make the first move."

"And if he doesn't?"

"Then I shall have kept my pride, if nothing else."

Winter arrived, bringing its gloomy shroud of cold, winds, and dreary rain. *At least David is back*, Jane mused one day. She was curled up on the window seat in her room, an unread book in her lap, gazing out the leaded windowpanes at a gray day of steadily falling rain. *Rain that matches my mood*, she thought, thinking of how she had rejoiced when she heard that David was coming home, then lamented when she learned that Lord Dashmont had summoned Lady Cavendish to London to fetch the child.

"Why did he send for Lady Cavendish?" she had indignantly inquired of Lord Harleigh. "He knows perfectly well David is happiest in my care. When he's with his grandmother, he shuts up like a clam." With a scowl she'd added, "And furthermore, why didn't he bring his son back himself?"

Lord Harleigh appeared not the least perturbed. "The man's loathe to face you after that debacle. But I note he hasn't left for Jamaica yet, so give him time. I wager he'll come riding up the driveway sometime soon, claiming he wants to see David, but it'll be you he's after."

She had informed Lord Harleigh how mistaken he was. Now, staring gloomily out the window, she mused, *he'll never come back while I'm here. If he wants to see David, he'll send for him.* But it wasn't only Lord Dashmont who was causing her malaise. She worried constantly about her family. Letters from the tiny cottage near Hedley Hall were ever more heart-wrenching, mainly because of Mama's being close to her lying-in and feeling poorly. Jane was feeling increasingly concerned and desperate. If only there was something she could do. But there was nothing. Thank heavens, she had David to keep her busy as well as Lord Harleigh, who in his own unique way kept her spirits buoyed and made her believe that somehow, some way, there might be hope for her future.

Mary entered and curtsied. "Came to tend the fire, Lady Jane."

"Mary, how many times must I ask you not to curtsy to me?" Jane asked gently. She missed their old friendship and felt uncomfortable being mistress again.

"Yur lookin' in low spirits, jes' sittin' there," said Mary. "Has Lady Cavendish been nasty again?"

"She's the least of my troubles," replied Jane. It was almost laughable, the way Lady Cavendish kept casting hateful glances at her when no one else was looking. Jane could understand, though. The poor woman was still smarting over that terrible humiliation at the hands of her son-in-law. "Her ladyship has been quite horrid, but I pay no heed."

"Mayhap you should." Mary's voice held a warning. "She's mean and full of vitriol. I wouldn't put nothin' past her."

Sighing, Jane traced a raindrop rolling down the windowpane with her finger. "Ah, Mary, I cannot waste time worrying about a vengeful old lady. It's my family I worry about."

Mary knelt to build up the fire in the fireplace. "What ya need is to find the treasure," she said, casting the words over her shoulder.

Surprised, Jane asked, "You know about that?"

Mary nodded eagerly. "Everyone does. Hundreds of years ago those old monks buried a heap of gold 'n pearls 'n diamonds, and some old gold cup—a chalice, they call it. 'Tis all down at the ruins somewhere, everyone knows."

"But where?" Again, Jane thought of the map she'd found, then lost. "Once I found what could have been a treasure map, hidden in the binding of an old manuscript."

Mary's eyes opened wide. "Oh, my stars! Where is it?"

"I lost it." Jane told of the night that James had burst into the study with the news that Lord Harleigh was ill. In the excitement she had put the map somewhere—but couldn't remember where.

"Well, put yur thinkin' cap on. You've got to find it."

"I have tried."

"Well, try harder." The fireplace and her lowly position forgotten, Mary sank down on the window seat next to Jane. "Jus' think—if you found the treasure, your family would be rich again."

"I wish it devoutly, but . . . hmm . . . let me see." Jane closed her eyes and tried to envision that moment when James burst into Lord Harleigh's study. "James came in—said, 'His lordship has fallen ill.' I gasped and said, 'Oh dear,' or something similar, and then . . ." Jane tried to conjure up the vision of which book she had slipped the map into, but nothing came to mind.

There was a light knock on the door. Mary answered it, let in Hortense, made a quick curtsy, and hurried away. Jane was pleased that, of late, Hortense had begun to visit her frequently in her new bedchamber. It reminded her of the old days when she and Christabell used to try on dresses and hats and jewels, and chat and giggle for hours. Now she could do the same with Hortense, who lately had revealed a merry laugh and bright intelligence.

"Did you know about the fortune hidden at Linneshall?" she asked Hortense.

"Who doesn't?" Hortense replied. "Is there something new?"

Jane proceeded to relate her conversation with Mary,

wherein she had mentioned finding the map and was racking her brain to remember what she had done with it.

Hortense thought a moment. "If you checked all the old books and it wasn't there, mayhap you didn't put it in a book?"

Something stirred in Jane's mind. For a long moment she remained silent. A light slowly dawned, and excitement welled within her. It was all coming clear. "My sewing basket!"

"That's where you put it?" asked Hortense.

Jane slid from the window seat and rushed to her marbled armoire, painted with angels and roses, that stood in the corner. She pulled open the two paneled doors and bent to where her sewing basket had stood neglected in the corner ever since that night. She opened it and reached inside, saying, "I haven't touched my embroidery since the night Lord Harleigh took ill, but"—she groped inside the basket—"I must have stuffed it in here somewhere . . . aha!" She felt a piece of parchment. "Found it," she exclaimed as she pulled it out.

Hortense clapped her hands together. "Oh, Jane, you'll be rich."

"Wait, there's many a slip . . ." Forcing herself to calm down, Jane seated herself on the window seat again. "Let me read this." With great care she unfolded the thin, fragile piece of parchment across her knee. The writing was dim. She held the paper to the window and read,

> *Hark ye to where our hearts are buried*
> *Go ye forthe through the nave, to the east transept.*
> *From the northe side of Brother Osbert de Guees*
> *Looke ye IV foote to the cross and fleur-de-lis.*
> *Thence VI foote east to the priest's grave marked with a*
> *chalice, thence southe to the knight's marker.*
> *In the middle of these, search ye the chambre beneathe*
> *that conteyneth the treasure of Linneshall.*
> *All is loste in this year of our Lorde, 1536.*
> *Abbot Wulfric.*

When Jane finished, she silently folded the paper again. "What do you think?" asked Hortense.

"It sounds as if . . . yes, it could be the treasure, but I mustn't let myself get carried away." Full of suppressed excitement, Jane stood purposefully. "I must show this to Lord Harleigh."

Jane found the old man in his study. He was coughing as she entered, and James, looking concerned, was offering hot tea and honey, which his stubborn master, at his crotchety worst, was waving away. "James, stop coddling me. And stop telling me I should be in bed." He spied Jane. "Well, girl, I see you're about to burst like a thunderbolt. What is it?"

"I found the map, sir, the one that was in the binding. Take a look and tell me what you think."

Lord Harleigh took the scrap of parchment in his shaky fingers and for a long time pored over it. She could not gauge his reaction until he raised his eyes. They were gleaming with excitement. "By gad, girl, I think you've found it. That it was signed by Abbot Wulfric most definitely indicates the treasure was hidden at the time of the Great Suppression. Well, let's find it." With a labored grunt, he pushed himself up from the table. "Get your cloak, Jane. James, get my greatcoat, hat, and boots, and my cane. Best get a lantern, too."

"But, sir, it's raining," protested Jane, exchanging a worried glance with the valet, "and you're not well."

"Don't be a goose. James, get moving, and mind you keep this to yourself." Jaw set stubbornly, the old man looked at Jane. "I know what you're thinking, but I'm fine as five-pence. A little rain won't hurt me. Just think, within the hour the treasures of Linneshall could be within our grasp. And it's yours, Jane, I promise you that."

She gasped in disbelief. "All mine? But I thought—"

"I'm an old man with all the wealth I need. I have no need of treasure. But you? You're young and you have your family to think of. Upon my death, the property goes to Anthony, of course, but as for anything of value found upon it"—he awarded her with the most heartwarming smile she'd ever seen on his face—"come, my dear girl, let's go find your treasure."

*   *   *

Jane and Lord Harleigh, aided by James, followed the wooded pathway to the remains of Linneshall Abbey. Though the rain had let up by the time they arrived, they were soaked half through by moisture from the wet grass and dripping trees.

Despite the warm kerseymere cloak she was wearing, Jane shivered from the cold. "We must hurry, sir. It's started raining again and 'twill be dark soon."

Lord Harleigh, wrapped in his greatcoat with a shawl over his head, paid her no heed. In the gathering darkness, amidst the debris-strewn nave of the church, he squinted over the parchment. "Hold the lantern higher, James. Hmm . . . we shall go through the nave to the south transept."

"Beneath which somewhere lies the chamber," said Jane. Concerned, she added, "But can you climb through all that debris?"

"Confound it, of course I can. Once we get there, we shall start at the knight's grave marker, as indicated by the map, then count paces."

True to his word, the old man, aided by James, looked almost nimble as he made his way through the nave over the rough stones and other debris. Jane scrambled easily, but as they came closer to the east transept, she felt an unease.

"How can we find the north side of Brother Osbert de Guees, m'lord?"

"Don't know yet." Lord Harleigh's enthusiasm had diminished. He wore a worried frown. "If 'tis to the left, it's clear and we shall find the treasure. But to the right . . ."

When they reached the east transept, Jane's heart sank. To the left was clear. But to the right, the floor was covered several feet deep by tons of rocks and debris from the fallen roof. "We had better take another look at the map, sir."

James held up the lantern while Lord Harleigh peered at it once again, turning it around and around in his hands. "From the north side of Brother Osbert de Guees," he muttered. He looked toward the huge pile of rocks and scowled. "Damme, we've been foiled."

Jane took one look and knew he was right. The chamber that contained the treasure, if in truth it was there, was covered by tons of rocks and debris. "Is there any way?" she asked forlornly.

"No," replied the old man stoutly, "although 'tis not impossible. We could, of course, hire a crew of workers to clear off all the rocks and sell them to a quarry." At Jane's look of alarm, he continued, "Rest easy, dear girl. I shall not have anyone disturb the beauty of Linneshall." For the first time ever, he put his arm around Jane's shoulders. "Who are we to tamper with destiny?" he said with a sympathetic squeeze. "The treasure's been hidden away for centuries. Perhaps 'tis God's will we leave it be."

Jane nodded willingly. "We shall leave Brother Osbert de Guees in peace, as well as brave Abbot Wulfric."

"In the event the treasure is found someday, after I am gone, remember it belongs to you."

"I am most grateful," she said, not for a moment believing she would ever see it.

"Don't be," he said, surprising her. "That treasure may turn out to be a mixed blessing. You may have a quandary on your hands—finding what honor decrees and what your heart decrees are not the same thing."

She wondered what he meant by that, but it didn't matter. It was obvious the treasure was buried forever.

Later that night, Lord Harleigh took ill with chills and fever. Three days later, Jane, shaken and sad, knelt by his bed. "If only I hadn't found that map. Then we would never have gone out in all that cold and dampness and you'd not have caught a bad humor."

The old man feebly reached for her hand. " 'Tis but fate, my girl," he whispered, "don't blame yourself."

"You are going to get better," she told him, concealing her rising concern at his drawn face and labored breathing.

"Don't be daft. Before I go . . ." His voice faded. She waited while he caught his breath again. "You must tell Anthony you know . . ."

"That he saved my father?" asked Jane.

With an effort Lord Harleigh nodded his head.

"I shall consider telling him if I see him, sir, but it's been months now, and he has obviously been avoiding me."

The old man actually chortled. "Then something good will come of my death. Anthony's sure to come home for the funeral."

Shortly thereafter, Lord Harleigh fell into a coma. Jane sat all night by his bedside and watched with silent tears as toward dawn, with a small sigh, her beloved mentor slipped away.

Chapter 13

Beneath leaden skies, Roger, Lord Harleigh, was laid to rest in the family plot at Fairfield Manor. Jane stood at the graveside, fighting back tears of sorrow. What would she have done without that irascible old man? How could she have survived those first horrible days at Fairfield Manor without his support?

A somber Lord Dashmont had arrived the night before. He had greeted his small son with a warm kiss and a hug; granted the semblance of a smile to Lady Cavendish and Hortense; but when he turned to Jane, his face became as unreadable as a stone. "I trust you are well," he stated with excruciating politeness, accompanied by a stiff, unyielding bow.

"Quite well, sir," she answered with a curtsy equally as stiff, "although greatly saddened at your loss." His final words in the music room came back to her: *Have no fear I shall further annoy you. I cannot imagine any circumstance under which I would return to Fairfield Manor any time in the near future—or distant future.*

As if he'd read her mind, he said in a wintry tone, "It appears I was wrong. I am, lamentably, back sooner than I thought."

How could he have known? she thought with a stricken heart. *If only I hadn't said what I said.* Now, as she stood by the newly dug grave, she felt a triple weight of grief: for Lord Harleigh, who had been the brightest ray of sunshine in her life; for her stricken family; and now this latest—she must bear the hurt of Dashmont's obvious disdain. She must conceal her dismay, though. Heaven forbid her aching heart might show. She wanted desperately to tell him she knew the truth, but how?

After his curt greeting, he had turned away, eyes full of remoteness.

After the service, the sizable crowd of friends, and a few relatives, gathered in the grand salon. Jane, dressed in somber black with a white cameo brooch at her throat, dutifully mingled with the guests. At first, she had hoped she might find a moment alone with Dashmont, but he seemed to turn his back whenever she approached. It soon came clear he was avoiding her. As a consequence, her misery grew until she was hard put even to keep a pleasant expression upon her face as she desperately wondered what to do.

Let it go, advised the wise, practical inner voice. *You cannot chase after him. Mama would be horrified.* Yet she heard another voice—that yearning, reckless voice that also dwelt within her—saying, *you must get him alone—tell him how you feel or you will lose him forever.*

All evening Jane observed Dashmont acting the gracious host, sincere, yet reticent in his grief, as he chatted dutifully with guests, kept an affectionate eye on David, and even endured, with the utmost civility, his mother-in-law's counterfeit tears of mourning.

The evening dragged on. Finally Jane, in an ever more woeful state of mind, reached a decision. She would make no further attempt to talk to Lord Dashmont. Poverty-stricken or not, she was a lady, and a true lady never chased after a man, nor gave the slightest indication she wished to do so. If she did, she would be ostracized from society. She had never made a fool of herself over a man. This was no time to start.

Finally, when all the guests had retired or departed, she returned to her bedchamber with head held high, suspecting that with her thoughts in such a turmoil she would have difficulty getting to sleep.

She was right. She was so perturbed she could not even think of lying down. Still dressed, she went to the window and peered pensively into the night. The skies had cleared. The stars were out, a full moon just visible over the horizon. How beautiful it must look, she mused, rising over the ruins of Linneshall. She had never seen the ruins at night, especially under a full moon. A rebellious thought struck her: there was nothing to prevent her from going right now to view the ruins of Linneshall. Of course, Mama would not approve of her venturing out alone at night. Aunt would doubtless throw a fit. But why should she not? She was a woman now, entitled to make her own decisions. Besides, if ever she should go, it should be tonight. She would feel closer to Lord Harleigh, finding solace in the ruins he had loved so dearly. She would sit on his favorite bench near the sundial, meditate in that beautiful, peaceful place, hopefully dispel the dark cloud of gloom that hung over her, and find the strength to carry on.

Yes, she would do it. She reached for her cloak.

The night was chill without the slightest breeze. Except for crickets chirping, there was silence as Jane pulled her cloak closer about her and walked the wooded path to the ruins. At the top of the hill she stopped in wonderment. *What an enchanting sight*, she thought. Like a bright precious stone, the yellow moon hung over ancient stone walls that reached, in jagged silhouette, toward the twinkling black sky, speaking hauntingly of the inexorable passage of time. Through the mist of centuries her imagination took her back to when others must have stood in this very same spot and viewed with the same wonderment this magical scene. They were gone now, all of them, their triumphs and tragedies, their laughter and sorrows all forgotten, buried in the past for eternity.

Just as yours shall be some day, missy.

Lord Harleigh. She could hear his voice clearly. It was as if he were standing at her shoulder, smiling that taunting little smile of his that cut through all her petty vanities.

. . . and when you go, will you ask yourself, "Did I live my life the way I wanted, or did I stay a ninny, blindly following society's witless rules?"

She felt humbled, and very, very small. *Why am I so worried about what other people think?* she wondered. Lord Dashmont deserved an apology, and she, caring more about her own selfish feelings than what was moral and just, was acting the conceited fool. *He shall have his apology*, she decided, *if I have to throw myself at his feet to get his attention. Even if he laughs at me, it's the fitting thing to do. And if, just possibly, he does forgive me . . .*

Again, for at least the thousandth time, her pulse raced at the memory of his impulsive embrace that day in the hallway at Chalton House. Long since forgotten by him, she supposed. *But what if he did remember? What if he did still care?* Perhaps she had only to apologize . . .

Stop imagining, you foolish girl. She watched the moon for a while, confident she had made the right decision, then found her way amidst the tumbled ruins to the tangled garden, where she sat on Lord Harleigh's favorite bench near the sundial. She sat there for a time, immersed in her thoughts, until . . .

"Good evening, Lady Jane. Should you be here alone?"

Dashmont. His deep, masculine voice flooded over her like honey, causing her heart to twist in response. She stood abruptly. He was standing only a few scant feet away, but she, deep in her thoughts, had not heard him approach. The night was silent now, not even crickets chirping, as if all the world was holding its breath, waiting for her reply. "I . . . I didn't expect you here."

"After I returned with my parents from Jamaica, I came here often," he replied in a quiet, wistful voice. He looked out over the ruins. "Uncle's favorite spot . . ." After a long pause he continued, "I can remember trying to imagine what Linneshall was like back then, how it must have bustled with activity—the choir singing, the monks doing their writing, studying, meditating along those beautiful arcades."

She answered softly, "To think, this very same moon we're standing under now, they stood under back then."

"The very same," he answered in complete rapport. "Sad to think it all came to an end nearly three centuries ago."

She was surprised. The rake of London had just revealed a compassionate, reflective side of his nature she had never seen before. "I never thought you cared about these ruins."

"Of course I care," he said with quiet emphasis. "More every day. Of course I always acted the opposite, just to vex my uncle. It was my way of standing up to him, though if you knew Uncle, you would know he would not have wished it otherwise. I . . ." He paused, as if a thought had just occurred to him. "But

I shan't disturb you further. I was out for a stroll and saw you sitting here. Incautious of you, Lady Jane. 'Tis after dark. You should not be out alone."

"I can take care of myself, m'lord," she answered with an obstinate toss of her head.

"Of course you can," he conceded flatly and started away. "I shan't bother you further," he called coolly over his shoulder. "Good night."

He was leaving. *Oh!* As yet, despite her resolution, she had not been able to bring herself to apologize. The words refused to leave her mouth. Instead, she had sounded like a child, offering up silly protestations when he chided her for being out alone at night. No wonder he was avoiding her. But could she apologize? She, the daughter of a once-powerful earl, hardly knew the word *humble*. Most certainly, never in her life had she felt obliged to apologize to a man.

He was nearly out of sight now, disappearing into the shadows. *But if I don't call him back and apologize, he will return to London, not ever knowing how I feel, and thence to Jamaica, and I shall never see him again . . .*

More words from Lord Harleigh popped into her head. "*Be yourself, Jane. Don't let society's rules confound you. No one should tell you what you ought to do but you.*"

"Lord Dashmont!"

The receding figure stopped and turned. "Yes?" he called.

"I . . . I . . . there is something I wish to say."

He returned immediately and stood close in front of her, so close she caught the tantalizing, slight scent of musk from his eau de cologne.

"Well, what is it?" he asked when she remained silent.

His voice was cool. Doubtless, after she offered him her agonized apology, he would give it short shrift and walk away. *Well, so be it.* She was in for it now and would not change her mind. She took a deep breath. "I owe you an apology, m'lord."

Was it her imagination, or had she heard a sharp intake of his breath? "Do tell me why," he said lightly, "I am all ears."

" 'Tis not amusing, sir."

"I never said it was," he answered, now deadly serious.

In a torrent of words, she plunged ahead. "I have discovered the truth about my father—that he . . . he . . . tried to take his life and 'twas you who prevented him, and that was why you told him he could sail to America and start a new life. I am most grateful for that, and I shall never, ever again call you a blackguard and a devil."

There, 'twas done. She had let the words out in one long stream and had to pause to catch her breath. If he wanted to upbraid her, now was the time. She would force herself to stand and listen, no matter what he said.

She could hear the soft sound of his breathing, faster now, as she waited for his response. He then surprised her by turning away. He walked a few feet, and with his back to her placed his hands on his hips, propped one booted foot on a convenient stone, and gazed upward, as if seeking advice from the moon. "Good God," he finally erupted.

She knew he'd be angry. "I am sorry, m'lord. Had you but told me"—she stopped, warning herself not to make excuses—"I mean, I should not have been so . . . so . . ."

"Idiotically stubborn?" He turned. She could feel his probing eyes upon her. "Shall we add unreasonable? How about childlike and hardheaded?"

"You are angry," she said, "and I know you have every right to be."

He strode back to her. "I am *not*," he began forcibly, then continued, this time in a softer tone, "I am angry, but not why you think." He paused; she could see his pained expression in the semidarkness. "I shall be blunt. That night we met—"

"At Lady Ponsonby's ball, yes, I remember."

"From that first moment when I saw you across the dance floor, I was taken with you." From his lips came a bitter laugh that seemed directed at himself. "Taken with you? I've been obsessed with you. You are the reason I fled to Jamaica, where, to my utmost disgust, I found I still could not stop thinking about you. Time and again I told myself this was madness, that I must obliterate you from my mind. Nothing worked. You, Lady Jane, are the reason I returned to England. God help me!"—he glanced upward at the moon again—"can you imagine how hard this is on my pride?"

She was stunned. Never had she dreamed such words would come from his lips. "But why—?"

"No," he interrupted, "let me finish. My first wife, Georgiana, was also a London belle, much like you. I took her to Jamaica, thinking she would learn to love plantation life, but instead she loathed it. God rest her soul, but I would never go through a wretched experience like that again."

"So what are you trying to tell me?" she asked, bewildered. "That you . . . you like me, but want nothing to do with me?"

"In essence, yes. After our last 'discussion' in the music room, wherein you did a thorough job of castigating me, I returned to London, determined to forget about you."

"And did you?" She waited for an answer, but he was silent. "No matter," she went on. " 'Tis not as if I expected you to marry me. No man would want me now. I have no dowry."

"God's blood!" He gripped her upper arms and shook her slightly. "Do you think I care about dowries?"

Tight in his grasp, she was overwhelmed and hardly knew how to answer. "I only meant—"

"I do not give a groat what you meant or did not mean," he replied hoarsely, his face only inches away from hers. She could feel his body trembling as he continued, "I want you. Do you know how utterly illogical that is? How absolutely insane, after what I went through with . . ." He paused, then words burst from his throat. "Logic be damned. At this moment all I can think of is to feel your beautiful body against me and to kiss you."

His arms encircled her, slipping beneath her cloak. She felt their power as he pulled her even closer, so that every inch of his lean, hard body pressed tight against her. It made her pulse pound, made her wonder how she could possibly resist. "Wait, let me think," she cried.

"No. You think too much. Thinking gets you into trouble." She felt his warm breath upon her cheek. "Ah, Jane . . ."

His last words were smothered as his lips crushed hers with savage intensity. He bent her back over his arm and continued the kiss hungrily, as if he could never get enough. She returned his kiss, her head spinning, aware that this was not one of those hasty, stolen kisses that she, totally in charge, had permitted to be bestowed by one of her beaux. She was not in control here. This was not child's play. This was a man's kiss—savage, demanding, signaling a passion she might not be able to allay. Nor did she wish to. She knew a reckless abandon as she relaxed in his arms, a spurt of hungry desire spiraling through her as she felt the warmth of his hand through the thin material of her dress. At first his hand rested at her waist; slowly it slid up her side until it touched her breast. A moan of pleasure escaped her. At that, as if returning to reality, he broke from the kiss and with a mighty curse clasped her shoulders and thrust her at arm's length, as if pushing temptation away. "No, I cannot do this," he said, his voice shaking with intensity.

She could hear his ragged breathing. She took her own deep, fervid breath and stared at him in the semidarkness, her heart full of loving and longing for him. "Oh, Anthony—"

"No." He was silent for a time, biting his lip, staring deliberately at the ground, until he was breathing normally again and back in control. "My apologies," he said in a brisk voice. "You cannot imagine how tempting you are standing there in the moonlight, but that's hardly a reason for me to take advantage."

Tempting? Was that all? Suddenly all pleasure left her. She pulled herself tall and rearranged her cloak. "You did not take advantage, m'lord. I daresay I've a mind of my own." She managed a breezy voice as she continued, "But no harm done. What was it but a kiss?"

"It was more than that," he answered bluntly. Tenderly his finger traced the line of her cheekbone and jaw, then moved to finger a loose tendril of hair falling over her forehead. "We shall go on a picnic tomorrow," he said finally.

"Where?"

"Here, at the ruins, of course. Uncle will be here, at least in spirit." After a thoughtful pause he asked, "Have I really been forgiven?"

"I don't say things I don't mean."

"Yes, of course." His hands took her face and held it gently. "I have never been in love, Lady Jane."

Her heart leaped. Did he love her? Was that what he was trying to say? Carefully, she answered, "I, too, have never been in love, m'lord."

"Forgive me for being cautious," he replied. "I am not reckless with other people's hearts, nor would I put up with people
who are reckless with mine. I need time to think. Come, I shall
walk you home."

As they walked the wooded path homeward, Jane felt like
dancing, not walking sedately by his side. It was hard to believe
that the unconquerable Lord Dashmont, object of countless
broken hearts, had kissed her urgently, shaking with passion in
her arms. It could be only lust, she supposed, but she didn't
think so. She might be young and naive, but she knew his ardent kiss had been beyond lust.

Such a night of revelation this had been. She had at last seen
that Dashmont was not the degenerate rake who was the talk of
London. Rather, through their discussion about his uncle, and
the ruins of Linneshall, she could see he was a man of deep sen-
sitivity and caring, though indeed he hid it well.

But aside from all that . . .

Her pulse raced when she recalled the ecstasy of being held
tight against him. Indeed, the sheer masculine attraction of the
man had sent her senses reeling. She wondered if she loved him
and decided, yes, she did. But what would happen next? After
the sad events of the past months, she was almost afraid to expect anything good might happen to her. But what if he proposed tomorrow at the picnic? *How glorious.* She knew he
would be generous, and her family would live in their accustomed style again. As for herself . . . her spirits soared at the
thought of marrying a man she truly loved—sharing his bed,
sharing his life.

It was such a joy to contemplate, she tried to put it out of her
mind. She hardly dared to think an impossible dream might
come true.

It was past midnight when they entered Fairfield Manor's
barrel-vaulted entry hall and, to Jane's chagrin, discovered
Lady Cavendish standing on the first step of the grand staircase,
every inch of her thin self uptight with disapproval. To Anthony
she said, "Out rather late, are you not, sir?" She fixed Jane with
a look layered in blackness. "Wherever have you been at this
hour?"

Anthony responded icily, "Lady Jane was just going up to her bedchamber, madam. I trust you'll soon be retiring to your own."

Jane made a brief curtsy. "Good night, sir, your ladyship." Swiftly, she started up the staircase. As she passed Lady Cavendish, the look she received from the older woman was full of jealousy, hatred, and seething rage.

She wants to hurt me, thought Jane, though she was not overly alarmed. Lady Cavendish might despise her, and that was obvious, but with Lord Dashmont wise to her ways, what could one old, embittered lady possibly do?

Chapter 14

There was no picnic. Early the next morning a message arrived for Jane.

> *Dearest Sister,*
> *The baby lived only hours. Mama is very sick, perhaps*
> *dying. We need you.*
>   *Christabell.*

"I must go to my family," said a shaken Jane to Lord Dashmont when she showed him the message.

"You must leave immediately. I shall put my coach at your disposal."

Jane accepted Dashmont's offer gratefully. After anxious hours of traveling, she arrived at the yeoman's cottage. It was worse than ever she had pictured. The thatched roof was in a state of disrepair, the yard and bushes unkempt, as was the slovenly female servant who answered the door. Inside was even worse: shabby furnishings, the children poorly dressed.

"Oh, Jane, I'm so glad you have come," Christabell cried after hurling herself into her sister's arms. Jane was shocked at her appearance. The rosy bloom had faded from her cheeks. Her face was thinner now, dark circles beneath her eyes.

"How is Mama?" Jane asked anxiously.

"A trifle better, but as you can see . . ." Christabell gestured about her ". . . our life is hideous here. Our food is barely adequate . . . and we're cold . . . and Aunt Eugenia won't ever come out of her room."

"Any word from Papa?"

"It's as if he disappeared off the face of the earth."

With vast relief, Jane found her mother better, though grieving for the baby girl she had lost.

Jane spent the next days by her mother's bedside, as well as helping with the children, giving what comfort she could. A week after she had arrived, a concerned Christabell took Jane aside. "There's something I've been wanting to discuss. Lord Bradbourne has taken to staying at Hedley Hall much of the time. He comes here often to visit me."

"*You?*" Jane felt a chill over her heart.

"I do have the feeling he has some interest in me, but now he's heard that you are here. He has sent word he will come for tea this afternoon and most especially wants to see you." Christabell clasped her hands together. "Oh, Jane, do you suppose it's another proposal? I know Lord Dashmont said bad things about him, but Lord Bradbourne has been quite nice to me. As far as I'm concerned, he's a gentleman—a very rich gentleman whom you ought to consider." She smiled at her sister sweetly. "Because if you don't, I will."

Though Jane had not said a word about Lord Dashmont, she felt that now was the time to be candid with Christabell. "I could hardly consider Lord Bradbourne when it is quite possible that Lord Dashmont and I . . ." In spite of herself she smiled. "I don't wish to speak too soon, but—"

"Oh, Jane, you and Lord Dashmont?" Christabell beamed. "He's richer than Bradbourne. How wonderful. When will you know?"

Jane took Christabell's hand. "I'm almost positive we needn't concern ourselves further with Old Bony Fingers. Since Mama is so much better, I shall be returning to Fairfield Manor soon, and when I see Lord Dashmont—"

"Don't say it." Christabell lightly pressed two fingers to Jane's lips. "We daren't put a hex on your wonderful news before it happens."

"If you say so," Jane laughingly agreed, "though truly, I'm not the least concerned about a hex."

"It's good to hear you laugh again." Christabell regarded her sister thoughtfully. "You've changed. You seem so much more grown up somehow, not so—"

"Frivolous and shallow?" Jane sobered quickly. "I suppose I

have changed. It's strange—I yearn for the old days, yet I could
never go back to being what I was. We've been through a lot,
haven't we? After Papa's flight, the future looked so bleak I
thought I'd never smile again. But I've gathered my strength
these past few days, perhaps because I'm so confident Lord
Dashmont will propose next we meet. But even if he doesn't, I
know somehow we'll cope."

"But he must propose," said Christabell. "Our happiness de-
pends on it."

"I'm almost positive he will."

When Lord Bradbourne arrived, Jane found he was not quite
as odious as she remembered. His complexion did not appear
quite so pasty in the dim, late afternoon light of the small parlor. Too, his offensive air of superiority was nowhere in evi-
dence; he was all sympathy for the loss of their infant sister.
During tea, which she had been dreading, he had been almost
charming, entertaining them with light *on-dit* of the neighbor-
hood. Now, at his request, she faced him alone, Mama and
Christabell having withdrawn.

She was curious. On the low table between them lay a mysterious package, securely wrapped, which had earlier been
carefully carried in and deposited there by Lord Bradbourne's
coachman.

"You are wondering what the package contains?" asked
Bradbourne, who had noticed her inquisitive glance.

She would not deign to admit to the least curiosity. "What is
it you wished to see me about, Lord Bradbourne?" she asked
with solemn dignity.

He gave her a smile. "Perhaps you should open the package
first. Then I shall tell you."

She opened the package—and gasped with delight.
"Timmy!" Tears sprang to her eyes. In her hands was her
beloved ormolu clock. "I . . . I thought I would never see it
again."

"'Twas Christabell who mentioned how much the clock
meant to you. You should have told me." He smiled benignly.
His mouth did not look so cruel after all. "I must confess to a
great fondness for you, Lady Jane. Though you may have a

scurrilous opinion of me, you must know it was never my intention to deprive you of something you loved."

"I hardly know what to say, sir," she said, clutching the porcelain elephant tight, feeling a nostalgic lump in her throat for that little girl in that innocent world long gone who had loved Timmy so much.

"You need not say a word." Here came his kindly smile again. "I asked you to marry me once. The offer is still open." With a look of distaste he gazed about the shabby parlor. "You are meant for finer things than this, as is your dear family. It is my heartfelt wish to establish them again at Hedley Hall."

If I marry you, thought Jane. Clearly he was offering a bribe, and yet, she did not feel the burning resentment toward him she'd felt before. Mama and Aunt Eugenia had never spoken of the shocking disclosures concerning Bradbourne that Anthony had revealed to them that day in the library. Whatever they were, could he have been mistaken? Or, perhaps, exaggerating? But all that didn't matter. She was going to marry Anthony, and had better apprise Lord Bradbourne of that respect. "Sir, I am flattered beyond words at your kind offer, but—"

The truth struck her. What was she thinking? Dashmont had not yet proposed. Until he did, she would be a fool to utter a positive no. "I shall have to think on it, sir, if you don't mind."

"Not at all, my dear. Take your time." His expression was that of reasonableness and complete unconcern. Again, it occurred to her that perhaps she had been mistaken about the man.

Later, when Jane was alone, she chided herself. Why had she not told Bradbourne the truth? Without a doubt she was going to marry Lord Dashmont. He would propose upon her return to Fairfield Manor.

But within her, a little voice nagged, *You ought not be too sure of yourself.* But why shouldn't she be confident? What could possibly go wrong?

Two weeks later, Jane said good-bye to her family and set out for Fairfield Manor. The tragedy of Lord Harleigh's death, along with the loss of her infant sister, still dampened her spirits. But at least Mama had recovered. Also, she had managed to set her nagging doubts aside. Now, whenever she thought of Anthony and his expected proposal, she felt a bubbling joy.

The coach ride went quickly. A mile before the driveway to Fairfield Manor, she spied a heavy wagon carrying stones, rolling toward the highway along a road that was hardly more than two tracks in the ground. It was the little-used road that led from Linneshall Abbey.

"Stop," she called up to the coachman, feeling a sudden unease. When the horses halted, she jumped quickly from the coach and confronted the driver of the wagon, who was just now turning onto the main road. "Where are you getting those stones?" she asked, shading her eyes as she looked up at him.

With a sweep of his hat the driver answered, "From the ruins of the old abbey, mum. Taking 'em to the quarry."

"Have you taken many?" she asked, bracing herself for the worst.

"Not just me, mum. There's been wagons running this road for the better parts of two weeks now. But this is near the last of all the debris. They'll be used for road stone, most likely. 'Twill fetch his lordship a pretty penny."

"That's all then?"

"Far from it. Now they be knocking the arcades down, then the church, then every building left standing." With a disapproving shake of his head, he continued, "Those old monks'd be rollin' in their graves if they was to see this." With a flick of the reins he moved on.

Oh, no, oh, no. The abbey lay just over the hill. The coach forgotten, Lord Dashmont, everything forgotten, Jane gathered up the skirts of her dove gray traveling dress and started running up the old road to the abbey. When she reached the top of the hill, she stopped to look at the sight below. At first it didn't seem too bad: the walls of Linneshall's church still stood, but the tons of debris that had covered the nave and north and south transepts had nearly all been carted away. Not so bad, she thought, the debris had indeed been unsightly. Then she froze in horror. The beautiful arches that had formed the arcades had been leveled. Now, as she watched, laborers were loading wagons with the last of the stones from the arches, while others were applying picks and sledgehammers to the church walls, preparatory to knocking them down.

"'Tis a sickening sight, is it not?" came a man's sad voice.

"Brother William," Jane exclaimed. In her horror, she had not noticed the slight, brown-clad figure of the old Cistercian brother standing forlornly next to the stream. She went down the hill to stand beside him.

"'Tis a good thing Lord Harleigh did not live to see this day," said Brother William with a dismal shake of his head.

"Who ordered this?" Jane asked, her voice shaking.

"Lord Dashmont owns the property now." With a helpless shrug Brother William held out his hands palms up.

Jane felt sick at the pit of her stomach. "It can't have been Lord Dashmont. Only Lady . . . someone else . . . could do anything this deplorable. Good day, Brother William, I . . . I have business to attend to." She ran back to the coach and ordered the coachman to drive on to Fairfield Manor at top speed.

"Lord Dashmont is not here," Barkley announced when Jane arrived. "Lady Cavendish is in the small salon."

Seconds later, yanking off her bonnet, Jane stormed into the small salon and found Lady Cavendish at her harlequin desk, writing letters. Her chest heaving, Jane managed to gasp, "I must talk to you."

"I see you are back," said Lady Cavendish, lifting a haughty eyebrow. "I trust your mother has improved?"

The old harridan didn't care a fig about her mother. Jane opened her mouth to speak, realizing just in time she was about to raise her voice at the woman who sat so smugly before her. But no, she could not sound like a fishwife. She willed herself to speak in a low voice, tight under control. "I have come to talk about the destruction of Linneshall. How could you?"

"How could I what, my dear?"

"Destroy the abbey. I saw it coming home—the arcade gone—wagons carrying the stones away—and now they're hammering at the church. What sacrilege. If Lord Harleigh saw what you have done, he would—"

"Lord Harleigh is dead," Lady Cavendish interrupted harshly. With a false smile and passionless eyes, she arose from her chair. "For years we have been obliged to put up with that unsightly rubble. Now, thank heaven, those ugly ruins shall all be carted away, down to the last stone."

Jane gave a heartsick cry. "You can't."

"Indeed, I can. It was only out of the kindness of my son-in-law's heart that he postponed the inevitable until his uncle died. Life moves on, my dear. Lord Dashmont will be paid a tidy sum for those stones, as well as for the lead from the roof that was not already salvaged. Aside from that, he wishes to build a guest house and clear the land for new tenants."

She was stunned. "So it was at Lord Dashmont's orders?" She held her breath waiting for the response.

"Of course Lord Dashmont's orders." The older woman peered down her nose at Jane. "You do not believe I acted alone, do you?"

Still Jane could not comprehend. Dashmont's sentimental words came back to her: *I can remember trying to imagine what Linneshall was like back then* . . . Vividly she recalled that night they kissed at the ruins, and his touching reminiscences. He had seemed so sincere—so genuinely attuned to the precious, irreplaceable, little piece of English history that had lain before him. Lady Cavendish had lied before. Surely she was lying again. "Where is he?" Jane asked.

"His lordship has been in London these past weeks, but is returning today." Lady Cavendish slanted a lofty look at Jane. "But if you think you'll get a different story from him, you are sadly mistaken."

"So you've made up your mind *not* to propose to Lady Jane?"

Tatton Fulwood, sitting across from Anthony in the coach bearing them to Fairfield Manor, quizzically regarded his friend.

"Don't tell me you're surprised," said Anthony.

"Frankly, yes. Never have I seen you in such a state as you've been in these past weeks. Did she cast some sort of spell over you? You've not once gone gambling. You've avoided all your former lady birds, who are, as you very well know, dying to recapture you. If you want the truth, you've become a bore, walking about London as if in some sort of daze. And it's all over a girl you're *not* going to marry?"

"I have no idea what you're talking about." With a great show of casualness Anthony stretched out his legs and regarded his polished Hessian boots.

"Yes, you do."

Anthony sighed. "I admit, I was rather attracted to the chit for a time. My decision not to propose wasn't an easy one." *Not easy?* No need for Tatton to know how he had returned to London devoid of all rational thought—that he could not eat or sleep for thinking of her—that his mind was still full of that kiss in the moonlight and the intoxicating feel of her soft breast through the thin bodice of her dress. A tremor ran through him. He was like a schoolboy, sick with longing. *Jane, Jane . . .*

He must pull himself together. "Of course, you, Tatton, would understand my plight better than most."

"Only too well, having seen at close hand your travails with Georgiana." Tatton sighed. "Which leads me to ask, are you sure? Jane is not Georgiana. She might not hate Jamaica as Georgiana did."

"I cannot accept that risk."

"And I thought you were a gambler. Ah, well, our choices are all half chance at best. You are wise to forget about her."

"I heartily agree, Tatton." *Forget about her?* When his body ached for her touch; when his heart swelled just thinking of her delicate face and the way her blue eyes flashed when she was angry, and that charming lilt in her voice when she wasn't angry; and the way she carried herself, as graceful as a willow bending in the wind. But what was beauty? True, she had displayed courage in the face of great adversity. Generosity, too, when she stood up for Hortense. But had that vain creature he'd met at Lady Ponsonby's ball disappeared forever? His heart told him yes, but his sensible side told him absolutely no. He would be a fool to think otherwise.

Tatton regarded him from under heavy-lidded eyes. "Admit it, you're mad for her."

"I must deal with this in my own way, Tatton," he answered sharply, then thought better of it. Perhaps he should explain. He *wanted* to explain, as if to clear up the doubts in his own head.

"When Georgiana died in such a horrible way, I felt responsible."

"Water under the bridge, Anthony."

"I *was* responsible. I knew she should not be driving that phaeton, but by then I'd grown so weary of her giddiness . . . her selfishness . . . her low moral character." Anthony paused, seeing the surprised expression that crossed Tatton's face. "You think I didn't know of her affairs? Of course I did. But by then it didn't matter. I let her have the phaeton because I didn't care. I shall take that to my grave, Tatton. If only I'd said no."

"So what has this to do with Lady Jane?" asked Tatton.

"She and Georgiana are much alike. Both raised to live a life of idleness—both selfish and vain."

"But you said—"

"Oh, I know what I said concerning Lady Jane. Since her father left, she has conducted herself in an exemplary manner. I've been impressed. But what if I should marry her? How do I know she wouldn't revert back to the silly little chit she was the night we met? I cannot go through that again, Tatton. Better that I marry Miss Wentworth. She may not be beautiful, or charming, but she's solid, and reliable, and . . ."

"How about punctual?" Tatton interjected sarcastically. "There's every man's dream, Anthony—to bed a woman who's solid, reliable, and punctual."

"You'll never understand," Anthony answered, then made a point to concentrate on looking out the window. They were almost home. Their coach was passing the old road that led to the ruins of the abbey. *Strange*, he thought, it looked as if it had recently been used. Idly, he recalled a conversation he'd had with Lady Cavendish, back when he was still married to Georgiana. In her usual annoying fashion, his mother-in-law had been complaining about those "unsightly ruins."

"Nothing can be done at present," he had informed her. "They belong to my uncle and are most dear to his heart."

"And after Lord Harleigh's demise?"

Anything to silence her. "If it means so much to you, when Linneshall is mine, you may order those 'unsightly ruins' as you call them, cleared away."

Now Anthony flinched inwardly at the callous words he had uttered back then. How witless and unthinking he had been, so immersed in his own problems that he hadn't understood the full meaning of the priceless, irreplaceable ruins of Linneshall that now belonged to him.

"Her ladyship is in the small salon," Barkley announced when they arrived.

Anthony noted that his flawless butler had a warning look in his eye. "Is she alone, Barkley?"

"No, m'lord. Lady Jane is with her, having just arrived back from her visit to her family."

"We shall go in directly. Come, Tatton."

Despite himself, at the thought of seeing Jane again, Anthony's pulse quickened. When he and Tatton stepped inside the drawing room, it began to pound, and he was hard put to maintain his implacable composure. How beautiful she looked, standing there in her simple traveling dress. He gave a perfunctory nod to Lady Cavendish, then said to Jane, "What a pleasure to see you again. I trust your mother is better?"

She remained silent. It was only then he became acutely aware of the strained atmosphere hanging over the room: Lady Cavendish standing stiff, unsmiling; Jane unsmiling too, clenching her bonnet tight. "Is something wrong?" he inquired of her.

In a shaking voice she replied, "As we speak, the priceless remains of Linneshall are being carted away. Lady Cavendish says you are responsible. Is that true?"

He felt as if a lightning bolt had just struck. She looked so stricken he wanted to take her in his arms and comfort her. But that wouldn't do, since he was the cause of her distress. If he could just explain . . .

A thousand explanations swirled through his head. A thousand explanations he rejected.

Lady Cavendish declared, "I was merely implementing your wishes, m'lord. You had clearly stated the ruins would be disposed of upon your uncle's death. Is that not so?"

That was years ago. God's blood, woman, you should have known I have changed my mind since then. It was all he could do to suppress his fury. Suppress it he must, though. Much as she deserved a scalding rebuke, he could not, in all honor, demean a lady in the presence of others. "You are correct, madame, in that I did at one time mention the ruins should be destroyed, but . . ." Words failed him. He would like to throttle that prunelike neck of hers, especially since he was positive she had done this out of pure jealousy and spite. He turned his attention to Jane. "Allow me to explain," he began, wondering how he could possibly explain without sounding like a self-serving idiot.

She looked at him as if he were a stranger. "So you did say it."

"Yes."

"Then there's nothing left to say. I shall take my leave now." He noted her set face as, with a graciousness inborn, she curtsied, murmuring to Tatton a quick "A pleasure to see you again, sir," and hastened from the room.

I must get to my bedchamber, thought Jane as, devastated, she half ran across the foyer. She wanted to scream—to cry—to pound her fists upon her pillow. A hand gripped her arm. *Dashmont.* She jerked her arm away. "Leave me alone."

"No." He spun her around and clasped her upper arm in a viselike grip. "Listen to me—"

"No, no, I won't listen." She pushed at his chest, but he wouldn't let go. "How could you? To think I cared about you! That dear old man's whole life was centered on those ruins, which you, with your greed and complete callousness, have chosen to plunder."

"You don't understand. I loved my uncle. If you will allow me to explain—"

"It won't do any good." She could see the pain in his eyes, but it didn't matter. "You have done the one thing that I can never forgive you for, not ever."

He started to reply, but thought better of it. Instead, he dropped his hands from her arms and backed a step away. "Regardless of how you feel about me, I trust you will continue to tutor my son?"

Her mind was spinning, but she knew she must give an answer. "For the present I shall continue to teach David, but I may soon have other plans."

"What other plans?"

"You do not understand, sir. You have never lost your wealth. You have never seen your family poverty-stricken, your mother ill, your aunt demented. If there's any way in this world I can help, then believe me I shall, for I shall never turn my back on my family." She paused to control her shaking voice. "Mama is pining away, yearning for Hedley Hall, the home my father gambled away, aided and abetted by *you*." She knew the accusation was false—she had even apologized for it—but made it again anyway.

"That's not fair, and you know it," he said.

"I don't care if it's fair or not," she answered, tears beginning to spill.

"I hate to see you cry," he said gently. He reached to touch her cheek, but she knocked his hand away.

"You'll never see me cry again," she answered proudly, wiping the tears away with the palm of her hand.

"I am glad you've chosen not to leave right away," he said, attempting to be casual, but she could see his dismay. "Perhaps we can talk later when you've . . . under calmer circumstances. Meanwhile, I can assure you, the dismantling of the abbey shall be halted immediately."

"For that I am grateful. However"—she knew this would hurt him and she *wanted* to hurt him—"I shall probably be gone soon, as I'm considering a proposal of marriage."

His mask lifted. He looked as if he had just been struck. "Bradbourne?"

"Lord Bradbourne has promised to return Hedley Hall if I agree to marry him. If I don't, he will probably propose to my sister, and that, of course, is unacceptable." She could hardly get the words out, but with a quiet, desperate firmness she continued, "If anyone is to marry Lord Bradbourne and save my family, it shall be me."

There was nothing more to say. She turned away and hurried up the staircase. This time he did nothing to stop her.

*   *   *

Shown to his bedchamber, Tatton could not resist a satisfied grin as he shut the door. He was quite pleased with himself for having fooled Anthony—not a minor feat considering Anthony was usually so astute, so discerning, that sometimes Tatton suspected Anthony was reading his mind. Not lately, though. These past weeks Anthony had been naught but a lovesick sod, so distracted by the Sperling chit he could hardly distinguish night from day.

It was downright amusing that in his dazed condition Anthony had not noticed that Tatton, too, had been struck by Cupid's arrow. Naturally, Tatton had struggled to conceal it, hoping he would awake one morning to find his obsession with Lady Hortense Cavendish had gone the way of all his infatuations, of which over the years there had been too many to recall.

But so far, nothing of the sort had occurred. He had thought of Hortense constantly since that dinner when she, having changed miraculously from a shrinking violet to a full-blooming rose, had stood up to her overbearing mother in a magnificent show of bravery.

Tatton had been delighted when Anthony again invited him to Fairfield Manor. This visit would provide him the opportunity to see Hortense again, and no doubt ascertain that his eyes had played tricks that night, her sudden transformation only an illusion. Fervently he hoped so. He was rooted in contentment with his life as a London bachelor. It was unthinkable that one small, insignificant, mealymouthed girl could get the better of Tatton Fulwood.

After his valet arrived with his clothes, Tatton bathed and dressed in a stylish serge spencer jacket, worn over a waistcoat and drill trousers. *Not bad*, he thought, as he turned this way and that before the mirror. With wry humor he asked his valet, "How could I waste all this splendor on just one woman?"

"You could not, sir."

No. He most certainly could not. Tatton stepped from his bedchamber. His heart leaped. She was coming down the hallway, a vision of loveliness in a white gown trimmed with cherry ribbon. Now she stood in front of him, her face aglow.

"Ah, Mister Fulwood!" Hortense exclaimed. "How kind of you to visit us again."

Her words were ordinary, but when he looked into the depths of her warm emerald eyes, he saw tenderness—passion—an aching longing. "It must be difficult," she continued, "tearing yourself from the delights of London, to visit us simple country folk."

"Indeed not, Lady Hortense," Tatton answered, silently amused at his own banal words. "I am delighted to be back," he continued, sending a message with his own eyes: one of admiration, pent-up longing, and burning desire.

I am lost, he thought, but he didn't care.

In the dimness of her room, Jane lay on her bed, feeling desolate and heartbroken. How cruel life was. Only hours ago she had thought herself in love with a wonderful man. Now she knew the truth. Anger surged within her time and again, just thinking of his treasonous behavior—his disrespect for all that Lord Harleigh held dear. *I told him I shall never forgive him, and I won't*, she thought bitterly. *And for my family's sake I shall marry Lord Bradbourne.*

A small knock sounded at her door, followed by its discreet opening. "Lady Jane?" a small voice called.

David. She felt another stab at her heart, knowing how she would miss the little boy. She sat up, fumbled for her lace handkerchief, and dabbed at her eyes. "Come in, David."

He came in saying, "It's dark in here."

"Oh, dear, so it is." Jane hastily arose from the bed and lit a lamp. "Is that better?"

"Yes. Oh, Lady Jane." The child appeared almost to be dancing with excitement.

"Mercy, what is it, David?"

"I thought of something. Do you remember the treasure and how you and Uncle looked for it, only it was all buried beneath the stones?"

"Yes, of course I do. I—" Jane stopped as the significance of David's words struck her. "The rubble—it's cleared. That means—"

"That means we should be able to find the treasure." David's gray eyes were bright with excitement. "Do you still have the map? Uncle left that treasure to you, you know. If we can find it, you'll be rich."

If they found the treasure, she could save her family—not marry Bradbourne. It was almost too beautiful a dream ever to come true. She went to the window and peered out, but all was darkness, and she remembered there was no moon tonight. "We shall go to the ruins first thing in the morning."

"Please, can't we go now?"

"It's dark out," she answered, "and it's cold. And your father would most definitely not approve."

"He needn't know. I cannot bear to wait till morning. No one will see us go out. Please?"

David's lips curved into a smile full of his father's devastating charm. It touched her heart. The child was so eager—how could she turn him down? Now that she thought about it, she, too, would be hard put to wait. Besides, it might snow tonight, making the site impossible to find if they waited till morning. Not only that, the workmen would be there in the morning, and this was something that must be done in secret. "I'll get the map, David. You get your coat and boots. We shall find that treasure tonight—if it's there."

A chill wind blowing in from the North Sea threatened snow as they arrived at the ruins and huddled near the cloister walls for shelter, Jane with a lantern lighting the way. "You have the map, David. Read me the first line."

She lifted her lantern as David peered at the old parchment and in his high, child's somewhat hesitant voice read, "Go ye forthe through the nave, to the east transept."

"That's easy enough if it's cleared. Come along." Leading the way, Jane entered the long nave, center of the church, which had previously been filled with debris. "It's clear now," she said with delight. "We can walk right through."

As they passed through, Jane felt a sadness that Lord Harleigh could not have seen this sight. "Look, David," she said, holding the lantern high, "the nave is full of altars to saints and shrines to archbishops who lived centuries ago. Too bad it's so dark. In the morning you can see them better."

"Aren't you scared?" David asked with a shiver.

She hadn't thought to be afraid. "No, David," she replied in a comforting tone, "and you mustn't be. Think of all those kindly saints who are watching over us."

They came to the east transept, a huge room to the north of the main altar. "David, read the next line."

"From the northe side of Brother Osbert de Guees."

"Hmm, that must mean his grave." Jane lowered the lantern. The floor had been broken and depressed by the falling masonry, yet the remains of elaborate tiles were still visible, interspersed with grave markers. "Let's look for Brother Osbert," she said, keeping the lamp low to the floor.

After a short search, David called, "Here," pointing excitedly to a broken stone marker, much in the shape of a coffin, that was marked with a cross and the name, "Brother Osbert de Guees."

Jane felt a mounting excitement. "Next line, please."

David held the parchment close to the lantern. "Look ye I . . . V foote to the cross and fleur-de-lis."

"I . . . V?" she asked. "Oh, you mean four. We must work on your Roman numerals, David," she muttered as she looked four feet to the east and saw a grave marked with a cross and fleur-de-lis. "There it is. What's next?"

"Thence VI foote east to the priest's grave marked with a chalice."

"VI means six," she informed him. She lifted the lantern and saw a plain stone marked only by a chalice. "We're getting close. What's next?"

"Thence southe to the knight's marker."

She found it immediately—a grave marker with no name but marked with a cross and a sword. She was beginning to understand now. The four grave markers were roughly in a square. The spot must somehow relate to all four. "The rest of it," she cried, trying to contain her excitement.

David obliged with, "In the middle of these, search ye the chambre beneathe that conteyneth the treasure of Linneshall."

Jane immediately swung the lantern to the spot that lay equidistant from the four grave markers and saw a small stone, not nearly big enough to mark a grave, that was engraved with only a small cross. She felt her heart beating as she knelt to examine it, setting her lantern on the knight's marker. The stone was about four feet square. She tried to wedge her fingers underneath it, but it wouldn't budge. "Drat! It's not moving, David."

"The workers left their picks," he said, then grabbed up the lantern and hurried away. While he was gone, Jane knelt in the darkness. A blast of wind hit her. She tugged her cloak closer around her in the increasing frigid air. Something cold and wet splashed her cheek. Snow. They must hurry.

David returned with a pick. Jane took it and slipped it beneath the edge of the stone. Together they worked at prying it up, but it refused to move. "Let's put all our weight on it," she cried. Now snowflakes swirled about their heads as they pushed harder. Suddenly the stone broke loose, and they were able to push it aside. A large, hollowed-out hole lay underneath. With bated breath, Jane lowered the lantern into the hole. A casket, lid closed, rested inside.

"Open it," David shouted, his voice filled with excitement.

"Take the light," Jane said. With David holding the lantern, she reached into the small chamber and grasped the lid. *Was it locked? Would it open?*

It would.

Easily, she swung the lid back and there, sparkling and glittering even in the dim light were the rubies, pearls, emeralds, diamonds, silver, and gold that the doomed Abbot Wulfric had buried nearly three hundred years ago. They had found Linneshall's priceless treasure.

Chapter 15

The casket had proven too heavy for Jane and David to even lift, let alone carry. They had been obliged to move the stone back over the hole, leave the casket overnight, and in the morning retrieve it, aided by no less than three footmen.

Now, in the dining room at Fairfield Manor, Jane could hardly suppress her delight as she and David pulled each item from the casket and placed it with care on a linen cloth laid upon the long dining room table. The treasure was magnificent, far beyond her wildest dreams—Lord Harleigh's, too, she imagined. There were heaps of crosses, some plain gold or silver, others encrusted with precious stones, hanging from heavy gold chains. There were gold plates and silver goblets and dishes—and the gem of them all: the solid gold chalice, embedded with sapphires, emeralds, and rubies.

"Feel the weight," Jane said, handing the heavy chalice to David. "No wonder we needed help. And look at this"—she held up a dish of silver, decorated in black-and-turquoise mosaic with the head of a saint—"Saint Bacchus, I should guess."

"Who was he?" asked David.

From memory, Jane quoted, "Beneath Saint Bacchus doth lie two heavenly powers: Dominion and Might."

"What's this?" came a sharp voice from the doorway. Lady Cavendish entered. "I shall have none of that papist nonsense in this house." Her thin nose was more pinched than usual.

Not even this humorless woman could curb her own joyous spirits this morning, Jane told herself. Besides, there was no sense arguing with someone who had not the wits to understand. "David and I were simply looking at the Linneshall treasure, madame," she replied equitably. "We discovered it last night."

"I heard," came the peevish reply. "Servants' tittle-tattle travels with the utmost speed." Her ladyship strode to the table and scrutinized the treasure practically piece by piece. It was obvious she was endeavoring to maintain a straight face, but her greedy grasp of each priceless object gave her away. "Pagan rubbish," she muttered as she picked up the precious chalice. "I don't want it in the house. I shall inform his lordship it should be melted down immediately and sold."

"But it's not yours, Grandmama," David spoke up. "It all belongs to Lady Jane."

Thank heavens for the blunt honesty of children. Jane had been unable to sleep last night, so excited was she that her family could live in comfort once again. Her one fear was that such fantastic luck was too good to be true. Were Lady Cavendish's heedless words just now bearing her out? A wave of anxiety swept through her. She knew that as a woman she had few rights, so if Dashmont decided the treasure belonged to him, there would be little she could do. And why wouldn't he claim it for his own? She had, after all, done a thorough job of alienating him. "What David said is true, Lady Cavendish," Jane stoutly replied. "Lord Harleigh left the treasure to me, should it be found."

"And we found it," David chimed.

"On Lord Dashmont's property, let me remind you," the older woman sourly replied. "I hardly think the treasure belongs to you, Lady Jane, much as you might wish to think so. By all that's just and legal, it belongs to his lordship. David should eventually receive his share, of course. I, as David's grandmother, am also entitled to a share, not only as the mother of his poor dead wife, but for the time I have put in caring for the child."

"Enough." From the doorway came a voice brimming with indisputable authority. Followed by Tatton Fulwood, Lord Dashmont entered the room, both men splendidly dressed in brass-buttoned hunt coats of bright scarlet, carrying black top hats, leather whips, and gloves. Dashmont's expression was grim as he confronted his mother-in-law. "The treasure belongs to Lady Jane, madame."

"But look at it." Lady Cavendish made an angry sweep with her hands. "Lord Harleigh was expecting only a simple chalice. He had no idea the treasure was this enormous and worth . . . well at the very least, thousands of pounds."

"No matter." Dashmont's voice was firm, final. "Uncle left the treasure to Lady Jane Sperling, and so it shall be hers—all of it."

What a relief. Jane felt like dancing again. The treasure was hers. Dashmont had said so, and rebuked the greedy woman. Jane actually felt a scintilla of gratefulness. *My first kind thought about him since yesterday*, she thought with irony. But her disgust with him, and disillusionment, still rankled. She would never forgive the man.

In a martyred voice Lady Cavendish spoke again. "Very well, Anthony, if you choose to give your son's inheritance away, there is nothing I can do."

Anthony ignored her and turned to Jane. "My heartfelt congratulations." He smiled sincerely and gestured toward the treasure. "I know what this means to you."

She could at least be polite, she supposed. "Thank you, m'lord. I must first find out how much it is worth."

"I daresay a great deal," contributed Tatton, "melted down, of course."

"I can only hope it's enough to rent a London town house for my family," Jane replied, "and buy them some decent clothes, and a carriage and horses, and—"

"And resume your social life?" asked Dashmont.

"I . . . suppose."

"Why the hesitation?"

In all the excitement, she hadn't thought. Now she could return to her old life, and that meant balls, beaux, soirees, the Season. The thought did not excite her, but she would die before she admitted it. "I have no hesitation. I am thrilled at the thought of returning to London." She thought of David and rested an affectionate hand upon his shoulder. "I shall miss your son. When he visits you in London, may I see him?"

He regarded her strangely. "I shall be leaving for Jamaica

soon. I'm taking David with me. With luck, we shall not be returning to London for a lengthy period of time. Never, as far as I'm concerned."

Never to see Anthony again? His shattering words caused a pain around her heart that took her totally by surprise. How strange she should feel such devastation, especially after she had just decided she despised him. But she would make sure her dismay would remain well concealed. She searched for a disdainful answer, but before she could find one, Barkley announced, "A visitor to see you, m'lord. A person from the monastery."

"Brother William," Anthony exclaimed when the wizened old monk hobbled into the room, "it's been years since I've seen you."

"Peace be with you." Brother William bowed low to Lord Dashmont and all in the room, his arms crossed and invisible in the voluminous sleeves of his simple brown robe. His sweet smile filled the room. "I have heard the wonderful news. I—" He caught sight of the table. "The treasure." His voice was buoyant. "Forgive me, m'lord, I would not dare think of disturbing you, but over the years I have dreamed that through some miracle the treasure hidden by Abbot Wulfric on that terrible day three centuries ago would be found. I dreamed, too, that I might gaze upon it just once before I died." He cast longing eyes at the chalice and humbly asked, "If I could but hold it, m'lord?"

Dashmont smiled. "Of course."

The old monk limped to the table and lifted the golden chalice tenderly, as if it were the most precious object he had ever held. His eyes glistened as he looked at Jane. "I have heard 'twas found by you and the young master. Tell me, please, m'lady, how did you find it? And where?"

Brother William listened attentively, almost reverently, as Jane related the story of the map that had fallen from the ancient book binding—the search she and David conducted for the grave markers—that ecstatic moment when they opened the casket and saw it was filled with gold, silver, and precious jewels.

When she finished, Brother William made the sign of the

cross over the treasure. "Bless Abbot Wulfric who hid it there. Did you know he was sent to the Tower? He gave his life rather than surrender the precious treasure of Linneshall. He was a true martyr." The old monk sighed gently and replaced the chalice. "We live in poverty now, our glory and riches gone, but no matter. Abbot Wulfric still protects us. He looks down on us from heaven, knowing we still remember his great sacrifice and honor him for it. May I ask, m'lady, where the treasure will go? Could you find it in your heart to donate at least some small part of it to the poor?" His gaze turned upward, toward heaven. "Abbot Wulfric would have wanted it so."

Reality struck. Since she'd found the casket, something had been bothering her. Now she knew what it was. "I . . . I'm not sure, Brother William. I shall have to think on it."

The best—the only—place to think was at the ruins. Jane hastened there shortly after Brother William's visit. *At least the workmen are gone*, she thought as she sat, totally alone, on the bench near the sundial. *What have I been thinking?* she wondered. Lord Harleigh was at her shoulder again, his words ringing in her ear.

"That treasure may turn out to be a mixed blessing. You may have a quandary on your hands—finding what honor decrees and what your heart decrees are not the same thing."

That old devil. Now she knew his meaning. Her heart told her, keep the treasure—help her desperate family. But honor told her that the treasure rightfully belonged to the poverty-stricken brothers of the Cistercian monastery. She should give it back, all of it. She had no right to one single part of it, and if Abbot Wulfric was truly looking down from heaven right now, he was wondering, who is that selfish young chit who claims the treasure of Linneshall as her own? Without the slightest doubt he would want all of it returned.

Mama—Christabell—Brother William—Lord Bradbourne— her poor little sisters—Lord Dashmont. Such a quandary. She lost track of time as her thoughts coursed wildly pro and con, this way and that, until, in the peace of the monk's old garden she knew what she must do.

*   *   *

"Most exhilarating," exclaimed Tatton as he slid from his horse at the front entrance to Fairfield Manor. "Even the snow obliged us by melting. It was the kind of hunt I like—short, sharp, decisive, and enjoyed by all."

"Except the fox," Anthony replied dryly. Relieved to be back from his neighbor's hunt, he swung from his horse. "It will be my last."

Tatton raised his eyebrows. "You're through with fox hunts? But you used to love to hunt. And you're such a superb rider, I am astounded."

Anthony handed off the reins to the stable man. "I ride all day in Jamaica, but for a useful purpose, not for my own supposed amusement, riding a helpless animal to ground."

"Confound it, man, it's only a fox." Tatton examined him curiously. "You've been out of sorts all morning, for some reason . . ." Realization lit his face. "Lady Jane—that's it. Oh, priceless. You stoutly declare you are *not* going to propose, yet it's obvious everything she does deeply affects you."

Anthony had no reply as he and Tatton strolled into the entry hall. He had enjoyed the hunt even less than he'd let on. Thank God, he'd soon be back in Jamaica where he, like the rest of the plantation owners, could direct his energies toward productive work, rather than such nonsense as fox hunts. Meanwhile, he assured himself he could rest easy. Lady Jane had found the treasure and would, along with her family, be secure. His conscience would not have allowed him to rest, otherwise. Now he could get on with his life.

He heard a light footstep and lifted his gaze. Lady Jane, with a grave expression on her face, but looking stunning in a simple white muslin morning dress, was descending the staircase in such a lithesome, graceful way it made him ache to touch her. He would give her a cool greeting and pass by, but before he could, Tatton spoke up.

"Good morning, Lady Jane. You're looking beautiful as always, but rather solemn, I should say. Have you forgotten your newfound treasure?"

"No, indeed, Mister Fulwood." Jane arrived at the bottom of the staircase and gave him a wistful smile. "But it's not my treasure anymore."

Anthony stopped, totally caught off-guard, and listened as Tatton asked, "What do you mean?"

"I have decided the treasure should go where it rightly belongs—to the poor brothers of the Cistercian monastery."

"But . . . but . . ." Words failed Tatton.

"All of it?" asked Anthony.

"All of it. I have no right to one single piece."

Slowly, incredulously, Anthony shook his head. "Oh, Jane, you foolish, foolish girl," he said, so shocked he forgot the formalities.

She drew her shoulders back with great dignity. "It was not an easy decision."

Damn the woman. A wave of anger replaced his astonishment. Through gritted teeth he told her, "Step into the salon. I wish to speak to you in private."

"No," she promptly answered.

"Er . . . need to change," said Tatton. He tossed a quick "If you will excuse me" over his shoulder as he made a hasty retreat up the staircase.

Anthony silently watched him disappear. "I said I wished to speak to you alone," he repeated.

She tilted her little chin defiantly. "There is nothing to discuss, sir. The deed is done. Unless, of course"—her face clouded with uneasiness—"you won't fight me on this? The treasure belongs to the monastery, as surely you must know."

"But what of your family?" he asked in indignation. "Here you had the means to give your family a good life again, and you . . . you . . ."

"I did what honor decreed." A look of despair crossed her face. "Do you think this was a quick decision? Do you think I didn't agonize over this? But how could I, in all good conscience, take a treasure that was so clearly theirs? I would be nothing better than a thief if I did."

His heart melted as she gazed up at him, those amazing blue-gray eyes full of such unquenchable spirit that he knew the shallow little twit he'd met at the ball was gone forever. *I love this woman. I want this woman*, he thought, feeling such a pull of attraction toward her that he was compelled to press his arms to his sides so they wouldn't reach out for her. Yet how could he tell her? He, the breaker of hearts, the chased, never the chaser, who had never been compelled to go after a woman in all his life. "You are still angry," he said finally.

"Yes," she answered.

"And you will never forgive me."

"Never."

He smiled bitterly. "So quick to agree?"

She did not smile back. Her eyes filled with a deep sadness. "It's no use. I must admit, there was time when I . . ." she stopped and bit her lip, seeming to reconsider her words ". . . but no matter." Anguish crossed her face. "I have tried to overlook what you did, but I cannot. I told you yesterday I could never forgive you for your attempt to destroy the abbey. That hasn't changed, and never will. You should know I intend to leave as soon as possible, as soon as . . . certain arrangements have been made."

He felt his heart grow numb. To cover it, he raised his eyebrows in mock amazement. "Don't tell me you're back to Bradbourne again."

"I intend to marry Lord Bradbourne, if he'll still have me."

He was losing her. A sensation of intense despair swept over him. Careful to maintain his cool facade, he remarked, "How unwise."

"He is not so bad as you have painted him." Remembering Bradbourne's return of the ormolu clock, Jane continued, "I find him to be most generous and kind."

"Good Lord!" he exploded, "can't you see the man's deceiving you? He will go to any length—"

He stopped abruptly, and with a curse turned and walked away, thrusting his hand to his hip. After a moment of deep thought, he turned and asked, "If you would but consider my offer to increase your stipend?"

"Absolutely not." She looked puzzled. "Why are you making such an offer?"

He wanted to tell her he loved her. He wanted to get down on his knees and beg forgiveness for his part in the near destruction of her beloved Linneshall. He opened his mouth to tell her, but the words would not come out. Pride prevented them. Stupid pride, he knew, and yet . . . even if he did tell her, what was the use? No matter what he said, she would never forgive him. "I promised your father I would do what I could for his family," he said gently. "Therefore, I could hardly allow you to marry Bradbourne without interfering."

Sadness filled her voice as she answered, "*You* will not allow me to do anything, Lord Dashmont. I shall do what I think best, with no interference from you."

"You may rest assured there are no strings attached to my offer to increase your stipend."

"Never," she firmly said and backed away. "I shall never take your charity. As for the rest, there is nothing you could do that would ever cause me to forgive you."

"Very well," he told her coolly, "let me know when you are leaving, and I shall put my coach at your disposal."

"It will be soon, sir."

Terrible regrets assailed him as, wordlessly, he spun on his heel and left her standing in the hallway.

"You mean you gave it all away?" asked David, his eyes wide with astonishment.

Poor child, thought Jane. She had come to his bedchamber to explain. "You see, it wasn't mine to give. It belonged to the abbey, and it would have been wrong of me to take it."

David thought a moment, then looked up at her with those wise eyes that were so like his father's. "I do believe you are right," he said finally, his voice solemn. "But I am still sorely disappointed."

Her heart went out to this wise, compassionate little boy. How she wished she could have him for her own. "Then you forgive me?"

"But of course," he replied with a maturity far beyond his years. "But now what will you do?"

It was so hard to smile, but she did so and answered, "I shall be leaving soon."

"But you don't have to." David's face brightened. "I know! If you're not going to be rich again, and return to London, then you should come to Jamaica with Papa and me. He likes you a lot. Maybe he could marry you. I should like that."

"Oh, David." Fighting tears, Jane knelt in front of the child and clasped his arms. "That would make me your stepmother, and I should love that. But some things are simply not meant to be, I'm afraid."

He reached his fingers to her cheek, a gesture that touched her heart. "You're not happy, are you, Lady Jane?"

There was no way she could lie. "Not so very."

"Your eyes are all red. You've been crying."

"Yes, I have. In some ways I hate to leave."

"Will you miss my papa?"

How observant he was. How could she answer? "Yes and no. Your father is a compassionate man, wise and generous in many respects. There were just some things we didn't agree on." *There, that was truthful enough.* How could she further explain when she, herself, could not understand how she could despise him for what he had done, yet feel devastated she was leaving him? "I shall write to you, David. Will you write to me?"

"Of course I shall," he answered solemnly, "and please . . . I want you to be happy."

"I shall try," she answered. *But could she?* Even though Bradbourne's thoughtful gift of the ormolu clock now sat on her mantel, the thought of marrying Old Bony Fingers was so distasteful she could hardly bear to think of it. Still, what choice did she have? It was clear Lord Dashmont offered to increase her stipend out of pity. Pride alone would keep her from accepting, let alone his callousness in destroying part of the abbey.

The future lay before her like a huge black hole. Nothing could help her now. There was no way out, and she was doomed.

Chapter 16

As their coach rolled toward London, a bored Tatton glanced over at his silent friend. "So, Anthony, you'll be off to Jamaica soon," he remarked, attempting to spark a conversation. No answer. He nudged the toe of Anthony's boot. "Good heavens, man, can you pull out of your funk long enough to answer?"

Anthony shifted his gaze from the window, where he'd been staring out, unseeing, for the entire length of the ride. "What did you say?"

"Nothing. I shall leave you to your deplorable mood and not disturb you further."

Good. Anthony wanted to be left alone—left to ponder how he, the so-called rake of London and breaker of a dozen hearts, had lost the only woman he truly loved, or would ever love. *What irony*, he thought, his misery so acute it was like a physical pain. He had made a fortress of his heart, that fateful night at Lady Ponsonby's ball, because the very thought of another Georgiana had been so totally loathsome. What a fool he'd been, rejecting Lady Jane on that account. Worse, even after that night, when she had been so brave in the face of total ruin, he had been too proud and stubborn to see the strong, compassionate woman hidden beneath her frivolous facade. The sad truth was, from the very beginning, Lady Jane Sperling had conducted herself with honor and integrity, while he, steeped in his own arrogance and groundless fears, had not the wits to see it.

Now it was too late. She had made herself abundantly clear on that point. *You have done the one thing that I can never forgive you for, not ever.* Her words rung in his ears, magnifying his misery. But was it really too late? Was he not the rough and ruthless rake of London who could always get what he wanted?

An hour went by, Tatton napping, Anthony in deep thought, until at last he smiled to himself, nodded, and said softly, "I've got it."

"What, what?" said Tatton, awaking with a start. "Got what?"

"A way to win her back."

"Lady Jane? But last I heard—"

"Forget what I said." A jubilant gleam shone in Anthony's eyes. "She told me she could never forgive me, but she will."

"Are you sure?" asked Tatton.

"Not only sure, I'm positive."

That night, as they strolled up Saint James's Street, approaching Brooks, Tatton's expressive face grew even more somber. "I cannot believe you're doing this," he said, "it's insane. In all the years I've known you—"

"In all the years you've known me, you have never seen me as anything other than utterly selfish," Anthony replied. "Now, for once, I am doing something for someone other than myself."

"But win back Hedley Hall?" Tatton paused in the street, incredulous. "How can you be sure you'll best Bradbourne? With all due respect, he's as good as you are, possibly better. *Probably* better, if you want the truth."

"Now there's a true friend," Anthony commented dryly.

"God's blood!" Tatton could hardly contain himself. "I am put in mind of Sir Charles Stepney. Remember? He was detected cheating at cards, and after the trial, which, as you recall, did not terminate in his favor, he died of a broken heart."

"I am aware of that," Anthony answered agreeably.

"To be caught cheating is the one deadly sin for which society will never forgive you. You'd be ruined—totally disgraced. No sense thinking you'd be safe in Jamaica—your reputation would follow you to the ends of the earth."

"Well stated, Tatton." They were at the entrance to Brooks. "Now be a good fellow and open the door, will you? I have it on good authority that Bradbourne will be here tonight."

*   *   *

Elderly Sir Godfrey Hatton, seated next to Tatton Fulwood in Brooks gambling room, looked more puzzled by the minute. "Has Anthony gone mad?" he inquired, words carefully shielded behind his hand.

With dazed exasperation Tatton whispered, "I hardly know, Sir Godfrey."

The older man shook his head in disbelief. "I would as lief play cards with the devil as that villain Bradbourne." His bushy white brows rose in disapproval as he gazed at Lords Dashmont and Bradbourne, seated across from each other at a nearby faro table. A huge pile of markers and coins was stacked in front of Bradbourne. In front of Dashmont, nothing.

Sir Godfrey continued, "How could Dashmont play that scoundrel for hours—for ever-increasing stakes—and lose so heavily? My word, such idiocy. Why doesn't he just get up, accept his losses, and walk away?" His forehead creased in a troubled frown. "I'm troubled by those rumors."

"Concerning Bradbourne's cheating?" whispered Tatton.

Sir Godfrey nodded. "You know very well it's been rumored for years he's the master of the table pass, but how could Anthony not know? He's always avoided Bradbourne like the plague. So why is he playing with him now?" He scratched his head. "Perhaps Anthony's spent too much time in the Jamaican sunshine—yes, that must be it, the sun has scrambled his brain."

"If Bradbourne cheats, he's good at it," commented Tatton.

"Oh, I agree. Those long fingers of his are lightning swift— all the better to make his table passes with, I'll wager. That knave should be banned from the club."

Sir Godfrey grew silent as Lord Bradbourne gave Anthony a look brimming with scornful triumph as he scooped up his winnings from the latest hand. "So, Dashmont, are you done?"

Dashmont returned a slightly amused smile. "Not by half." He dropped his chips on the ten, which, two turns of the cards later, Bradbourne won.

"Still more, old man?" Bradbourne inquired with an ill-concealed sneer. "Must say, you're a glutton for punishment." He indicated the markers. "Forty thousand pounds at least.

Perhaps we had better call it a night. I hate to take advantage of someone so obviously . . . unskilled."

"Uh-oh," murmured Tatton, bracing for excitement. Anthony would not tolerate such an insult. Surely, at the very least, he would grab Bradbourne by his cravat and slam his pasty face into the table.

To Tatton's surprise, Anthony did no such thing. Instead, he smiled pleasantly and said, "Let's raise the stakes, shall we?"

"By all means," Bradbourne answered, "up a hundred pounds? Two hundred? Although I do believe you're over your head, old fellow—"

"Hedley Hall."

Although Lord Dashmont had spoken in an ordinary voice, a heavy, tense silence immediately settled over the room, all eyes fixed upon the two men at the faro table.

"Hedley Hall?" Bradbourne's laugh was scornful. "Is this your idea of a joke?"

"Not a'tall." Anthony gave him an easy smile. "Hedley Hall against Fairfield Manor, all on the next hand."

An astounded murmur rippled through the room. Tatton blanched and took an extra deep gulp of his brandy. Sir Godfrey, an inveterate gambler who thought he had witnessed every reckless bet known to mankind, fell back in his chair, shocked and silent.

Bradbourne retained his composure. "You are serious, aren't you?"

"Indeed I am. I repeat, Hedley Hall against Fairfield Manor." Anthony dropped a chip on the six of spades embedded on the table. "All on the six."

Bradbourne's lids came down over his eyes, but not before a crafty look of greed flashed through them. "As you wish, sir."

Sir Godfrey, recovered from his initial shock, sat straight again and whispered urgently to Tatton, "Your friend should be hauled off immediately to Bedlam. Fairfield Manor is worth ten Hedley Halls. With Bradbourne dealing, Dashmont might as well sign over the deed right now."

Tatton, his face clouded with concern, whispered back, "I cannot argue. This is sheer insanity."

A tense silence hung over the room as all eyes watched Lord

Bradbourne's long, swift fingers expertly shuffle the cards. With a flourish, he set them in front of Anthony, who cut them into two nearly equal stacks. Bradbourne picked them up swiftly and was drawing them toward himself when Anthony lifted a finger. His friendly smile had disappeared, replaced by a frosty look in his eyes. In a voice deadly calm, he said, "Wait."

Bradbourne paused, lifting a curious eyebrow.

"I am changing my bet," said Anthony. He flicked the chip aside, picked up a copper penny, and dropped it on the six of spades. "The six, to lose."

"He's coppering," exclaimed Sir Godfrey in amazement, this time not remembering to lower his voice.

Tatton, too, was astounded. Putting a copper on the card reversed the bet. Anthony was betting on himself to lose. Tatton watched in horror as Lord Bradbourne made a move to shuffle the cards again.

Fast as a striking snake, Anthony's hand shot out and grabbed Bradbourne's wrist. "You have already shuffled," he said in a voice ruthlessly hardened.

Bradbourne pulled away. "I have every right to shuffle again."

There was a stir in the room. The two men glared at each other, caught in a deadly dangerous tableau, until old Sir Godfrey rose to his feet and with commanding presence proclaimed, "No, you have not the right to reshuffle, Lord Bradbourne."

"Handsomely put, Sir Godfrey," called Lord Carlisle, also one of the club's oldest and most venerated members. "Once the cards are shuffled, no need to shuffle again, what?"

A chorus of approval echoed through the room. Someone shouted, "Why shuffle again? What have you to hide, Bradbourne?"

"Deal," demanded Anthony.

Lord Bradbourne clutched the cards, his face, previously implacable, growing white with barely bridled anger. He slid off the top card, the soda, and fairly hurled it away. Next, biting his lip, with the greatest reluctance, he reached for the second card. With unwilling fingers he slid it off and turned it over . . .

A six.

A collective gasp filled the room. After a pause during which his face hardly moved a muscle, Anthony, with magnificent aplomb, arose from the table and addressed Bradbourne. "A six—how remarkable. To think, if I hadn't switched my bet you would have won. How's that for a stroke of luck! You know my solicitor. Kindly send him the deed to Hedley Hall in the morning. Now there's a good fellow."

With a congenial bow to one and all, and with a small, amused smile, he left the room.

Tatton, who had followed Anthony out, could hardly contain himself until they were out in the bustle of St. James's Street again. "You won! I thought my heart would stop when you put up Fairfield Manor. How could you? Such a risk."

Anthony grinned. "Not really. I played with Bradbourne long enough to make sure those rumors about his cheating were true. He's clever, fast as light, but it soon became obvious he was engaging in table passes. You need a quick eye to see how he picks up the lower half of the deck after the cut, seems to place it on top, but instead slides it underneath in what I must say is one admirably smooth action."

Tatton said incredulously, "But still, how could you have risked your estate?"

"How could that second card not have been a six?" Anthony countered. "Knowing Bradbourne's greed and utter ruthlessness, 'twas hardly a gamble."

Hardly a gamble? Anthony thought to himself. He had taken some risks in his life, but tonight's was by far the most foolhardy and perilous. Easily, he could have lost the family estate. *And all for love.* He knew now that he was madly in love with Lady Jane Sperling. Although his pulse had not yet returned to normal, a buoyant joy swirled through him. He had won Hedley Hall for her. In truth, he would have risked everything to win her back.

"So what next?" asked Tatton. "I should imagine you'll be on your way back to Fairfield Manor by first light." He slanted a knowing gaze at Anthony. "You're in love, Anthony. You did this for the little Sperling chit, and don't tell me otherwise."

"Not Fairfield Manor yet, Tatton. First there's something I must do."

As they strolled down St. James's Street toward their carriage, Tatton remarked, "Now that we're away from all ears, you can tell me the truth. Would you have cheated, had you not caught Bradbourne's table passes?"

The beginning of a smile tipped the corners of Anthony's mouth. "Cheat? Really, Tatton, how could you think such a thing? Cheating is the one deadly sin that society will never forgive. Is that our carriage over there? Come, let's go home."

"Jane, I shall never comprehend how you could have done such a thing," complained Lady Cavendish.

Jane groaned inwardly. Ever since she'd given up the treasure, Lady Cavendish had constantly berated her. Now, in the dining room at Fairfield Manor, in the midst of dinner, the older woman had burst forth again.

"What's done is done," said Hortense, trying to placate her mother. "How many times must Lady Jane explain?"

Lady Cavendish cast vindictive eyes in her daughter's direction. "Jane has yet to explain in a satisfactory manner what madness possessed her." She shifted her indignant gaze to Jane. "As if you could possibly have an explanation for such outrageous, incomprehensible behavior . . ."

Jane listened dutifully as Lady Cavendish rambled on. It had been two weeks now, and still the selfish woman could speak of nothing but the treasure and what a fool Jane had been to give it away.

"Brother William will sell some of the treasure and keep the rest for the church," Jane answered equitably, for, it seemed, the thousandth time. "The money from the items he sells will go to the poor. Now could we talk of something else?" How she missed those lively meals with Lord Harleigh, filled with wit and intelligent conversation. She wished she could tell him how right he had been—that she would be much better off dining with the servants, rather than be forced to listen night after night to all this ignorant vitriol.

"The poor," sneered Lady Cavendish, "what will they spend it on but gin? And furthermore . . ."

Jane let her mind drift, as she usually did through these miserable dinners, and thought of the letter she'd received this morning from Christabell. What of Lord Dashmont? Hadn't Jane been madly in love with him? Wasn't he going to propose?

What irony, thought Jane. Time and again, she had told herself, forgive him. So what if he had given orders to tear down the abbey? It really didn't matter. If she tried hard, she could forget it. But then, inevitably, she would picture dear Lord Harleigh and how heartbroken he would be to see the abbey walls torn down—by his very own, beloved nephew. At that, her opinion of Lord Dashmont would plummet. The man was without heart, greedy, and had earned his place in hell for tearing down a sacred, irreplaceable piece of history. Would Lord Harleigh have eventually forgiven his nephew? She didn't know. She only knew that she never could.

Christabell had mentioned Lord Bradbourne was visiting in London, but would soon return to Hedley Hall. *I can stand no more of Lady Cavendish and shall leave for the cottage tomorrow*, thought Jane. *And when Lord Bradbourne returns, I shall be there to finally, humbly, accept his proposal.*

The next morning Jane began to pack her possessions— everything, for this time she would not return. She hated leaving David, but at least she would always know she'd played a major part in his remarkable recovery. As for Lord Dashmont . . . *ah, Anthony* . . . she could never forgive him, but despite herself she knew she would never forget a single detail of his face, or the burning desire she had felt under the full moon, at the ruins of Linneshall, when his mouth hungrily sought hers. It was a memory that would always be with her.

Her valises were packed. *I feel as if I'm going to my own funeral*, she thought as she sat at her dressing table, halfheartedly attempting to arrange her curls. Even now, after months of caring for herself, she lamented her lack of a lady's maid, although the arrangement of her hair styles was vastly improved over those first, disastrous attempts.

There was a knock on her door. It was Barkley, announcing, "Lord Dashmont wishes to see you, madame."

"He's here?" she blurted, her heart suddenly racing.

"In the study. He asks that you bring your cloak and bonnet."

"Very well." Overwhelmed with curiosity, she knew she must retain her calm. "Tell him I shall be down directly."

After Barkley left, Jane's first impulse was to change out of her drab brown traveling dress into something more attractive. *But no, don't you dare*, she admonished herself. Why should she care what he thought of her appearance? But still, she turned to her mirror once again and made one more attempt at her less than perfect coiffure, pinning her hair up in back and coaxing curls down over her forehead. Good enough, she finally decided, commanding her racing heart to slow down. If only . . . despite herself, she found herself wishing that somehow, in some way, a good fairy would appear, wave her magic wand, and somehow make all the terrible things he had done disappear forever from her memory. *What a foolish wish.* She would go downstairs to see him, but nothing would come of it, no matter what he asked, or said, or did, or gave, or offered her.

As she came downstairs, she saw he was at the bottom of the staircase, awaiting her, in that engaging, masculine stance of his with feet apart, elbows out, thumbs hooked on the waist of his trousers. He was grinning up at her, as if he had totally forgotten she had clearly stated she would never forgive him. What could he be up to? Although he appeared casual and relaxed, there was a near imperceptible tenseness about him, as well as a strange, determined look in his eyes.

When she arrived at the foot of the stairs, he said, "We're going for a stroll, you and I."

She immediately bristled. "No," she answered bluntly. "I have no wish to go any place with you."

"It's important. You must come."

"And if I don't?"

He gave her a broad smile. "Then I shall toss you over my shoulder and carry you."

She thought a moment. "Well, there's no sense creating more juicy *on-dit* for the servants." Swinging her cloak about her shoulders, she continued, "Very well, I shall go, but I have no idea what this nonsense is all about. And furthermore, I have no interest in whatever it is you wish to show me."

"Well said, madame," he said with a small, mocking bow. "Now, if you will accompany me . . ."

*   *   *

The air was crisp, but the sun shone brightly as they silently climbed the wooded path that lead to the ruins of Linneshall. All the way, Jane struggled to find a reason for his asking her here, but could find none. He halted at the top of the hill. She felt his intent gaze upon her as she looked down at the ruins and saw that workmen were swarming over the alleys where the arcades had stood. "Oh," she cried. Her hand flew to her heart. "What are they doing?"

"Putting the arcades back," he said, "exactly as they were, with the very same stones, which, by the way, I have bought back—every last one—from the quarry. They are taking pains that each stone shall be replaced in precisely the same location it was in before. Given time, and a little ivy, you'll have your arcades back, good as new."

She stood there, blank and incredulous. "That's . . . most gratifying," was all she could think of to say. Truly, it was wonderful that the arcades would be restored, but considering the circumstances . . . "Of course, it's the least you could do, considering 'twas you who had the arcades torn down in the first place."

He smiled wryly. "How I marvel at your persistence, though some might call it single-mindedness. So it's not enough, eh?"

"Not really," she flung at him, and without another word followed the path to the ruins, found Lord Harleigh's bench by the sundial, and seated herself. Her thoughts were in such disarray she didn't know what further to say, but when he appeared and stood before her, she remarked, "It will be lovely to have the arcades back."

He smiled down at her. "This is only the beginning. I am planning a complete restoration of Linneshall. First, I shall reconstruct the church, preserving every inch of its architectural detail. Then the rest of the buildings, along with a complete excavation of the garden."

"Are you serious?" she asked, flabbergasted. Even Lord Harleigh had never talked of such a vast plan as this.

"It will take years, of course. But I'll see to it that after three centuries of neglect, Linneshall shall finally be safe from all further destruction, be it by the simple forces of nature, or man's plundering."

Was this the callous, heartless man she had detested? She was silent, unable to take in the scope of what he had told her.

"I see you need further persuasion," he said.

"Persuasion to do what?" she asked.

"To see I'm not quite the devil you think I am."

With a little smile she said, "That would still take some effort."

"Really?" A faint light twinkled in his eyes. "How's this for a good beginning? As of yesterday, your family is occupying the home that is rightfully theirs."

Was this some sort of cruel joke? "Hedley Hall? How is that possible?"

"I now own Hedley Hall. Only temporarily, though. I shall deed it over to you as soon as possible." He continued on, explaining that he, personally, had overseen the joyous return of her family to their former home. "Your mother, especially, was pleased, and your great-aunt seemed to perk up and be aware of her surroundings."

Jane listened quietly, in a state of complete bewilderment. Now she asked, "How did you do it?"

"I acquired Hedley Hall in the same manner your father lost it—in a card game."

She gasped. "You played Bradbourne and won? But what did you risk?"

"Fairfield Manor," he said off-handedly.

"But why?" she asked, astounded.

"Perhaps I felt sorry for you."

"If you did this out of pity, then I cannot possibly accept."

"What would you have me do?" he asked in amusement, "lose it back to Bradbourne?" Anthony sat beside her and drew her hands into his own. The humor in his eyes had disappeared, replaced by a tenderness she had never seen before. "My dear, sweet girl, I'm going to marry you. You have gone through enough. I want to take care of your family. I want our children to cherish Linneshall, as my uncle did. I want our children's children to cherish it. I want—"

"Our children?" she interrupted. An amazing thought flashed

through her mind, so startling she spoke it aloud. "Why, Lord Dashmont, you love me, don't you?"

He burst into laughter. "That's priceless. I risk my estate. I risk my reputation. I have just pledged countless sums for the restoration of a half demolished old ruin of a monastery. Now you ask me if I love you?"

He moved closer, slipping one hand round the back of her neck, entwining his fingers in her hair. "I don't just love you, Jane. I adore you. Since we met at the ball, I've been obsessed by you. Would you like to hear what torment I've been in? How I cannot eat or sleep for thinking of you?" He spoke lightly, but she knew he spoke the truth. And she knew, too, that a man who could do all those things for her was a generous, warmhearted man of honor, not at all the debauched gambler she had once thought he was.

"I have no need to hear any more," she said, "I think . . . oh, yes, perhaps I can forgive you after all." His fingers were warm against her head. Without thinking, she moved closer, wanting to feel warm and safe in his arms, wanting . . . she looked at him and her heart lurched madly. "I love you, Anthony. It started the night we met, at the ball." Before she could say more, he crushed her to him and took her lips with a fiery possession. Shivers of delight ran through her. When he lifted his lips, he caught his breath and looked down upon her with a radiant smile. "You will be mistress of Montclaire"—he frowned—"that is, if you think you can endure Jamaica."

"I shall adore Jamaica." She kissed his chin. "But forever? My family—"

"We shall come back from time to time," he went on. "Eventually, when our children are of an age when they must return for their education, we shall settle permanently in England. Here, if you like. Then you can rummage around these ruins to your heart's content. Will that be acceptable?"

He had just described a completely heavenly life. Her heart swelled with feeling. "That will be quite acceptable, m'lord," she said, and lifted her face so he could kiss her again.

Epilogue

On a warm, sunny day in August, 1824, a three-masted clipper ship glided through the broad entrance to Kingston Harbor, Jamaica. Tatton Fulwood stood at the railing, Hortense by his side. Two little girls, aged two and four, stood between them, eyes bright with excitement. As the ship cut through the sparkling waters, Tatton nodded toward the distant docks that lined the shore. "I wonder if Jane and Anthony will be there," he remarked.

"Of course they will," Hortense replied. Smiling, she gripped the railing and breathed a satisfyingly deep breath of the bracing salt air. They would be there because she wanted them to be there, she was sure of it. Since that long-ago day she had defied her mother, everything she wished for had come true. Her happy marriage to Tatton—her two darling girls and another baby on the way—Mama now safely ensconced at her estate in Cornwall—far, far from London.

Tatton pointed toward a spit of land that extended into the harbor. "That's Plumb Point, where the old Port Royal stood before it was destroyed by an earthquake."

"Where the pirates lived, Papa?" eagerly asked his older girl.

"Yes, Elizabeth." He laughed wryly. "I told Anthony once he would never find me on this hot, uncivilized, little island of his."

Hortense slanted her husband a glance warm with affection. "Now it will be our home."

Tatton slipped his arm around her shoulders. "Do you think you'll like it here?"

"On our very own plantation?" Hortense looked beyond the sparkling water, to where the spectacular Blue Mountains rose—those special mountains of Jamaica that could be seen fifty miles from shore. "I shall love it here."

As the ship drew closer to the docks, five figures that at first had resembled tiny specks, began to emerge.

"It's them!" Hortense cried, "I knew they'd be here."

Lady Jane Dashmont stood on the dock, her gaze held steadfast on the clipper ship cutting toward her across the bay. She was surrounded by her family: her husband, Anthony; her two small sons; her stepson, David, fifteen now and taller than his father. She held her baby daughter in her arms.

"Look, Mama—Papa—it's them!" cried the older boy, five-year-old Roger, namesake of his great-uncle, Lord Harleigh.

Jane shaded her eyes and looked out to sea. "Yes it's them." She glanced at Anthony with glowing eyes. "There's Tatton and Hortense and Elizabeth and little Emily." Her heart swelled with feeling. "Oh, how good it will be to see them again!"

Anthony cast her a teasing glance. "I daresay it will take at least a month for Hortense to apprise you of all the London *on-dit*." He, too, looked out to sea. "Tatton at last," he remarked, shaking his head with wonder. "I told him once he'd never get more than a mile from St. James's Street."

"You were wrong," Jane answered, laughing. "Tatton will make a fine plantation owner. How lucky that Isabelle married and moved away. He was able to buy the Wentworth Plantation for a song. Just think, they'll be right next door."

"I'll give him all the help he needs—until he gets the hang of it," Anthony replied. "But then"—he put a loving arm around Jane's shoulders—"it's back to England for David's education—and Roger's and little William's."

Jane nodded agreeably. "Indeed, we have waited much too long."

England! Jane's heart leaped at the thought. She had loved these years in Jamaica, but always in the back of her mind was Hedley Hall and her family, and Fairfield Manor, and . . . Linneshall! Over the years she had followed closely the reports on the progress of the restoration of the old abbey. Now, not only would she soon see for herself, but she could play a part in restoring dear Lord Harleigh's beloved ruin.

England, I am coming home! she thought, and her joy knew no bounds.

Miss Haycroft's Suitors by Emily Hendrickson

Against her will, a lovely young heiress is about to be married off to a man she doesn't love—to satisfy her uncle's gambling debt. All seems lost until a dashing lord takes interest in her plight. Lord Justin creates make-believe suitors for the woman to keep her uncle at bay, but the ardent feelings in the lord's heart are all too real....

0-451-19834-4/$4.99

The Misfit Marquess by Teresa DesJardien

While fleeing the embrace of a false lover, a beautiful young woman is rendered unconscious in an accident. Discovered by a handsome lord, the marquess frets over her reputation and pretends to be a little daft. The lord's suspicions of her arise with his desire to help her...and to have her. But the villain who pursued her will not surrender her without a fight....

0-451-19835-2/$4.99

To order call: 1-800-788-6262